8 Seconds to Die

by

Loretta C. Rogers

A Doc Holliday Mystery, Book 5

"They say it's not *when* you get hurt bull ridin',
it's how bad!"

~ *8 Seconds*

Chapter One

There's nothing like springtime in Kentucky, especially in Enigma. The landscape is alive with showy flowers, and the land in the front pasture rolls away with rich green grass. After a difficult winter, the near-fatal injury to my dad, and the trial that sent Bonny Cowen to an asylum for the criminally insane, I was relaxing in my front porch swing, enjoying a cup of hot chai tea.

I'm not generally given to nostalgia, especially when it involves my high school years. Most times, being half Cherokee and half Irish caused me emotional grief, which often led to bullies meeting the happy end of my fist. I was fourteen when Dad became sheriff of Enigma. He taught me to solve my own problems and to never tattle, but he also reminded me that I was his daughter, and that I could come to him, anytime. I tried hard to never hide behind the protection of his badge. And, sometimes, he had to remove his father's hat and be the lawman that he was—daughter or not.

A particular picture in my high school yearbook resurrected a flood of hurtful memories. I closed the book, not wanting to revisit a particular not-so-funny practical joke.

My name is Dr. Tullah Crow Holliday, veterinarian. I live with a black Labrador Retriever, named River, and his sidekick, a gray teacup donkey named Rascal. My father, John Henry Holliday, is Sheriff of Enigma

County. When he's serious, he calls me by my given name or Dr. Holliday. However, most times he calls me—Punkin.

Although I am a veterinarian and lead a fairly sane life. I was born with the innate gift of being contacted by spirit animals that lead me to crimes that have happened or are about to happen. While I wouldn't wish this curse on anyone, it does help me assist my dad in solving difficult cases.

The closed Enigma County High School album sat idle in my lap as I washed away the hurtful memories of the past. I looked across the yard to where my friend and partner, Dr. Ella Sanders, resides in her newly constructed ranch house. Her yard was rife with azaleas. The sweet fragrance of purple wisteria drifted across the yard to tickle my nose. It was a great day to be alive.

River lifted his head from the porch step and woofed. He and Rascal scampered down the steps to meet a vehicle barreling down the driveway toward my house. At the sight of Dad's 4Runner, both animals always raced to meet the truck. Dad parked under the sprawling oak tree and hurried to the passenger door to assist my grandmother, Mayor Tanti Crow, to the ground.

My grin widened when I spotted the box from Sweets 'n' Eats in her hands. I held the door wide and invited them into the kitchen. Grandmother immediately set the coffeepot up in record time. Dad looked pensive as he settled in a chair, opened the box, and helped himself to a powdered lemon curd donut.

While the coffee was brewing, I mulled my selection and settled for a Boston crème eclair. Grandmother filled our mugs with aromatic, hazelnut coffee. We gathered around the kitchen table. When Dad spotted the album I had placed on the table, he opened it and flipped through a few pages before settling on the page showcasing a few photos of Enigma High School's rodeo events.

I watched him sit back and square his shoulders; his finger marked a page. A deep dread skittered over me as I looked into his craggy, tanned face. A very handsome man, dressed in his tan uniform with his badge pinned to the shirt pocket. My instinct said that his visit was more than Sunday donuts with his daughter and mother-in-law.

I didn't need a sixth sense to tell me I didn't want to hear whatever it was he was about to spring on me. I decided to beat him to the punch. "Dad, you're always telling me to relax, unwind. That stress is a killer. Whatever it is, the answer is no! I'm on vacation from crime."

"Yep," he spoke blithely, and smiled. "I didn't say a word."

Grandmother picked at the flakes on her glazed donut, while her gaze went back and forth between Dad and me. We sat in silence, savoring our sweet treats and coffee. Dad's finger still held a place between the pages.

"Okay, Dad, I give. Why are you finger-marking the page filled with shots of my high school rodeo blurbs and bloopers?"

He was thoughtful for a moment. "Does the name Caleb Calloway ring a bell?"

Righteous anger iced my heart as I grabbed the album and pointed to a picture of my gray mare standing in the middle of the football field. "If you mean the Caleb Calloway that painted black zebra stripes all over Venus's body, and then hung *that* sign around her neck"—by now my insides trembled—"yes, I remember him. And if you also mean the Caleb Calloway that purposely buried a stone beneath the underside of her frog, causing a painful bruise that lamed her so badly she stumbled and fell... She was in so much pain she limped when I led her from the arena, costing us the barrel-racing championship! Then, oh, yeah, I remember him."

My fury demanded another donut. This time, I chose a chocolate-covered glazed one and chomped into it.

Dad waited. He's all too familiar with the Irish side of my temper. To fuel my fire, Grandmother swiveled the album to look at the picture of my beautiful zebra-striped gray mare standing in the middle of the football field, during half-time, with a large cardboard sign hanging around her neck. Emblazoned in dripping red paint were the words—squaw horse.

Obvious indignation filled my grandmother's ebony eyes. "That was a sorry day. Especially when we found you tied up in the girls' locker room with your face painted and your beautiful long hair butchered. Your mother and I were livid."

She arched her eyebrows. "Those boys should have been horsewhipped."

The fact that the principal and the football coach had acted quickly to lead Venus off the field, and Dad had sentenced Caleb and his buddies to several hours of mucking out stalls at the various horse farms, didn't erase the humiliation I'd suffered the remainder of my senior year.

The words I spoke didn't seem to come from my mouth. "You're here because he's in trouble." Not tasting the sugary sweetness, I finished off the donut and, shaking my head, said, "No, Dad. Just plain *no!*"

His voice was gentle. "It was twelve years ago, Punkin. You're a good detective. He needs your assistance." Dad glanced at his watch. "Tanti, if you're ready, I've got to get back to the office."

My head itched with anger as I walked them to the porch. Before climbing into his vehicle, Dad said, "I told Caleb to call you. Listen to him, Punkin. Think about his dilemma before refusing to help."

As an afterthought, he turned back and said, "You've always loved the rodeo."

You've always loved the rodeo. Those words rattled around inside my head while I watched the 4Runner disappear down my long driveway.

I planted myself in the porch swing and used my feet to furiously push myself back and forth. Day was slipping into dusk. I thought about Dad's last words. I also wondered how bad Caleb's problem could be. After all, no spirit animals had appeared—no owl, raven, buzzards, or wolves to warn of an impending death. I sat, thinking about…nothing.

The melodious chime of my cellphone interrupted my reverie. Without looking at the caller ID, I knew it was Caleb Calloway calling. This was not going to be a fun conversation.

I didn't bother to hide the terseness in my voice. "What do you want, Caleb?"

"Ah, um, I see you've spoken to Henry."

"Sheriff Holliday, to you. Just because you're an adult doesn't mean you can get all palsy-walsy with him."

"Sorry, Tullah. Really. I'm sorry."

"Just cut to the chase, Caleb. I'm busy."

Silence.

He whispered, "Maybe this was a bad idea."

The line went dead.

I experienced thirty seconds of regret. As if it had happened yesterday, I clearly saw my raggedy hair, hacked off in haste by Caleb as three of his buddies held me down, and the zebra stripes painted on my gentle mare.

I walked inside to the kitchen and turned on the faucet to splash cold water over my face. A loud bellow and River's frantic barking drew my attention. I leaned against the sink for a better look. A Brahma bull was chasing my little donkey around the yard. I owned Black Angus and Belted Galloways, better known as Oreo cows. No Brahma cattle. I grabbed my broom and raced outside to open a corral gate. To escape injury, Rascal dashed through the gate, followed by the bull. I held the snorting bovine at bay until the little donkey raced to safety, and by the skin of my teeth escaped being hooked by one of the bull's horns. I recognized the broken triangle brand, and once inside the house, I called the owner to come get his wayward bovine.

My heart was still racing when my cellphone pinged. I didn't recognize the number. My finger hovered over the answer key. "Okay, okay," I said aloud. "The bull must be the omen."

To calm my voice, I sucked in a deep breath and let it out slowly. "Dr. Tullah Holliday, how may I help you?"

"Tullah, please don't hang-up. It's Caroline Tupper. I hope you remember me. We were on the cheerleading squad together." She hastened on. "I'm Mrs. Calloway, now. Please, Tullah, Caleb is in big trouble. What he did in high school was stupid and wrong, but, please…"

I relented. The pleading in her voice sounded genuine. "What kind of trouble, Caroline?"

"Caleb is outside with our son and daughter. They're nine and six years old and the delight of our lives." I heard her draw a breath, and I waited. "Tullah, Caleb and I own Triple C Ranch and Stock Company in Oklahoma. We breed some of the finest bucking bulls in the nation."

I had stopped following rodeo news years ago and had not heard of or thought about Caleb and Caroline in years. I wanted to say, *So what...big whoop!* Instead, I spoke through clenched teeth. "Why do you need my help?"

Her voice dropped to a whisper. From the hush, I knew she had placed her hand over the phone's mouthpiece, and wondered who it was that she didn't want hearing our conversation. She said, "Someone is juicing up our bulls, making them extra mean. Two top riders have been seriously injured."

"Caroline, call your local vet to do a serum sample, then trace it to the source."

"No, you don't understand. We can't trust anyone. Last night, someone poisoned the children's pet goat. Caleb called the sheriff. He said he'd investigate. Here's the thing, though—he's been known to consort with a few shady characters."

"Caroline, I live in Kentucky. There's nothing I can do from here."

"Hold on, Tullah, Caleb wants to speak to you. Don't hang up, please...please."

"Tullah?" Caleb's voice held the same note of fright that had filled his wife's. "We have the PBR Unleash the Beast rodeo in Louisville, Kentucky in May. From there, it's on to the Cheyenne Frontier Days in Wyoming. I've followed you and Henry, ah, um, *Sheriff Holliday* in the news and know you have a special knack for solving crimes. I'm not a man to beg, Tullah, but whoever killed my kid's pet goat and cut off its head is sending a serious warning. Understand?"

I did. All creatures big or small, human or animal, always touched my heart. My restraint was about to slip. This was a dilemma. "Caleb, I have a busy career. I can't just walk off and leave my clinic for goodness knows how long. Plus the moment anyone sees me with my medical bag will know I'm a veterinarian and the reason I'm examining bulls."

"That's the beauty of it, Tullah, we'll be in your neck of the woods. You could go under cover. You were once an accomplished barrel racer. In fact, you would've won the high school championship if I hadn't—" His voice trailed off. "We were stupid teenage football jocks and full of ourselves. No amount of apologizing can excuse the hurt we caused you."

He gave a heavy sigh. "I'll supply the horses, the equipment, whatever you need. I'll even pay your travel expenses, hotel expenses, entry fees, and make sure you get on the competitor's docket. It's only three days, Tullah. Three days of guts and glory."

When I continued to hesitate, he added, "I'm a wealthy man. If it's money that's holding you up, then name your price."

Outside my kitchen window, I spotted the Brahma bull trying to climb over the corral fence. Brahmas are mean and dangerous by nature. I envisioned a rider being gored to death by a bull that had been injected with a serum to drive it mad.

Dad and Grandmother were continuously hassling

me about taking a vacation. I'd always loved the rodeo, and there were days when I missed competing. However, a three-hour drive to Louisville wasn't exactly in my "neck of the woods."

"Caleb, I'll need to make arrangements with my business partner to see if she can handle the extra workload. I'll also bone up on rodeo protocol, and I'll even try to fit a little barrel practice in. Tell me when to meet you in Louisville."

"I'm beholden to you, Tullah. What name should I register you under—probably not Holliday, as anyone could look you up, as I did?"

To honor my mother and to have her spirit with me on this dangerous journey, I wanted to say *Josie Waya Crow*. Despite the space of time since her death, thirteen years, it seemed like only yesterday. Because she was a world-acclaimed artist, and a Native American woman, for weeks her brutal and unsolved murder had made all the news channels and newspaper headlines. I feared someone might remember her death, put two and two together, and figure out my true identity.

"Tullah?"

Chapter Two

I knew I needed to answer Caleb. I'm not sure why the words stuck in my throat. Maybe I was still harboring old resentments, or maybe I was doubting my ability to compete in a rigorous sport. Like bull riding, barrel racing isn't for sissies.

A distant wolf's cry drew me out of my quagmire of uncertainty. River's black hackles stood on end as he and Rascal raced through the kitchen's doggie door. They, too, had heard the unsettling bay. There are no wolves in Kentucky. Years ago, human population had driven them out of the state.

A yip and the following long, eerie series of howls had the hairs on my arms prickling. My spirit animal was speaking, and it either meant that a murder had already taken place or was about to happen.

In a soft, doubt-filled voice, Caleb said, "You haven't changed your mind, have you, Tullah?"

My words came slowly. "No, Caleb. I'll do what I can to help. You can register me as Chenoa Waya."

He spelled it out, "C-h-e-n-o-a…W-a-y-a?"

"Yes. In Cherokee it means—wolf."

Regret rippled over me the moment I disconnected the call. I didn't want to do this, yet at the same time I felt compelled. Less than thirty days to get barrel-racing fit was impossible. None of my three horses were barrel trained. I nixed asking Ella if I might borrow her Jupiter.

It had been at least two years since she'd run barrels with him. Sure, Caleb had offered to supply me with a selection of his horses, which were probably the best of the best running Quarter mounts. Still, once the animal went through quarantine after crossing state lines, and then a rest period after standing for hours in a horse trailer, that ate into my training time. I don't exactly fall into the spring chicken category, and twelve years is eons when it comes to being rodeo fit.

I grabbed the last two chocolate donuts, refreshed my coffee, and headed back to the porch swing to collect my thoughts and figure out a workable plan. One thing for certain—I refused to make a fool of myself at a world-renowned rodeo event, in front of thousands of spectators, media outlets, and television cameras.

Maybe if I used Ella as a sounding board, I'd come up with a solution to help Caleb while staying out of the limelight. I set my empty mug aside and walked down the steps. A white picket fence separates our properties, and to shorten her trek to the clinic, she'd installed a gate, which makes it convenient for both of us. I was mere steps from the gate when I spotted Deputy Andy Kemble's sleek black truck. Once upon a time, I'd envisioned the two of us as a couple. It turned out we were better suited for a platonic relationship than a romantic rapport.

I trudged across the yard and returned to the porch. Before entering the house, I stood listening to the eclectic symphony comprised of a woodpecker's rat-a-tat-tat against a tree, a red-winged blackbird's *conk-la-ree,* and a mate's answering call of *oh-ka-lee.* It seemed everyone I was close to had someone, including the birds. To all appearances, the lovebug had bitten Ella and Andy. Dad and Dr. Sunny Sanders' relationship continues to blossom. Grandmother had her group of lady friends. In fact, she and Patty Sweet, former owner of Sweets 'n' Eats pastry shop and café, are completely giddy about their up-and-coming all-girls cruise to Europe.

Once inside, I ambled to the kitchen and peered out the window at the bellowing brahma bull still trying to escape the confines of my corral. As much as I wanted to shrug off the heavy cloak of loneliness, it clung tenaciously against my shoulders.

The raucous barking and braying alerted me to a truck towing a stock trailer pulling into the yard. The driver did a U-turn and expertly aligned the trailer with the corral's gate. Elwood Yates, owner of the Broken Triangle Ranch, stepped from the cab. His son, Woody Yates, a lanky, sixteen-year-old, raced to join his father.

I commanded River and Rascal to hush their racket. "Hello, Elwood...Woody."

Elwood hitched his denims a little higher. "Sorry as I can be, Doc Holliday. Hope King George didn't cause you any trouble. I'm sure you don't want to contaminate your Galloways with Brahma blood." The senior Yates emitted a disgusted snort. "This is the third time Woody and me have had to round up that aggravatin' critter since we bought him last week. If I hadn't paid a hefty sum for him, I'd have him castrated. But I'm lookin' to improve my herd." He shrugged his skinny shoulders. "You know how it is."

I assured the rancher that King George would be mighty disappointed if he'd managed to get in with my Oreo cows, because they were all steers. That brought a hearty round of guffaws. "I'm way too busy with my practice to increase the size of my herd."

Ella trotted to stand beside me. She huffed. "I heard the bawling, and saw the truck, and thought I'd check to see if we had an emergency on our hands."

"Not an emergency, but I'm glad you're here. Do you have time for a little girl-talk?"

"Sure, do. Andy's on duty tonight, so I'm all yours. What's up?" She also greeted Elwood and his son.

"I'll tell you later." I rushed to help Woody Yates lower the trailer's tailgate while his dad unlatched and swung the corral gate wide. Like most Brahmas, King George dipped his head, slinging a string of salvia across the dirt. With his head lowered, he pawed the ground and snorted. King George didn't mind letting us know he was two thousand pounds of dynamite.

As soon as the bull charged, Elwood jumped behind the wooden gate, barely missing a horn aimed to hook him in the crotch of his faded jeans. He removed his battered cowboy hat and waved it toward the trailer's entrance, and shouted, "Git on in there, bull. I ain't got all day."

King George backed off, gave all of us the stink-eye, bellowed, then made a run for the fence. I knew he intended to do his best to jump it. I whistled to River, and pointed toward the gray bovine. "Load 'im up, River."

My black Labrador raced toward the bull's hind legs, nipping and yipping. Bless my little gray donkey, he thinks he's a dog. Rascal mimicked River by rushing in and nipping at King George's hind legs also.

With a loud bawl, the agitated bull bolted forward. I swear the ground beneath our feet trembled. Once he was inside the stock trailer, Ella and I rushed to help Woody and his father lift the heavy tailgate and latch it before the Brahma realized he was a prisoner and headed for home pasture.

Elwood and Woody thanked us for our assistance. The senior Yates said, "Son, it looks like we might need to invest in some electric fencing." Before climbing in his truck, he offered me a smile. "I sure hope ol' George earns his keep and sires some good calves."

"If not, you can always sell him."

"Might just do that, Doc."

Ella and I waved goodbye and, before walking to the house, watched the truck and trailer disappear down my long driveway. Once inside the kitchen, I rewarded River and Rascal with their favorite homemade critter biscuits and hugs for a job well done. I also didn't miss Patty Sweet's signature pink box under Ella's arm. I lifted my eyebrows. "What have we here?"

"Andy knows how much we love Patty's donuts." She grinned. "There's a couple missing. I couldn't help myself." She opened the box while I filled glasses with ice cubes and tea. "Want to sit in the kitchen, or enjoy our goodies on the porch?"

"It's getting a bit chilly. Let's stay inside."

I set the glasses on the table, then excused myself, saying I'd be right back. I returned with my high school yearbook. As I sat, I assured Ella we weren't about to take a trip down memory lane. Instead, I opened to the page and showed her the picture of my zebra-striped mare. I also gave Ella the long version of what had happened at the homecoming game that year. She merely shook her head. "That's awful, Tullah. I can't imagine how you got through the rest of the year without enacting some serious revenge on those guys."

We sat in silence for a few minutes. "Here's the thing, Ella. Caleb is in trouble. He reached out to my dad for assistance. Dad thinks I should use my empathic abilities to help Caleb find out who's behind juicing up his bulls to make them killing machines."

"What do *you* want to do, Tullah?"

"Honestly, I'm conflicted. Part of me thinks it's the right thing to help out an old enemy, and the other part is angry at my dad. My gift isn't for sale. How dare he think I can just conjure up spirits out of thin air to lead me to unscrupulous degenerates!"

I'd been angry plenty of times, but never to the point that I felt the need to disrespect my father, even though he had overstepped his parental boundaries. I'm an adult, a doctor licensed to treat both humans and animals. He had no right to even hint that I'd come to Caleb's aid.

Ella refilled our glasses. "Wow, Tullah, this is a real dilemma. There's no way you can get ready to barrel race in less than a month. I'd offer Jupiter, but, like you, he'd need lots of practice. What are you going to do?"

I sniggered. "I don't know. Maybe the answer will come to me in a dream."

"What do you know about this Caleb guy? Other than the fact that it appears he's royally pissed off some very bad people."

I shrugged. "After graduation, I left Kentucky to study at the University of Georgia. I put Caleb Calloway out of my mind and concentrated on my studies."

"Whatever I can do to help, Tullah, you know I'm up for it. If you need to take some time off, I can handle most of the patients; and with Jeff's help, we've got the office covered."

She grinned at she divided the last glazed donut and handed it to me. "C'mon, I'll help you feed the horses and cows before it gets too dark."

Chapter Three

You may have guessed that I'm not a regular run-of-the mill woman. Nope, far from it. My name is Tullah Josie Crow Holliday. My grandmother, Tanti Crow, is full Cherokee and the Mayor of Enigma, a small rural town in southern Kentucky. Josie Waya Crow Holliday was my mother. A renowned artist of Native American art. She was murdered while in New York presenting her work at a major museum. It was shortly after her death that spirit animals began to visit me, sometimes in dreams, sometimes in reality. More often than I'd like, crimes that have already happened or are about to happen come to me in visions. My father, John Henry Holliday, is Enigma's sheriff. He often relies on my gift to help him solve crimes.

Don't get me wrong when I say that I'd prefer not to possess this—whatever it is—gift or curse. Nonetheless, it seems I'm stuck with it. Grandmother says I was given this ability long before I was conceived, and that I should treasure it because the Great Spirit Father, from all those born into the *Waya* (Wolf) clan, chose me to possess this skill.

In spite of the chill outside, the house suddenly felt claustrophobic. I gathered a shawl and walked to the porch to settle in the swing. In the stillness, I listened to the tiny trill of a songbird, and its answering call. At times, most often at dusk, I've seen the spirits of warriors doing battle, or slaves toiling in the fields. They are visions from a long dead past.

I looked at the purpling sky and lifted my arms upward. "Oh, Father Spirit, and Earth Mother, I have malice in my heart against an old enemy that seeks my help. What should I do?"

Wind blew across the open field. I hugged myself against the chill. It was as if the rustling leaves had a voice and were speaking to me. *You take the bull by its horns and a man by his words.*

Of course. The bull showing up in my yard was deliberate. It was the messenger, and Caleb Calloway had reached out to me, a girl of ethnic difference whom he had wronged many years ago. I wanted to abandon my need for revenge, but caution was the only path I could choose to follow.

I thanked the Great Spirit Father and asked for his guidance and protection on this journey I was about to take. That settled, my thoughts hinged on a cup of coffee and my computer. While I waited for the coffee to brew, I sat at the kitchen table and opened my laptop.

I typed Caleb Calloway's name in Google's search engine, and got more than I'd anticipated. The biggest surprise was when I spotted Caleb's name in a newspaper clipping titled *Teen Sentenced for Vehicular Manslaughter.*

I read the article with interest. The report stated that at the age of nineteen and while driving drunk, Caleb had driven off a bridge. None of the passengers were wearing seatbelts. Two passengers had been killed and one passenger paralyzed for life. Caleb had been sentenced to serve not less than one year and no more than ten years. After serving three years of his five-year sentence, he was paroled for time served and good behavior.

I printed off several documents and articles about Caleb. Apparently, while in prison, he had been part of the bull-riding rodeo team. He'd also won the coveted silver buckle. After his release, Caleb's father had financed the purchase of a ranch in Oklahoma where he and Caroline now raised premier bucking bulls. I continued to read about the altruistic deeds sponsored by Caleb and his wife. He'd had a hospital wing at a children's hospital named for him, and he helped sponsor a prisoners' rodeo rehabilitation team.

I closed my laptop and rubbed my tired eyes. All of these do-good deeds didn't give me a clue how to help the Calloways with their current problem. On the way to answer nature's call, I spotted the stack of neglected magazines. I riffled through them, and one slid to the floor, so I bent to retrieve a copy of *Rodeo and Cowboys*. The front cover featured Pablo Santiago showing off his bull-riding championship belt buckle. The photo sparked a light-bulb moment. I had the solution to helping Caleb without my having to barrel race.

I looked at the clock. It was late, but this couldn't wait. I pressed speed dial on my cellphone. I counted to six before a male voice answered.

"Caleb?"

Skepticism laced his voice. "Yeah. Please don't tell me you've backed out."

"Out of barrel-racing, yes. Helping you, no. You up to listening?"

"Hell, yeah!"

"Good. Question—is this your house phone or cellphone?"

"House. Is that important?"

18

"I know it's late. Get your cellphone, go outside where no one can hear you, or get in your vehicle and drive to where no one can hear you. Then get out of your vehicle and return my call."

"You're scarin' the hell out of me, Tullah! You think my phone and truck are bugged?"

"Just do it, Caleb." I disconnected the call, grabbed a pen and jotted a note on the pad next to my recliner. *Get name of sheriff in Pittsburg County, OK. Have Dad investigate.*

Five minutes seemed like an eternity before my cellphone chimed. Caleb spoke in a hushed voice. "It's me. I'm at the end of my driveway and standing outside my truck. It's cold as a well-digger's…ah…never mind. This had better be good, Tullah."

"You can let me know after I finish. First, tell me the name of the sheriff in your district."

"Why?"

I rarely cuss, but sometimes it slips out when I'm extra aggravated. "Dammit, Caleb, you want my help or not?"

"Okay…okay. It's Sheriff O'Neal Coffey."

I jotted the name on my pad, making sure of the spelling. "Caroline indicated that Coffey might be into some shady dealings. True?"

Silence.

I was on the verge of disconnecting and blocking Caleb's number. His obstinance wasn't sitting well with me.

"Caleb, either you want my help or you don't. I have other things to do than wait around for you to play coy. What's it going to be?"

Silence.

To show him I was serious, I began to count, "One…two…thr—"

"Yeah, yeah, okay. It's just that I'm afraid for Caroline and the kids. There's no solid proof, but rumor has it that Coffey is dirty and hides behind his badge. If he finds out about you, we're all up shift creek without a paddle."

"Trust me. He won't. To protect your children, keep this conversation between us. If you have to put the fear of God into Caroline, make sure her lips are zipped. Got it?"

"Yeah, sure. By the way, I've already picked out three horses for you to ride. They'll be on their way tomorrow."

"Nix that. I haven't competed in twelve years. Your horses will need to go through inspections from state to state. They'll be weary by the time they arrive and will need to rest. All of that eats into practice sessions. You get the picture."

"There's no other way, Tulllah. I think—"

I interrupted him. "Today is Saturday. If I can get a flight, expect me Tuesday or Wednesday. I will stay at your place for a few days. You will introduce me as Chenoa Waya, a feature writer from *Rodeo Times Illustrated*. Get excited. Hype it up. Tell anyone who will listen that I'm shadowing you to find out what it's like to be a big-time stockman, run a ranch, et cetera. And, since I'm shadowing you as a writer, I'll also attend the rodeo with my trusty camera."

Caleb loosed an audible sigh. "You're a genius, Tullah. As a reporter you'll have better access to behind the scenes, and the bulls."

"Something else, Caleb. You might want to get a

burner phone. With today's technology, you never know if your cellphone has been compromised. Any calls you make to me, do it outside and away from the house."

"I understand, Tullah, but what about Caroline?"

"Don't worry. She can take me on a scenic trip around town where I'll fill her in. Also, plan to show me around the ranch, and maybe put on a little bull-bucking expo to impress this notorious reporter."

"You got it! And thanks, Tullah. Maybe I'll sleep a little easier tonight."

As soon as we disconnected the call, I shot my dad a text asking him to check Sheriff O'Neal Coffey's history—dirty or clean. My next order of business was to open my laptop and create a murder file which I titled "8 Seconds to Die!"

Victims: Caleb, Caroline Calloway, and children.

Crime: Someone is injecting bucking bulls with a serum that makes them extra dangerous. Two riders seriously hurt.

Reason: currently unknown.

Suspects: 1) Sheriff O'Neal Coffey.

I took another look at the news article and searched for the paralyzed victim's name. Unfortunately, it stated that, due to her age, her name was being withheld. Not quite a dead end; however, I made a note to follow up. It pays never to rule anyone out when crime is happening.

River nudged me with his moist nose and whined. This was his signal it was time to call it a night. Rascal gave me one of his silly snuffling brays. My body was stiff when I stood. "Okay, guys, race you upstairs."

Chapter Four

I lay awake in the darkness for a while, thinking over my phone conversation with Caroline and asking myself if there was an ulterior motive behind Caleb's contacting my father. Something other than the cock-and-bull story about an unknown person or persons sabotaging his bulls. We had never been friends in high school, and I didn't completely buy his story about following my career in the newspapers. True, there had been several articles in the news mentioning my name as having helped my father with solving crimes; however, I don't recall any mention of my unique ability, which we deliberately avoid to keep the loonies from seeking me out. Another thought crossed my mind—I truly doubted articles about a veterinarian in small town Kentucky had reached newspapers in Tulsa, Oklahoma. Needless to say, this last thought revved up my suspicious mind.

Across the fields, and off in the distance, a dog began to bark—at the moon, at a racoon, at a wandering cat or another dog. Who knew? I never allowed River the privilege of a woofing episode just for the sake of barking. Somehow the noise was fodder for my thoughts.

I found myself wondering how Caleb himself had changed, especially having been responsible for the death of his two best friends, and a young woman's permanent disability. Was she angry with him? Thinking back and recalling the zebra stripes he and his flunky buddies had painted on my mare, I knew that had angered me well into my college years. In my psychology classes I'd tried to understand the teens and the convictions they'd had in order to commit such a malicious act. And then, as if fueled by their fervor, the boys had cornered me in the girls' locker room and called it a—joke.

Fury had overtaken my seventeen-year-old self to the point that I was ready to call upon *a-sgi-na*—the Cherokee word for demons—to perform vile acts of retribution on Caleb, Caroline, and their buddies. Later that night my mother had held me in her arms as I wept over my horse and my raggedy hair. She had whispered, "It is not the way of our people to call upon evil spirits, Tullah. No, my sweet child, there is no need for revenge. Just sit back and wait. Those who hurt you will eventually bring harm to themselves, and if you are lucky the Great Spirit Father will let you watch."

At that recollection of her words, my eyes fluttered shut, for just a second of sweet oblivion. My anger against Caleb and Caroline slid off my mind, replaced with a sensation of calm.

I sensed sleep approaching, felt it stealing over me. The word *karma* danced in my subconscious. I held on to the thought that, good or bad, everything we put out eventually comes back to us. Caleb and Caroline had created their own karma. I looked directly at the sleep I needed and allowed my desire for revenge to slide away. Grandmother always said, "People may forget…karma will not." She also said, "Do good things and good things will come back to you."

Apparently, it was pay-back time for the Calloways. But who was behind these acts of vengeance?

****

Grandmother's voice was crisp when she opened the door to her apartment and said, "Good morning. So, what's new, Granddaughter?"

With the exception of Dr. Paul Ritter, our favorite curmudgeon, the usual Sunday breakfast group was gathered around her small dining table.

Patty Sweet scowled. The heavy wrinkles in her face lifted as she raised her eyebrows. "After all these years, I can't believe that young scamp has the nerve to ask you for anything except forgiveness. I hope you told him to go…go…" Her face pinked. "Well, never mind. You get my drift."

I glanced from my dad to my grandmother. She was trying an ingratiating smile, but it was sliding off the side of her face. I merely poured myself a cup of coffee. Dr. Sunny Sanders occupied Doc Ritter's chair. Except he was no longer with us. Age and ill health had finally taken its toll. We'd laid him to rest shortly after Thanksgiving. I sat next to Sunny.

Grandmother said, "Caleb Calloway always was the poster boy for bad behavior. I guess that's what happens when you're an only child born with a silver spoon in your mouth and with permissive parents. What did you decide, Granddaughter?"

I decided to not let myself get sucked into the moment. I'd made peace with my feelings last night. "Grandmother, remember what you've always said about karma?" I simply smiled.

She nodded, and I grabbed a blueberry scone and slathered it with butter. Between chews, I said, "Karma is beating down Caleb's door. I'm just sorry that his children are also caught up in this awful mess."

She reached over and filled my plate with scrambled eggs, bacon, and another blueberry scone. "Henry, we've raised our girl right."

Sunny flashed us a puzzled look. "Will someone tell me what's going on?"

While I enjoyed my breakfast, Dad filled Sunny in on the details. His mouth was set in a grim line when he said, "In the long run, we had to euthanize Venus. We'll never know if the boys purposely used lead-based paint or not when they covered her in black stripes."

I envisioned the woefulness in Venus's gentle brown eyes, and almost lost my resolve to help Caleb. My mare had suffered terribly before the vet had figured out that she was suffering from acute toxicity caused by lead poisoning.

For a few minutes the small room became a symphony of silence played at the same time as the practice session of an orchestra of forks against plates. It was as if everyone was waiting for the big finale. I emptied my cup and rose to refill it. I held the pot forward. "Anyone else?"

Grandmother's sigh was jam-packed with exasperation. "Are you going to tell us your plans or keep us in suspense?"

Patty Sweet cleared her throat as she accepted my offer to replenish her cup.

Dad cocked an eyebrow. "Tell us your plans and I'll tell you what I found out about O'Neal Coffey."

He had me and knew it. "Fair enough."

I explained that I planned to disguise myself as a journalist for *Rodeo Times Illustrated*, and that I had purchased airline tickets to Tulsa. "Grandmother, can you use your influence to get me a set of realistic-looking credentials? I'm using the name Chenoa Waya." My grandmother let out a small gasp at the mention of her mother's name.

I also related the news articles I'd discovered about Caleb's imprisonment and the reason. "The news article didn't give the girl's name, only that she was underage and that her injuries caused permanent paralysis."

Excitement twinkled in my grandmother's eyes. In her early years she was one of Kentucky's best crime reporters. "I suppose you also want me to find out the girl's name, and any other information I consider important."

"Absolutely, and with discretion."

She pulled a pouty lip, then smiled. "I'm the epitome of discretion."

I continued. "Remember how Bonny Brom wore a wig to disguise himself as his twin sister?"

Everyone around the table nodded. Bonny Brom had fooled all of us until his psyche had crashed and burned, which allowed my dad to nail Bonny for several murders.

"Anyone know where I can get a wig with short black hair? And, Grandmother, I'm not sure how a journalist dresses. Any suggestions?"

She ticked off a list of items and finished by saying, "Wear makeup, and earrings, and those fancy boots stuck in the back of your closet, oh, and perfume. You'll also need a small notepad, pen, and a camera."

"Why can't I use my phone camera?"

"Because it's not professional, and a phone camera might not capture details that you won't know you're looking for until you view the photos on your laptop."

Sunny offered a bright smile. "I have a wig. It's a short blonde bob with bangs. Sort of Cleopatra-ish in drag."

"But I…"

Grandmother waylaid my objection. "Great idea, Sunny. Tullah, as a blonde, you won't be recognized by anyone. Not even Caleb or Caroline."

After a second or two of small talk, Dad's cellphone rang before I had the opportunity to remind him that it was his turn to share information. By the way he wrinkled his forehead as he listened, I surmised the call was serious.

While still talking, he shoved from his chair. He signed off the call with, "I'm on my way." At the door, he grabbed his brown felt Stetson and situated it on his head. "Sorry, folks, duty calls."

In an instant, my dad had switched from easy-going guy to sheriff in charge. "Tullah, you'd better call Ella and have her meet you at the Trohill Ranch." Then he directed his attention to Sunny. "There's been a shooting; both human and animal. Tiny and Andy are on the way to the ranch as we speak. Deputy Ramsey related that Mrs. Trohill already called 9-1-1."

I might add that Tiny Goodbody had been elevated from deputy to under-sheriff, with Andy Kemble moving into the senior deputy position, and the newest on the force is Deputy Wayne Ramsey.

Don't go getting any ideas about a romantic interlude between me and the new deputy. As much as grandmother would like to see me married and with child, Wayne Ramsey is happily married and the father of two teenagers. The Ramseys have settled quite nicely into Enigma. Marilyn Ramsey teaches math at Enigma High School, and the thirteen-year-old twins, Phoebe and Liam, are active in 4-H.

Grandmother's small apartment had become a hive of activity. Dad, Sunny, and I scurried in different directions to meet the emergency head-on.

****

A festive Sunday morning had faded into a tragic dark-thirty. It was just past three in the morning when I parked under the carport. River and Rascal sat on the top step waiting for me to open the kitchen door.

The moment I flipped on the light, I spotted a large white note propped against the salt and pepper shakers. The note briefly said that Grandmother had let Uncle Charlie know about the situation and he'd left barbeque sandwiches, potato salad, baked beans, and a liter of cola in the refrigerator, and there was enough for Ella too.

I opened the fridge and spotted Patty Sweet's traditional pink box; too tired to open it, I closed the door and trudged upstairs. It was rare for me to resist stuffing my mouth with any type of Patty's pastries. Tonight, was the exception.

Chapter Five

While the tub filled with hot water, I sent Ella a text telling her about the sandwiches and pastries. She answered immediately that with the stench of blood in her nostrils, and nonstop surgery on three horses that had been shot at close range, all she wanted was a bath and bed. I totally understood. At least we'd have food for tomorrow's lunch.

I scooted deep beneath the hot water, allowing it to cover my chin. The shooting had been a senseless, random act of viciousness that left elderly Mr. Trohill in the Intensive Care Unit, his prized Thoroughbred stallion and two yearling colts brutally injured. Sadly, the filly succumbed to her injuries. I could feel the trembles and weepies looming, and reminded myself that this too would pass.

My mind filled with "why" questions, all of which remained unanswered. A moment of intense anger engulfed me. I hoped this act of violence wasn't a prelude to Caleb's situation. I asked myself what could happen in Oklahoma that would make it any worse than today.

I should have known better than to ask myself such a question.

****

When the phone rang at the crack of dawn, Ella's was the last voice I expected to hear. I awoke groggy and tried to focus on the clock. It was seven, and time for me to get up and ready for work. I offered up a silent prayer that Jeff, our office assistant, hadn't overly filled the appointment book for the entire day.

"You sound the way I feel, Tullah." Ella sounded apologetic.

"After yesterday—" I blew out a *pfft*. Ella wasn't a chatterbox by nature. She never called unless it was important. "What's up?"

"I called Jeff and asked about today's schedule. It's mostly routine visits...nothing serious. You have a lot to do before leaving for Lexington tonight. Anything I can't handle I'll refer to Dr. Redfern. Okay with you?"

I scrubbed a hand over my face. "That takes a load off, Ella. I'll check in before I head out."

After disconnecting, I washed my face and brushed my teeth and then opened my closet to begin the daunting task of filtering through my wardrobe for professional clothes appropriate for a journalist. As an afterthought, I decided to check the weather in Oklahoma, and mentally patted myself on the back. Genius. In the end, I opted for black jeans, a couple of pullover sweaters, black dress slacks, a silk lilac shirt, my favorite gold earrings, diamond studs, a pair of almost new boots for mucking around stock pens, the fancy pair of boots that Grandmother had mentioned, a light jacket, and a heavier one in case the weather turned colder.

I searched for a new notepad, several ink pens, and rather than my laptop, I opted to stuff my new and less weighty tablet inside my briefcase, which would also double as my purse. The one thing missing was the blonde wig Dr. Sanders had offered to lend me. I shot her a quick text asking if I could pick it up on my way to the airport.

She answered immediately that she'd leave it at the hospital's reception desk. One more item off my to-do list. I phoned the airport and asked for the rental car department. While I waited to be connected, I debated over the type of car I should reserve—luxury or budget?

Caleb had volunteered Caroline to meet me at Tulsa International. I declined the offer, thinking that if I needed a quick escape from who knows what situation, I'd be without wheels. Also, I liked the element-of-surprise idea.

A pleasant voice interrupted my musing. "Good morning, A-One Car Rentals, how may I help you?"

"Yes, I'd like to reserve a black BMW Coupe to be pickup at Tulsa International, ETA tomorrow, approximately three o'clock." While she was checking, I asked myself *What part of your brain just farted...A BMW?*

"I'm sorry, all we have available is a silver minivan."

At my hesitation, she added, "It's new, and fully loaded."

A minivan wasn't my idea of arriving in style, but it was certainly more suitable to my budget. The dollar gods were with me. "Thank you, I'll take it." And related all the information pertinent to reserving the vehicle.

I'd no sooner hung up than my cellphone chimed. Grandmother's picture popped up on my caller ID. "You're up early, Grandmother."

She chortled. "When you get to be my age, you'll need less sleep. Besides, I wanted to get this information to you before you leave for Tulsa."

"Okay, shoot."

"The girl in the article, you know, the girl paralyzed in the accident?"

"Yep, you found out her name?"

"I did, and more. Ready for this?"

My brain was screaming for a cup of coffee. Instead, I sat on the edge of the bed with pen in hand. "Fire away."

"Her name is Pamela Dorsey. She was fifteen on the night of the accident. According to my source, the only reason Pamela survived the accident was because she was stoned out of her head, which made her limp as a dishrag when the car crashed through the overpass guard rail and landed on top of a moving train. The rear-seat passengers were thrown from the vehicle and apparently died on impact; one boy landed on the tracks. Of course, the train couldn't stop. My source said he covered the accident, and to quote him, 'It was a bloody mess.' The boy's parents ordered a closed casket funeral."

"Did the parents file for a lawsuit?"

"Absolutely, for several million dollars. My source said there was an out-of-court settlement for an undisclosed amount."

I drew my eyebrows into a frown. "What about Pamela Dorsey?"

"Patience, Granddaughter. I'm getting to her," Grandmother chided. "This young lady's father was the sheriff. Apparently, he wasn't happy with the jury's decision to let Caleb off with a lesser prison sentence and accused the judge and members of the jury of being bought off by Caleb's father. Rumor has it that Sheriff Dorsey was forced to resign when he threatened to kill Caleb."

I heard Grandmother expel a breath before she

continued. "Apparently, Pamela wasn't exactly a poster child for the Girl Scouts. She miscarried in the hospital and claimed that Caleb was the father. Naturally, he denied it and refused to take a DNA test. However, my friend said an anonymous donor paid for all of Pamela's medical bills, physical therapy, electric wheelchair, and—although there is no proof, just rumor, mind you— a monthly stipend is deposited in a special account in Pamela's name; the benefactor remains unknown. Hmm!"

"Interesting, Grandmother." I did a quick calculation. "The accident happened twelve years ago. That would make Pamela twenty-seven. The secret benefactor is an interesting aspect. Could Caleb be that person, or his father?"

"Here's another interesting fact, Tullah. Caleb's father was gored to death by one of his own bulls."

"Wow! The plot thickens. Accident or otherwise?"

"Don't know, and neither does my friend. The sheriff, the one you've asked Henry to investigate, and the coroner both ruled it an accident."

"Who is your friend, Grandmother? I may need to contact him."

"Sorry, Granddaughter, you know I love you dearly and trust you with my life. However, a reporter always protects her sources."

I wasn't offended by my grandmother's refusal. In fact, I greatly admired her loyalty. "Anything else, Grandmother?"

"Nothing, except that Henry is driving Patty, Joyce, Flora, and me to the Lexington airport to catch our flight to New York. I wish you were going on the cruise with us. Anyhow, there's no need for you to drive when we're going to the same airport. Our flight to JFK airport departs at seven tonight."

I didn't need to be asked twice. I had already planned to spend the night at the airport hotel to catch my Tuesday morning flight to Oklahoma City. "Great. I do need a favor. Before leaving, we need to detour by the hospital to pick up the wig that Sunny is lending me."

"You needn't ask twice, Granddaughter."

"Thanks for getting Pamela Dorsey's name for me, and the other inside scoop."

She loved it when I used reporter terminology, and chuckled. "You are my favorite granddaughter, after all."

It was my turn to laugh. "Since I'm your *only* granddaughter, I'll take that as a compliment."

In a more serious tone, she added, "There's no need to drive to town. We'll arrive at your house around one o'clock."

"I'll be ready," I answered firmly.

I finished packing and hustled to the kitchen. I pushed the button on the coffeemaker and while it gurgled away, filling the kitchen with delicious aroma, I loaded River and Rascal's bowls with food and water. It was comforting to know that Ella would take care of all the feedings until I returned from my trip.

River's happy yaps drew me to the kitchen window. I spotted Jeff parking in his usual spot. Ella rapped on the kitchen door. She opened it with a cheery, "G'morning! All ready for your adventure?"

While I filled another cup with coffee, I pointed to the pink box filled with donuts. "Actually, no."

Ella selected a chocolate éclair. "Why not?"

"I can't quite explain it, but something about this whole scenario doesn't ring true. I feel like I'm being used. For what purpose, I don't know."

Ella shoved the box toward me and grinned. "As your friend, your partner, and a doctor, albeit for animals, I prescribe that you eat two of these delicious pastries, and do what you always do. Solve the case, then get the hell out of Oklahoma."

She licked the chocolate off her fingers, followed by a generous sip of coffee. "Seriously, Tullah. Be careful. Maybe Andy could go with you, as your assistant, just in case…well…you know…just because."

I grabbed the two bags of barbeque ribs from the fridge and handed them to Ella. "You and Jeff enjoy these, and don't worry, I won't take any unnecessary chances. Besides, my plans are to return on Friday."

I walked with her to the clinic. She handed the box of remaining pastries to our office assistant. "We've had ours, Jeff. The rest is yours to enjoy."

We spent a few minutes chit-chatting about the day's appointments, and about what I expected to learn from my visit to Caleb's ranch. I excused myself and strolled to the closet we use to store our pharmaceuticals. There I collected a small toxicology kit we used specifically to test for poisons in both equine and bovine. It would fit neatly in my carry-on case.

To pass the time while I waited for Dad to arrive, I opened my tablet to the file I had created on the laptop and transferred, then recorded the notes about the accident. I noted the following:

Caleb Calloway: charged with vehicular manslaughter.

Adjudication: Sentenced to five years; served three, released for good behavior.

Victim one: Pamela Dorsey, age fifteen,

permanently paralyzed from waist down. Miscarried in the hospital; claimed Caleb was the father, which he denied. Note: why would she lie?

Victim two: Howard 'Howie' Stanford, age nineteen, DOA; best friend to Caleb.

Victim three: Racine 'Race' Worthington, age twenty, DOA; best friend to Caleb.

Other: Lawsuit in the millions; paid in full; ongoing donations to Pamela Dorsey.

Death is never easy. However, I felt no remorse for Howie and Race. Having known them throughout my high school years, I was aware the status of their families seemed to have given them the right to bully kids considered "less thans."

Anger splintered through me as I recalled the vision of cradling my gentle mare's head in my lap, and listening to the death rattles caused by lead poisoning. The decision to allow the vet to put Venus to sleep was heart-wrenching.

River and Rascal roused from my feet and scampered out of the room. I was so engrossed in typing my narrative the intense flapping of the doggy door startled me. And then…a knock. Absurd, but the sound sent alarms racing through my bloodstream.

Dad entered the living room. "All set, Punkin?"

I shut down my tablet, set it into the briefcase, and nodded as he grabbed my small suitcase and wheeled it outside. An intensity gripped my insides when River *woofed* and jumped against the oak tree's trunk. I glanced upward. Seated on a limb was a great barred owl. Not just any barred owl, but the one that shows up as an omen. I touched my dad's arm and pointed. "He's here for a reason, Dad."

Dad gave me a sidelong glance. "Why do you think it's here?"

I watched the owl ruffle its feathers and stare at me with yellowish eyes. "Whatever it is, it can't be good."

Dad scowled as he opened the 4Runner's door. I greeted my grandmother and her friends. "All ready to set sail?"

Chapter Six

Grandmother reached over the seat to hand me a small package that contained a blonde Dutch-boy-style wig and another envelope that held a lanyard ID holder with credentials identifying me as Chenoa Waya, feature writer with *Rodeo Times Illustrated*.

While my grandmother and her friends chittered away about their upcoming adventures, I stewed about the owl and why it had visited. Dad concentrated on his driving with an occasional comment about the traffic and "where's a cop when you need one."

After Dad and I assisted Grandmother and her friends through airport check-in and security, my dad insisted, for their comfort, on hailing a tram to transport us to the boarding gate. With a little time to spare before venturing off to New York, and then a month-long cruise to Amsterdam and other exciting ports, Grandmother insisted we celebrate their adventure with a cocktail. Dad opted for a beer while the rest of us enjoyed pina coladas. I think we purposely avoided talking about the owl and what its appearance might mean to my visiting Caleb and Caroline. Instead, we chit-chatted about souvenirs and windmills and the Eiffel Tower, and ended with me admonishing my audacious grandmother and her equally adventurous friends to be cautious and to stay with their tour groups rather than venturing off on their own. I've known Patty, Flora, and Joyce my entire life. They are like family to me, and I felt very protective of them.

As soon as their flight was announced, including the message that all passengers were to proceed to their boarding gates, we ended our visit with hugs, well-wishes, and assurances that Dad and I would be at the airport when they returned home.

Dad and I stayed and watched until the plane taxied down the runway and lifted off. Dad said, "I don't know about you, Punkin, but my breakfast is long gone. How about I treat you to an early supper?"

We caught a shuttle to the airport hotel. I had already completed an early check-in via computer, and my room key was waiting at the courtesy desk. We made our way to the food court and settled on a seafood restaurant.

Once seated and waiting for our food to arrive, Dad glanced around the crowded room as if scoping out the space. He leaned forward, but hesitated when the waiter arrived with large mugs of coffee and a courtesy basket of garlicky cheese biscuits. Once the waiter left us, Dad said, "Tanti filled me in about Pamela Dorsey and the boys that died in the accident." He drew from his mug. I waited. He pulled an envelope from a jacket pocket and handed it to me. I unfolded the paper and spied the name O'Neal Coffey.

"Without me reading through all of this right now, how 'bout giving me the quick version?"

Dad took another sip of coffee. "It appears Sheriff Coffey operates on the shady side of the law, but not so shady as to be convicted of any wrongdoings. He has been admonished several times for excessive force when apprehending a suspect. On a couple of occasions, victims have claimed he didn't mirandize them."

I *pffted*. "I suppose he accused them of lying."

"Yup. And, he's been cited for failure to intervene when his deputies have used unnecessary force in breaking up a barroom brawl."

I glanced through the multiple-page report and was aghast when I read that Coffey had been forced to resign from his post in California on charges of sexual harassment, but was then hired in Wisconsin. "It seems the list goes on. I'm shocked this guy hasn't been banned permanently from wearing a badge."

"I agree, and whatever he's into in Oklahoma has got Caleb running scared. Watch your back, Punkin."

I sipped my coffee while I digested this information. I also needed to rid myself of a particular aggravation. Don't get me wrong, I love and respect my father. I also know that he'd give his life to protect me if push ever came to shove. "Dad…"

When I didn't continue, he waited before saying, "I know that look on your face. Whatever's eatin' at you, spit it out."

I heaved a deep sigh. "You know, I love and respect you, but Dad, my gift or curse is not for sale. I don't conjure up on a whim these spirit animals that contact me. They seek me out for a purpose."

I held up my hand to halt whatever he was about to say. "How did Caleb know about this special thing I have? He claims to have read about me helping you solve cases in the newspapers. I don't buy that. The cases I've helped you solve weren't exactly headlines for national news. I can't see Oklahoma media outlets printing stories about small-town Enigma, Kentucky. He also said you told him about me." I shrugged a shoulder. "The jury is still out on whether or not I believe him."

The waiter arrived with our seafood platters and

more garlicky biscuits. A young waitress arrived and replenished our coffee.

I lowered my eyes to avoid the hurt in Dad's expression. He reached to take both my hands. There was a huskiness in his voice. "I'm sorry, Punkin. I would never deliberately betray you." He heaved a sigh. "I'm afraid I've put you in a position where you felt you couldn't say no to Caleb. I was wrong."

He pulled his cellphone from his jacket pocket. "I'll call Caleb and tell him he'll need to rely on local law enforcement to help him."

"It's too late, Dad. The owl has appeared, and last night I heard a wolf's howl." I tried to suppress a shudder. It didn't work. "I don't know if it's a warning for my safety or for Caleb. Either way, I need to see this through. Let's just say that this is a *fishing* trip."

He knew I meant that this time around I was merely scoping out the situation and setting the scene for when I appeared at the upcoming rodeo as a feature writer.

He nodded grimly. "There are no wolves in Kentucky."

I shrugged to show my consternation. "And none in Oklahoma. I wish I knew what it all means." Again, a chill rippled through me.

"Perhaps I should go with you. I'll call Tiny and let him know not to expect me for a couple of days."

I plucked a bite of lobster from its shell, dipped it in butter, and savored it's luciousness. "The only reason I'm not backing away from this case is not for Caleb or Caroline but for their children. It takes a cold-hearted SOB to kill a pet goat and leave the bloodied head on the doorstep as a warning that the children are in danger."

As always, the differences between Dad and me

quickly melted away. We enjoyed the rest of our meal. While satisfying our sweet tooths with a shared serving of tiramisu and more coffee, we tossed questions back and forth—the who, the why—for personal gain or revenge?

I assured my dad that I would be extra careful. "You'd better get on the road, Dad. It'll be late when you get home. And thanks for the offer to stay with me."

"You're just so damned determined you are invincible that you can't bear anything that suggests you are weak." He smiled and stroked my cheek. "Just like your mother and Tanti."

I offered him a cockeyed smile. "Blame it on DNA; you know a mixture of Cherokee and Irish is a powerful combination of stubborn genetics."

He added a little cheer to his voice. "You may not be a cop, but you are a good detective, and I'm damned proud to be your father."

He stood and was thoughtful for a moment. "It'll be dark-thirty by the time I get back to Enigma." Before leaving he promised to meet me on my return date.

I watched him walk out. I checked my watch. It was about seven fifteen when I entered the elevator to my room.

Once inside, I slid the security lock in place, set my bags on the bed, and headed for the bathroom. After I'd relieved myself, I unzipped my briefcase and removed the envelope that held the wig, and a mesh cap. Thankfully, the wig came with a set of instructions. I returned to the bathroom. As I looked in the mirror, I wondered how I was ever going to stuff my thick and nearly waist-length hair under the wig and have it look natural. Worst case scenario, it might slide right off my head.

I followed the instructions by smoothing my hair and pinning it around my head, then I placed the mesh cap over it. Just as I suspected—too much hair. The mesh net popped off my head. I fished around in my briefcase for a pair of scissors. The thought of cutting my locks was like a death sentence. However, I gathered the length and snipped, allowing the strands to cascade around my shoulders. I've faced rabid dogs, rattlesnakes, dangerous bulls and horses, and all without as much distress as I felt cutting my hair. My hand actually trembled.

I returned to the room and opened my carry-on to remove my makeup bag and withdrew a mirror. Returning to the bathroom, I held the mirror and looked at my shorn locks which were now just above my shoulder blades. Once again I smoothed my hair and pinned it. This time the mesh cap fit firmly in place. Pulling the wig over my head as shown on the instruction sheet and adjusting it, I was amazed at the image that stared back at me. The blonde hair looked real, and I almost didn't recognize myself.

I spent the remainder of the evening wearing the wig, and swiveling my head in different directions, as well as doing a few minor aerobic moves—heaven forbid the wig fall off and blow my cover.

As if performing a ritual, I gently placed the severed black strands inside a plastic bag and laid them to rest beneath the clothes I'd packed. In the Cherokee culture, the women wear their hair long and only cut it when mourning the death of a family member. It had been nearly thirteen years since I'd last cut my hair, and that was when we'd buried my mother.

After completing my nighttime ritual of a bath and

drying my hair, I left a request for a morning wake-up call and settled in bed with a copy of my newest mystery novel, *Murder in the Mist*. It wasn't long before sleep shuttered my eyes. I prayed for a dreamless night because I didn't relish any spiritual visits foretelling about tomorrow.

Chapter Seven

I didn't realize how heavy my hair was until I climbed out of bed. My head felt light and airy as I slicked back my newly shorn locks and pinned them in place as smoothly as I could, then set the mesh cap and the wig in place. After carefully applying makeup, with an extra layer of lipstick, I dressed in a pair of black slacks and a black pullover sweater, which I adorned with an owl pendant on a gold chain and gold studs for my ears. I pulled on my new black boots, and as if hearing Grandmother whisper in my ear, dabbed on perfume.

"You look good," I told the blonde image in the mirror. "Pretty damn good."

I collected my luggage and left the room. After leaving the checkout desk, I double-checked my flight and hustled to catch the tram to the airport. I'm not crazy about flying. I'm the type that likes to know that when I stand up I have solid ground beneath my feet.

By the time I arrived, a line had already formed at the boarding gate. Once aboard, I stowed my carry-on, then settled in my assigned seat and opened to the page of my mystery novel.

In moments, a flight attendant announced that we should buckle up, and due to the short hour-and-a-half flight, only beverages would be served. I opted for coffee.

Once we landed, and after a satisfying breakfast and several more cups of coffee, I phoned the rental car company and asked them to deliver the minivan to the front entrance. A blast of cold air greeted me as I exited the airport and rushed toward the silver vehicle. I thanked the valet and handed him a generous tip.

Once inside the warm interior, I set my phone in the phone dock, then programmed the GPS with Caleb's address. After navigating through the airport parking lot and onto the highway, I asked Google to dial the Calloway's house phone.

"Triple C Ranch, Caroline speaking."

I checked myself before using my real name. Instead, I said, "Caroline, it's me...Chenoa Waya from *Rodeo Times Magazine.*"

I was met with hesitation. Then she said, "Oh, yes, of course, I remember. We hope you're still coming to do the...ah...the expo on my husband."

Good girl, I thought. "I'm just leaving the airport and expect to arrive at the ranch in about an hour." I chuckled. "That is if the GPS doesn't steer me to places unknown."

"Oh, Ms. Waya, when you pass through the little town of"—her nearly inaudible whisper left me thinking that I'd missed the name—"please observe the speed limit." It sounded like Caroline had placed her hand over the receiver as if she didn't want anyone to hear her next words. "The deputies are always on the lookout for out-of-town tags. Cletus Dodge is the worst of the bunch. Don't drive too fast or too slowly, if you catch my meaning."

"Thanks for the warning."

Her voice perked up a bit. "We're looking forward

to seeing you. Truly."

I drew a deep breath and tried to be equally as gracious.

We said our goodbyes and I disconnected the phone. Maybe the *truly* was Caroline's attempt to soften the edges of what had happened so many years ago. On the spur of the moment, I asked Google to dial my dad's number.

"What's up, Punkin?"

"Just wanted to let you know I'm on my way. I've talked to Caroline, and Dad, she warned me that Sheriff Coffey's territory is a speed trap, and that one deputy especially, a Cletus Dodge, is someone not to mess with."

"Did she elaborate?"

"No, sir."

"Cletus Dodge? Okay, I'll check him out, and Punkin, I'm sorry I got you into this mess. I should be there to watch your back."

It took all my effort not to give in and ask him to join me. Although my dad was college educated, he never wore an air of academia around him. He'd served in the military, fought in a couple of wars, received the medal of valor, and I knew he wanted to build a fort around me. I'd resisted him at every turn to become my own defender, yet he was my...superhero.

"Don't worry, Dad. Today's Wednesday. I'll take a bunch of photos of Caleb's bulls and other livestock, attend whatever social he and Caroline have planned; I'll play my part as a journalist, then plan to arrive at the Lexington Airport on Saturday."

I checked my speed limit, then pressed the gas pedal to move along the stretch of highway ahead of me.

"I'll be at the airport to meet you. And, Punkin..." His voice drifted off.

I smiled. "Yeah, Dad, I love you, too."

I drove through a stretch of desolate highway. A sign signaled that I was nearing the town of Ada. I kept my eyes alert for possible places where a deputy might park unnoticed, and I checked my speed.

I drove through the heart of the town, cruising through the single traffic light with ease. Like my town of Enigma, Ada was flat and unimpressive to a visitor. In a matter of seconds, Ada's main street was a reflection in my rental car's rearview mirror. According to the GPS, the Triple C Ranch was only a few miles away.

In a few minutes, I spotted the arched entrance with a large metal sign, featuring a bull on each side, identifying C & C Calloway as proprietors. The drive to the house seemed longer than my trip through the town. A white split-rail fence adorned each side of the paved road. Patches of green grass peeked through large swatches of brown thatch; an announcement that Spring was on its way. The Calloways' driveway curved up to an impressive two-story, log-cabin-style ranch house, complete with a wraparound deck, and an elevated landing with steps leading to what I assumed was guest quarters.

I had barely exited the minivan when a door opened and Caroline's windchime laughter greeted me. "Ms. Waya, I presume?" She skipped toward me with hands extended. "Welcome to our humble abode."

And then she leaned in close and whispered, "It is you?"

I supposed my blonde wig had cast a moment of doubt. I managed to nod. It was as if twelve years had melted away. Time had been good to Caroline. I returned her smile. "Yes, the trip was effortless." I glanced around. Caleb was nowhere in sight.

None of the earlier distress was in Caroline's voice, and I was amazed at the artfulness of my old nemesis' clarity. The scene inside the locker room of my senior year came back to me. Without much thought, I accepted her hand. Her blue eyes shimmered with tears.

"It's nice to meet you Mrs. Calloway. Is Mr. Calloway here?"

"We didn't exactly know when to expect you. I shot Caleb a text the moment I spotted the dust from your car." Her pouty little lip, the one I remembered so well, popped out followed by a self-deprecating laugh.

She had used that particular wile on most of the male teachers, including the principal, and it had worked. But I wasn't here to investigate Caroline's manipulation techniques. I was totally unprepared when a man emerged from the barn and trotted toward us. His hand shot out to grab mine, and pumped it up and down with vigor. He leaned close and whispered, "Thank goodness you're here."

And then he sobered, a grin barely lighting his face. His voice was soft. "Come inside. We have refreshments ready. I hope you like coffee, and Caroline requested that Sofia make a special coffee cake to welcome you."

There was a courtliness to Caleb that barely covered the true nature of the boy I knew in high school—a bottom feeder.

But from my quick observation of the ranch, a bottom feeder with a lot of dollar signs behind his name. I allowed him to cup my elbow and lead me up the steps to the house. Once inside, he guided me toward a stone fireplace dominating the living room. Caroline excused herself, saying she needed to speak with the kitchen staff and promising to return with refreshments.

I seated myself and watched Caleb remove his hat. Although he was a year older than me, his salt-and-pepper hair was impeccably trimmed to perfection, albeit thinning. A closer look at his handsome features revealed a haggardness, crow's feet evident at the corners of his brown eyes, which held an iciness. Their clarity was tempered by a hint of speculation, but their acuity had not suffered. He stood with a boot propped on the fireplace hearth and watched me carefully.

I was about to speak when a ranch hand walked in with my briefcase and wheeled suitcase. "Boss, where should I put the reporter's luggage?"

Caleb instructed the man to place my belongings in Suite A, and then he glanced at his watch—a Rolex, I guessed. I also didn't fail to notice the large diamond inserted in his wedding band. I noted the time on a wall clock—noon, straight up and down.

Caleb said, "Ms. Waya, are you up for a tour of the ranch grounds? I'd like to show off my bulls."

Caroline breezed in and a young maid followed with a silver salver. "There's plenty of time to show off your pride and joys, Caleb. Let Tu...ahm, Ms. Waya, catch her breath, for goodness' sake. Besides, you haven't even asked if she rides horses?" Caroline looked at me. "If not, we have a Mule UTV."

It almost felt as if she were challenging me. "I'd very much enjoy a tour, and horseback would be a treat. However, I'd like to change into more suitable clothes, and I'll need my camera."

Caleb shifted his position from the fireplace to a

large wing-backed chair. "Give us an hour and a half, Rex, and then bring the horses to the house. Saddle Dakota for Ms. Waya."

The ranch hand responded with a nod. He tipped his hat toward me. "Enjoy your stay, ma'am. Dakota is a bit feisty, but once he settles, he'll do you good."

"Thank you, Rex."

Without warning, the hairs on the back of my neck prickled.

Caroline motioned to the maid to fill the coffee cups. The sloe-eyed girl glanced at Caleb before lifting the lid to the cake server. I wondered if Caroline had also noticed the sly peek. Note to self: Perhaps Caroline is the perpetrator. After all, jealousy is a powerful motive for revenge. Another thought, if she is the guilty party, then why involve me?

Chapter Eight

My head itched and I yearned to snatch off the blonde wig. It was with great relief that I followed Caroline through an elevated, glass-paned alcove that led outside and to a series of guest rooms. "Here we are, Tullah. You're in the first room, what we call Suite A."

She opened the door and I followed her into a luxurious suite fit for royalty. My briefcase sat on top of the bed with the suitcase at the end. It occurred to me that the children hadn't appeared. "Are the children in school?"

Caroline opened a sliding door that led to a large deck, allowing a cool breeze to refresh the room's stale air. "Under the circumstances, we felt it best to send Maddie, Breck, and Caleb's mother to Florida. Marianne's sister lives in Arcadia."

"What about school?"

"Home-schooled. Have you forgotten that Caleb's *real* mother was a teacher?"

I suppose the puzzled look on my face prompted her to say, "His parents were divorced when we lived in Enigma."

Caroline lifted her shoulders and sighed. "Sonya, his second wife, and Clarise, his third wife, are no longer in the picture. And good riddance."

I'm not sure I ever knew that piece of information about Caleb's birth mother. I did, however, remember

Sonya, a Bridget Bardot look-alike. The boys on the football team went all googly-eyed when she'd come to watch football practice. "No longer in the picture—what happened?"

"Divorce. You know…the usual…rich, older man." Anger flashed in Caroline's eyes so quickly I almost missed it. She continued, "Carl doted on the bitch. Called her his honey-bunny. I can truly say that Sonya loved money, men, and bonking." Caroline winked. "Get my drift?"

"Uh-huh, she loved sex and didn't care with whom or when." I wondered about the third wife, but decided not to ask. I dismissed the idea of asking if she'd ever suspected Caleb of being involved with one of his young stepmothers.

Caroline interrupted my musing. She said, "The end suite is where Marianne lives. When Carl died, Caleb insisted his mother move to Oklahoma. However, she didn't want to live in the house. She said she'd lived alone for so many years she wanted to keep hold of a little independence—even with her arthritis. Below us is a heated pool complete with hot tub, which helps with her mobility. We call it our party room. Caleb does love his toys."

I totally understood about the independence thing. "My grandmother is nearing eighty, and she enjoys her freedom, too."

Caroline shrugged as if dismissing my comment. She pointed to a telephone. "If you need anything, Sofia's number is one-one-five." Before leaving, she said, "Meet us downstairs when you're ready."

I locked the door as soon as she departed, and then rushed to the bathroom. I snatched off the wig, and scratched through my thick mop of hair. Thoughts about new and possible suspects cluttered my mind. I resisted the urge to open my tablet. There wasn't enough time to make notes in my murder file.

The clatter of hooves on cement and the accompanying whinnies led me to the room's rear deck where I spotted Rex leading three saddled horses from a large barn. It didn't take long to figure out which horse I would ride. Dakota was a long-legged sorrel with a golden mane and tail. He pranced like he had springboards in his front feet.

After a last look in the mirror to make sure my wig was in place, I hefted into my jacket and slung the camera strap across my shoulder.

Once downstairs, I followed Caleb and Caroline outside and to where Rex held the horses. He looked embarrassed. To set him at ease, I said, "Don't worry, I'm not exactly green when it comes to riding."

He nodded, handed me the reins, and asked if I needed a boost. "He's got a hard mouth, ma'am, and he hasn't been worked in a while, if you catch my drift."

Rex held the cheek strap while I swung into the saddle. "Thanks for the warning. I'll be okay."

As soon as the sorrel tried to walk off, I checked him by applying pressure with my legs rather than pulling on the reins. This time he hunched and I knew he was going to buck. I pulled the horse's head around so that his nose almost touched my boot, then forced him into a circle before easing up on the reins. The sorrel quivered while I rubbed his neck and spoke to him in Cherokee. He still had plenty of pent-up energy, but he understood that I would tolerate no foolishness.

I tried not to scorch Caleb with a scowl when I said,

"What's the deal, Mr. Calloway? I thought I was here to take pictures of your bulls, your ranch, and to interview you—not prove my horsemanship skills."

Rex had turned in the direction of the barn. Still Caleb kept his voice low; the grin on his face reminded me of the same Cheshire cat grin he'd worn when standing over me in the gym with a paint brush. "It's a joke, Tullah." He guffawed. "Still can't take a joke?"

"Joke! You and your buddies' *joke* caused the pain and suffering of an innocent animal that never hurt you or anyone else. My mare died of lead poisoning, Caleb. And you call that a joke!"

Years of pent-up anger thrummed inside my head. "Obviously, coming here was a mistake." I dismounted, tossed the reins to Caroline, and hot-footed it toward the house.

Caleb promptly spurred his black gelding to block my path. "I'm sorry, Tullah. Truly."

Caroline had followed. "Please, Tullah." She skewered her husband with a glare that implied, *If looks could kill, you'd be dead.*

A hard edge tempered her voice. "Grow up, Caleb. this isn't high school. You're still on probation, remember?" She held the sorrel's reins toward me. "I don't blame you for being angry, Tullah. Sometimes Caleb is like two different people. Prison changed him." She added, "We really do need your help."

Caleb made no effort to admonish his wife.

An awkward silence fell, so heavy that it felt like I'd committed some kind of heinous social blunder. Caleb's face reddened, and Caroline's lips formed a tight line. We all stared at each other. The sorrel pranced around, flattened its ears, and tried to nip Caroline's palomino. I snatched the reins from Caroline's hand and swung into the saddle. I cut Caleb a sharp look, my voice hard, "Any hint of you pulling another one of your *jokes* and you're on your own. Whatever happens to you, your bulls, and the riders that draw them, is on you then. Got it?"

My simple logic seemed to stun Caleb. He blinked his eyes and nodded his head in agreement.

I extended my hand and motioned for him to lead the way. "A word of caution: if you continue calling me Tullah, you'll blow my cover and rouse unnecessary curiosity. Especially if one of your employees is out to get you."

The chill in the air wasn't completely weather related. As we gigged the horses into a canter, I noticed Rex standing at the barn's door. He had witnessed the entire episode. An ugly light crinkled at the edges of his eyes as we rode past. I wondered if he was watching to see if the fractious horse had tossed me from the saddle, and if was he another person of interest to add to my growing list of possible suspects.

We rode for the better part of ten minutes in silence. I clicked several pictures of the scenery.

"Tell me about your father's accident, Caleb. I understand he was gored to death by a bull."

"Yeah, about this time last year. As a matter of fact, it happened here."

We had approached a barn with an outside corral constructed of metal piping. Bulls are sometimes notorious for ramming fences. The metal pipes ensure the bulls can't break through the fence and escape, especially during breeding season. We dismounted and tied the horses. Caroline and I followed Caleb inside the stone barn. High brick walls separated the pens to keep the bulls from making contact with each other. I took more photos.

The aroma of fresh hay tickled my nose. From past experience, I knew sport animals are treated with the upmost care and accommodations. Some people are misled about the treatment of rodeo stock, or even thoroughbred race horses. Dedicated stock contractors make sure their animals are well taken care of and kept as healthy and comfortable as possible. I personally have recommended chiropractic treatment for a couple of prize thoroughbreds.

Several of the pens held bulls of various breeds, eating slowly and contentedly. A gray Brahma bull, the tips of its horns blunted, lifted his head and seemed to study me, not looking very dangerous, all slack-mouthed and benign.

"Doesn't look too mean, does he?"

I responded to Caleb's comment. "Not at all. But the look in his eyes tells a different story."

Caleb leaned against the metal gate. The Brahma ambled over. Caleb said, "This is Jackknife, one of the favorite draws by riders. Ol' Jack is gentle as a lamb until he gets inside the chute, and when the gate opens, he's all business, a real bucking machine."

I snapped more shots of the bulls as we moved on, with Caleb pointing out names and traits of each bull.

We stopped at another pen. "This is Do 'em In, another favorite among the riders."

I recognized the crossbreed of the muscled bull—a mix of Charolais and Brahma. "Does he live up to his name?"

"Better believe it. Once he's tossed his rider, the rodeo clowns and the pick-up riders rush in because

Do'em is a real cowboy stomper. He's sent more than one feller to the hospital."

A loud metal-on-metal clang vibrated through the barn. Caroline jumped as if she'd been shot. She grasped her husband's arm. "Caleb, are you sure he can't get out?"

I raised my camera and focused on the rambunctious black bull a little farther on.

"Don't worry, Babe. We've reinforced his pen with stouter pipes and heavier bolts."

Seemingly not reassured, Caroline gripped Caleb's arm while casting a dubious look toward me. "That's Diablo, Tullah…I mean…Ms. Waya. He's a killer. What he did to Caleb's father was…" Her voice trailed off as she grimaced.

We came to stand in front of a pen where a black bull with a wicked set of horns was pawing the ground with his forefeet, sending dirt and straw flying over his broad back. At the sight of us, the bull lowered his head and horned the ground. This animal was clearly telling us he wasn't one to be messed with.

I looked at Caleb. "Spanish fighting bull mixed with Brahma?"

Caleb simply nodded. "True to his breed, Diablo is the meanest and most dangerous bull on the ranch, and possibly on the entire rodeo circuit."

"Then why do you keep him, especially if he broke out of his pen?"

Caleb stared at the bull for a while. "Breeding purposes. It's my goal to perfect the Bramhan breed. Bodacious was the best bucker in the world. I'm shooting for having the best bucking stock in the world. I want a breed that's highly aggressive and a challenge to ride. I want another Bodacious."

I knew from my experience as a veterinarian that some bulls are bred to buck while others are bred to fight, and that it takes years of genetic mixing to get the perfect bucking bull temperament.

"But Caleb, Bodacious had to be retired because he became a killer. And if Diablo killed your father…I don't understand your reasoning." I shuddered at the thought.

"Money. M.O.N.E.Y."

Caleb looked startled at his wife's harsh emphasis on money, then narrowed his eyes and slowly nodded. "You bet, Caroline. What do you think keeps you in those fancy cars you drive, the roof over your head, the parties you like to throw, a housekeeper, a personal chef, huh?"

As if the loud voices had agitated the already agitated beast, Diablo emitted an earsplitting bellow and rammed the gate. He reared as if trying to climb over the six-foot-high enclosure. The muscles across my back and shoulders tightened. A stab of fear ran the length of my stomach and, for one scary second, I looked around for an escape route.

Two men raced into the barn. One grabbed a shovel and whacked the long handle across the bull's muzzle. "Hiya…hiya," both men yelled.

Snorts and bellows followed from the other bovine. I envisioned a wrecking ball effect from the massive shoulders of angry bulls as they each forced their two thousand pounds of sheer muscle against their enclosures.

It took several hard strikes before Diablo backed off. He backed off, but widened his stance and glared at us. The taller cowboy said, "We'll calm 'im down, Boss.

Better take the ladies and get out of here."

Caleb thanked the men for coming to our rescue, and we made a quick exit. Once outside, and in a tremor-laced voice, Caroline said, "I don't know about you, Tullah, but I need something stronger than coffee to settle my nerves."

Caleb said, "Yeah, I think we can forego the tour of the ranch until another time. Okay with you, ah..." He shot me a look that indicated he couldn't remember what to call me, for a moment. "Ms. Waya?"

I gathered the reins and settled in the saddle. The wind had kicked up and turned downright cold. I suppressed a shiver, and deep inside my spirit, I knew something bad was about to happen. "Sure, make mine a warm Bailey's Irish Cream." I added, "Caleb, I need to know exactly what happened to your father."

Chapter Nine

Once we were settled in the formal parlor with our drinks, I urged Caleb to relate the circumstances of his father's death. I watched the expression on his face, and for once there was genuine sorrow in his eyes.

Caleb rolled his glass between his hands. He took a moment to savor his whiskey sour before recounting the incident. "Tullah, believe me when I say that I hope to be a better father to my children than I was a son to my Pop." He heaved a sigh, stood, and stepped to the fireplace. "It was a year ago, on a Friday night, about ten o'clock. Pop said he was still wound up after the rodeo. Our bulls had done really well, especially Diablo, who was the super star outshining all the other stockmen's bulls. As you know, bulls are judged just like riders. All four judges scored Diablo with perfect twenty-fives. In fact, Diablo dumped his rider immediately out of the chute."

Caleb savored a swallow of his drink. He crooked a smile. "I'm sure you know what a score like that equates to in breeding fees. Anyhow, Pop wanted to retire Diablo. I didn't. In less than a split second, we'd racked up a half million dollars. Between Diablo and our other bulls, we came home millionaires. Dad and I argued. I'd had a little too much to drink, and said things better left unsaid."

Caleb stared into the fireplace's flickering flames.

He seemed lost in thought. I waited. Finally, he said, "We were still spittin' at each other when Pop received a phone call. I don't know from whom. There was something about the look on his face that caused me to ask if there was a problem. He simply shrugged and said he needed some fresh air and was going to make sure the bulls were bedded down for the night. I didn't give it another thought because when Pop had things on his mind, he'd visit the bull barn.

"Not long after, Caroline and the children went to bed. I stayed up nursing my anger with another bourbon. Several in fact. I passed out on the sofa. It was hours later when Caroline and Rex and Baily Strum, another ranch hand, rushed in here. The front of Strum's shirt was covered in blood.

"I can tell you, the sight of that blood and the expression on all their faces sobered me up really quick. Caroline was in tears and barely coherent. It took a few minutes for me to realize Rex was explaining that he and Strum had heard the bulls kickin' up a fuss and had gone to check on them."

Caleb's voice hitched, and Caroline mewled a sob. She continued where Caleb had left off. "It was awful, Tullah. When Rex and Baily finally entered the barn, Diablo had broken the chains on his pen and had attacked Carl. It took both Rex and Baily to fight the bull off Carl's body. Once they had him contained in another pen, it was too late. Carl was dead."

Caleb's jaw shifted. He walked to the wet bar and refilled his glass, this time with a shot of straight bourbon. He downed it and poured another. "My fault, all my fault. I shouldn't have argued with Pop."

The silence that permeated the room had never

sounded so loud. I finally said, "What happened then? Did you call the sheriff, or 9-1-1?"

Caleb poured another drink. It was half way to his mouth when Caroline admonished, "That's enough, Caleb."

He racked a trembling hand over his face before downing the bourbon. He grimaced. "Yeah, sure, it's just that I keep seeing Pop's mangled body." He heaved a deep sigh. "We rushed to the barn. Diablo had blood on both horns where he'd gored Pop. My ol' man lay in a heap like a broken doll. I wanted to shoot the bull. I guess it was a good thing Rex and Baily stopped me.

"We called Sheriff Coffey. He came with two deputies and the medical examiner, Reed Duckworth. Duckworth put Pop's death at approximately two a.m. He said it appeared almost every bone in Pop's body had been broken by the mauling."

I had to ask, "Was there an investigation…did you request an autopsy?"

Both Caroline and Caleb gave me owlish looks. Caleb said, "Investigation…what was there to investigate? The bull broke out of his pen. He gored my father to death. End of story. And no, we didn't request an autopsy. We knew how Pop had died. I don't understand why you're asking these questions, Tullah."

Not satisfied with the shortened version of the answer, I persisted. "From the way you've reinforced the pens with metal bars, how did the bull get out? Was your father gored in the front or in the back? Wasn't there a door or a ladder to the loft that he could've used to escape the attack? Was there any evidence of tampering with the latch on the gate of Diablo's pen?"

Caroline and Caleb sat silent. Their silence cued me

that there was more to the story. I waited. "Listen, you two, you've asked for my help. I'm getting a bit weary of the pranks and the evasiveness. What is it you're either hiding or not telling me?

"Was Carl's death an accident or murder? Does his death have anything to do with the threats you've received, and especially threats against your children? Have the perpetrators made demands for money or for something otherwise?"

I pierced both of them with a no-nonsense scowl. "Either come clean or I'm out of here." I stood, ready to return to my room, gather my belongings, and hit the road.

Caroline's cellphone pinged. She looked at it. "It's Sofia letting me know dinner is ready." Before opening the parlor door, she said, "Tullah, we did ask for your help, and we can't fault you if you leave. The truth is, we're not sure if we can trust you."

She bit her bottom lip, her eyes seeming to study a painting on the wall. My head itched, and it had nothing to do with wearing the wig. "Can't trust me? Explain."

"Because of what we did to you in high school." Caroline cast a glance at her husband. "Maybe you agreed to help us because it's an opportunity to seek revenge for our ridiculously cruel high school pranks. And...and what Caleb did this afternoon with Dakota was just plain juvenile. I don't care about the bulls, and regardless of Caleb's accusations about my needs for nice things, I don't care about that, either. It's the threat against my children that scares me."

Before I could answer, a knock sounded at the door. It opened, and the young maid said, "I'm sorry to bother you, but Sofia is ready to put the food on the table." She shut the door as quickly as she'd opened it, apparently fearing a reprimand for the interruption, I guessed.

I forced my angry quivers to settle. How dare Caleb and Caroline accuse me of seeking revenge on them! I decided to play nice and try to enjoy my meal. Before exiting the room, I said, "Let me be very clear. I'm not a vengeful person. The reason I'm here is because you asked for my help. I'm here to give it. I'll ask some hard questions, maybe some that you'll find offensive. If you're not up to being fully open, honest, and cooperative, tell me now! Got it?"

Caroline nodded. She slipped her hand into her husband's as we followed him to the formal dining room. I was surprised that steak was not on the menu. We were treated to jalapenos stuffed with a crabmeat cream cheese filling, then a bowl of silky New England clam chowder, followed with lobster mac-and-cheese as the main course, and every side dish imaginable, washed down with glasses of chardonnay, then topped off with chocolate cream pie for dessert.

I wiped my mouth with a linen napkin and sighed. "My compliments to the chef."

Caroline smiled. "I hope you aren't disappointed that we didn't serve steak."

Before I could answer, Caleb spoke up. "We're saving steak and ribs for tomorrow's barbeque. Complete with a junior bull-riding event. The sheriff, the mayor, and a bunch of other folks are coming to see what an important journalist looks like."

I thought to myself, *Won't they be fooled?*

He lifted his wine flute, but before taking a sip, he said, "Last year, I collaborated with the high school and local college to form a bull bucking school for young rodeo hopefuls." He rewarded his wife with a smile.

Caroline looked at me. "Breck wanted to learn how to ride bulls, too. He's six, and all cowboy. Trying to convince our little guy that he wasn't old enough, tall enough, or strong enough to ride bulls was like talking to a brick wall. We were honestly afraid he might try to ride a bull while we weren't looking, so, taking a cue from Caleb's venture, I approached a group of mothers to solicit interest in a peewee bull riding school."

Her cheeks pinked as if almost embarrassed to show her pride. "We gave it a try, and so far, we have riders from kindergarten age up to age tweeners and teens, and with a waiting list."

While I enjoyed the last bite of chocolate pie, I expressed my support of such a fine altruistic venture for children and teens. I glanced at the wall clock. It was still a few hours from bedtime.

Apparently, Caroline read my mind. She jingled a small silver bell. At the sound, the young maid entered the dining room. Caroline said, "We'll take coffee in the parlor."

The maid nodded and left. Caleb and I followed Caroline to the coziness of the parlor. I sat in the chair I had previously occupied, my mind filled with questions—hard questions.

Caleb seemed more relaxed than before dinner. I hoped the multiple glasses of wine coupled with his before-dinner whiskey sours had mellowed him enough to give me some straightforward answers.

The door opened and the young maid entered with a salver loaded with a large carafe and cups. She poured, then excused herself, closing the door as she exited the room.

I seized the opportunity. "Tomorrow will be a busy day, and I'm leaving the day after. Let's make the most of tonight." I forged ahead. "You asked why an autopsy was necessary. If your father was in good health, an autopsy would show that perhaps he'd been drugged, and that was the reason why he couldn't escape the bull, or that he might've had a medical condition that hampered his ability to ward off the attack."

The cup rattled against the saucer as Caleb grappled to keep from dropping it. "Oh, shit! Why didn't I think of that?"

I said, "A better question is why didn't the medical examiner or the sheriff suggest it?"

Caleb's face was flushed from all the alcohol he'd imbibed. It appeared he was having trouble collecting his thoughts. Finally, he said, "About Diablo getting out of his pen. When Pop bought the ranch, everything was old. We tore down the ranch house and built this one, remodeled the horse barns, rebricked and chinked the bull barn. There was so much to do that we never got around to upgrading the bull pens. Back then, the gates were held shut with a chain—a rusted chain. It appeared that Diablo had rammed against the gate with such force the chain broke. After Pop's funeral, we installed new gates with double-gauge slide-bolt locks."

Caroline dashed tears from her eyes. "I can still see Carl's broken body. What I don't understand is the importance of him being attacked from the front or from behind."

Anger laced Caleb's voice. "I can answer that. When I got to the barn, Pop was face down. But that doesn't prove anything. From the dirt on his clothes, his face, his hands, it appeared Diablo had rolled him several times, or maybe Pop was rolling to protect himself, while being stomped and gored to death."

Death is never pretty. I know because I've seen ugly death too many times, so I decided to shift away from the subject. "Here's another tough question, Caleb."

He sighed. He looked at his wife and motioned for more coffee. "Sure, ask away. I want to get this thing resolved."

"Okay. Tell me about the accident that sent you to prison, and your time in prison."

"Why is that important?" Caleb asked.

Caleb had blanched at the question. It was a tough question, and one I assumed he didn't want to relive. "Most of the time questions lead to answers, Caleb. The deeper we probe, the more likely we'll discover the why and the who. Once we know those answers, then we'll learn who's behind this, and theoretically an arrest will take place, a trial, prison, and then you and your family can move on with your lives."

Caleb set the cup and saucer aside. He rose to stand next to the fireplace. For a long time, he stared into the flames. I surmised he was gathering his thoughts, and I hoped he wasn't trying to think of ways to color the truth.

He strolled to an oil painting, a Remington, I believe. I waited while Caleb adjusted the painting's slight slant. When he returned to his chair, his voice was soft and worn; tears filled his eyes. "Before I relive my prison nightmare, tell me about your mare, Tullah. As I recall, she was white, I think."

Like Caleb didn't want to discuss his past, I didn't want to talk about my mare. I didn't want to recall the misery she suffered and the emotional pain it took for me to give the veterinarian permission to euthanize her.

"Why do you want to know?"

He shook his head. He seemed to study the palms of his hands. "My buddies and I were such shits in high school, so full of ourselves, thinking we owned the world." It took a moment before he looked at me. "I remember the horror in my daughter's eyes, and her scream when she'd opened the front door and found the head of her pet goat. I'd seen those eyes before, filled with emotional hurt. They were your eyes, Tullah, and they've haunted me for years."

I finished my coffee in three swallows and set my cup aside. "Her name was Venus. She was a seven-year-old, dappled gray Quarterhorse. She was a prize barrel racer. She was gentle." I didn't want to cry and choked back angry tears. "What happened to your rat pack, Caleb?"

Chapter Ten

Caleb flinched at the tone of my voice. "The night of the accident, Caroline and I had argued. We both made cruel accusations. Later, I met up with Eric, Davey, and his girlfriend, Pamela Dorsey. We hit every bar in town, plus a few out of county. Then we hooked up with another buddy and bought some weed. I was so high—" He stopped momentarily. "The next thing I remember was waking up in the hospital. It wasn't until then that I learned I'd driven off the bridge, that Howie and Race were dead and Pamela was in intensive care with a broken neck and would probably never walk again.

"I was twenty-one when sentenced to eighteen years for vehicular homicide. It was in prison that I got interested in bull riding. In his younger years, Pop was into rodeo, especially with him growing up in Arcadia, Florida. Football was my sport of choice." Caleb drifted away for a moment. Then he chuckled. "Even got a football scholarship, and like everything else in my hurrah days, I blew it."

He squirmed in his chair. "At the sentencing, Pamela showed up in a motorized wheelchair; paralyzed from the neck down. She called me a murderer and yelled that she hated my guts because I'd taken away her life and she'd never walk again." He shot his wife a quizzical look. "Why the hell was a fifteen-year-old girl out with college guys, huh? Where were her parents?"

Caroline rose to stand behind her husband. She massaged his shoulders. "Calm down, sweetie. You're a good father, and we're raising Maddie and Breck right."

She cast a look toward me. "Tullah, let's finish this tomorrow. Can't you see how upsetting this is for Caleb, and me?"

Before I could answer, Caleb interjected, "No...no, I need to get this out. If it'll help Tullah discover who's threatening to ruin our lives, then let me finish." He patted Caroline's hand. "I could use another cup of coffee. What about you?" He looked at me. I nodded in agreement.

The carafe was empty, so Caroline left the parlor, saying we should continue while she went to the kitchen. I suspected she needed a break from the tension and from reliving Caleb's confession.

I stared at Caleb. "Do you prefer to wait for Caroline to return, or continue without her for now?"

"We'll continue."

"Tell me about prison. My research revealed that you got an early release."

"Yeah, I did. I served three years, with fifteen on parole. Other than it not being a picnic, what specifically do you want to know, Tullah?"

I did a quick calculation. According to my math, Caleb still had eight years of probation left to serve. "Did you make friends inside? Who were they? What crimes did they commit? Or did you make enemies, and if so, what were their names and why did they target you? Also, I need to know more about Pamela Dorsey. Where is she now?"

Caleb seemed to have calmed down a little. He scooted forward, allowing his hands to dangle between his knees. "I can still hear her shrieking at me as the guard escorted me from the courtroom. She screamed, 'Look what you did to me. You're nothing but rich white trash. You killed my baby, and you've ruined my life.' And then her father rushed past the guards and grabbed me around the neck. Even as both guards pulled him off me, he pointed his finger at me and said that if I ever had children, he'd make me regret the day they were born."

I responded instantly. "Do you think he's the one making the threats and juicing up your bulls?"

Caleb frowned. "Nah, Sheriff Dorsey suffered a fatal heart attack some years ago. You asked where Pamela is. She had no family that wanted the responsibility or had the financial means of taking care of an invalid. She lives at Crestview Manor in New Haven, Connecticut. It's an upscale assisted-living facility."

I smiled. "So you're the anonymous benefactor. Does Caroline know?"

He nodded. "In fact, a few years back, my wife went to visit Pamela just to check on her and make sure the staff was seeing to all of her needs. It wasn't a good visit. Pamela said some terrible things to Caroline and told her to never come back—that she didn't need our pity."

Caleb's face reddened. "Doesn't the stupid girl realize that if I lose everything her life of luxury and lifetime medical care will end?"

"Do you think Pamela is behind this?"

He shrugged. "I don't see how, Tullah. I make sure all her monthly medical needs, clothing, and other comforts are taken care of, but beyond that there's not much left over, not enough for her to hire a henchman."

Caroline entered the room. "Sofia made a variety of

desserts for tomorrow." She smiled as she set the tray on a table and filled our cups with aromatic coffee. "I know we've just eaten, but I thought you might like cookies with your coffee." She seated herself and sighed. "Did I miss anything important?"

Caleb assured his wife that he had simply rehashed the trial and Pamela's and her father's threats toward him. He blew at the steaming coffee. We all sat silent for a few moments. It was as if our emotions needed a break from the drama. I thought about the tragedy of Pamela Dorsey's life. How horrible. I could almost pity her. Wheelchair-bound for the rest of her life, no family, depending on people to take care of her basic needs. However, nothing had been said about her brain being injured. I wasn't ruling her out as the perpetrator. With today's technology, Pamela Dorsey was perfectly capable of hiring someone to do her dirty work. Caleb and Caroline had enough worries. I decided to keep my thoughts to myself.

It took a second for me to realize that Caleb was speaking. "Like I said before, prison was no picnic. In high school, I considered myself a tough jock. On the football field, I could sack any opponent. Howie, Race, Phil, and I were the fearsome foursome. I didn't know what tough was until my first day in lockup. I can tell you I was scared shitless. I was introduced to the cellblock bullies—Earl the Pearl. He was in for murder one. Mousie Lee. Mousie really was a rat. He'd listen to conversations and report the juicier stuff to Earl, who would then use that information to his benefit. And then there was Dangerous Dan, who lived up to his name. After they'd finished with me, I spent three days in the infirmary. Every day afterward, no matter where I was, I was their target.

"Being on the rodeo team is what saved me and my sanity. After I'd won a gold buckle, Earl and his bullies laid off, and sort of took me under their wing. One night, I got wind they were planning to take out a couple of guards with homemade shivs.

"Pop was already working on getting me an early release, and honestly, Tullah, I was trying to keep my nose clean. The thing is, Earl and his bros were including me in their escape plans. I think they intended to use me as their scapegoat if they got caught. I'm ashamed to admit that I turned stoolie. I went to the warden and cut a deal. He promised to protect my identity.

"Long story short, Mousie was killed, and Earl and Dan escaped but were captured. Earl was transferred to another prison, where he was killed in a prison yard brawl, and Dangerous Dan spent ten years in solitary confinement for taking out two guards and another inmate that tried to escape with them. I learned he'd gone completely bonkers and was sent to a mental institution for the criminally insane."

"Interesting. Is this guy still institutionalized?"

Caleb cast a worried look toward Caroline and then to me. He said, "Honestly, I don't know, Tullah. I—that is, Caroline and I've been up to our ears improving the ranch, then travels on the rodeo circuit. Until now, I'd forgotten all about Dan."

"I'll have my dad run him through the database. Do you know the guy's last name?"

"Dangerous Dan is all I ever knew."

"That's okay. I have the name of the prison, and the year you were incarcerated. Checking for his name shouldn't be a problem."

"Tullah?" Caroline had her hands against her chest. "I'm frightened."

I didn't want to add more worry to her already fragile state. "I think you're safe. You have plenty of employees around. That usually deters criminals, who are basically cowards. By the way, you never did tell me why you don't trust Sheriff Coffey. Care to elaborate?"

Caleb and Caroline exchanged glances. Caleb said, "I'm still on parole. Right after I got out of the slammer and brought Caroline to the ranch, we were in town, and I was checking in with my parole officer. Coffey was in the office. He introduced himself, and while he was shaking my hand, he put the squeeze on it, saying to watch my step, and that if I ever needed a favor, he'd be happy to help me out. It was a threat. Then there've been little things like a deputy following Caroline for no reason. Coffey wasn't particularly thorough when investigating my Pop's death, and he completely shrugged off the incident with some creep killing my daughter's pet goat."

Caleb lifted one shoulder as he grimaced and said, "We've heard from others that he's fixed tickets and then used that to extort money from the victims. We've also heard that a couple of people that got on his bad side were put in jail and disappeared. Rumors, Tullah, but nothing we can prove."

Caroline hugged herself. "I don't like the way he tries to cozy up to me. I make sure someone is with me when Coffey comes to the house. He makes my skin crawl. His deputy, Cletus Dodge, tried to claim he had papers proving Sofia was an illegal. She's Quapaw and was born on the reservation in upper Oklahoma. Our ranch hands have been falsely stopped for speeding. And even though Caleb has a letter from his probation officer giving special permission to leave the state due to Caleb's involvement with rodeo travel, Coffey has stopped us numerous times claiming he needed to know where we were going and even when we'd return."

She expressed exasperation by spreading her hands. "Caleb never misses his check-in days with his parole officer, and he always lets him know, in advance, the day we're leaving and where we're staying, how to reach us. Caleb is not a threat to society and he's not a flight risk. Honestly, Coffey's treatment of us is ridiculous."

Caroline issued a concerned frown. "He'll be here tomorrow, Tullah. Be careful around him."

Her caution made my skin crawl. "The two of you had better heed your own warnings and remember to call me Chenoa or Ms. Waya."

We'd covered a lot of background history, but we hadn't talked about the bulls injected with an unknown substance, or the injured riders and the two deaths.

Still, we called it a night. Caroline escorted me to the stairs leading to the outside guest rooms. As soon as we'd said goodnight, I went to my room and locked the door. Although I was above the pool room, I locked the slider, too.

After showering and changing into a pair of pajamas, I propped against the bed's headboard and opened my tablet. I filled the murder file with copious notes and added Pamela Dorsey and Dangerous Dan to my suspect list. I also entered details about Carl Calloway's death with an asterisk to denote the lack of an autopsy, no investigation for fingerprints, and no follow-up on the suspicious phone call Carl received that caused him to go to the bull barn late at night.

After shutting down my tablet and turning out the light, I lay awake in bed a long time, my mind dwelling on the events of the day, and on Caleb's recounting of the accident that sent him to prison. Sorting through the information was like searching for the right puzzle pieces to fit into the correct spaces to form the perfect picture, or in this case, to solve a crime. It was often frustrating when pieces didn't fit.

It occurred to me that Caroline might be behind this. After all, jealousy or perhaps revenge is a powerful motive. And then there was Caleb. What if he was doing this himself? If so, what was his reason?

I also thought about the prank Caleb had pulled this afternoon, giving me a peevish horse to ride, and the way he'd guzzled several glasses of whiskey and wine. Caroline had commented that at times Caleb seemed to be two different people.

I tended to agree, and regretted committing myself to getting involved with his and Caroline's problems. The children and Caleb's mother were hundreds of miles away and, as far as I knew, were safe. I decided to see how tomorrow's barbeque and bull riding exhibition played out.

I'm not sure how long I'd been asleep when a sound woke me. I lay in the dark, listening. It'd been an extra-long day, and exhaustion kept me from crawling out of bed to investigate what sounded like sheep bleating, bawling cows, hammering, and bonging metal.

Chapter Eleven

I wasn't sure if I was awake or if I was dreaming. The Cherokee American woman standing in the dark shadows of the room appeared real, as if I could reach out and touch her.

I didn't feel frightened when I asked, *"Who are you?"*

"Do not be afraid, Ghigau. I am Shadow Woman, spiritual leader of your people. You are in danger, and I have summoned Shunkaha to protect you. He will not appear until the time comes."

"Is he of my mother's people?"

"He is a brave warrior. That is all you need know."

"He is not Cherokee? How will I recognize this valiant fighter?"

"Trust the spirit animal. His name is like yours."

"What danger am I in?"

"When the time comes, you will know. That is when Shunkaha will reveal himself."

I reached for the fleeting image and came face to face with a raging bull, its eyes sparks of fire as it pawed the ground, lowered its head, and charged. My mind was screaming. Time froze. A stallion, snorting puffs of smoke from its nostrils, reared. Its hooves struck my chest. I was driven backward, as though I'd been struck by a huge, invisible fist. I threw my hands up in a wild gesture and arced into a parabola, swiftly reflecting gleams of light as I spun end-over-end through the air.

I hit the ground, sprawling on my back, and in a flash I was watching the scarlet blood begin to pump, sending a jet of crimson to soak my white shirt. Like a miniature fountain it gushed, staining my heaving chest the brightest red I had ever seen.

I reached to grab an outstretched hand, only to have it disappear before it could rescue me. I cried out, 'Don't leave me!'

My eyes snapped open, revealing the dim outlines of furniture in the bedroom. My breath came in short gasps, but the vision of a Cherokee woman with long hair the color of soot, wearing a cape of eagle feathers draped over her shoulders, was still fresh in my mind.

In spite of the chill permeating the room, I was soaked in sweat. Shoving the thought of the charging bull and rearing horse aside, and to keep my mind off the details of the dream, I focused on preparing for the day.

In desperate urgency, I flung myself to the bathroom. The harsh, brilliant lights of the fluorescent fixture over the large, ornate mirror drove the images away. I removed my pajamas and stepped into the shower. The blast of cold water took my breath away. I stood under the stream until my body cooled and the water lost its shock.

Finally, I turned the water off, stepped outside, and dried myself slowly with a thick white towel. I moved carefully, trying to retain the details of the shaman's warning in my mind. It was still dark outside, but the glowing face of the clock next to the bed revealed it was a few minutes after six. Too late to go back to bed—even if I dared do so.

Prolonging the ritual of making up my face and

putting on the wig, I methodically followed my familiar routine while trying to recall the name of the person who was supposed to protect me. The name lurked somewhere in the dim corridors of my memory, probably waiting until I was relaxed before it would come back to me.

Yet the shaman had honored me by calling me *Ghigau,* war woman, which in certain circumstances also means beloved woman.

I opened my suitcase and fished out a pair of jeans and a long-sleeved shirt. Slipping the shirt over my head, I decided to decorate it with my favorite gold chain and the owl pendant. I quickly slipped on a pair of socks and work boots.

I don't consider myself a vain person. Perhaps it was the blonde wig that made me look more feminine than usual. A tall, shapely woman of thirty, with a pair of sky-blue eyes, deep-set in an oval face, stared back at me. My nose, I thought as always, is too hawkish, and my lips too plump. But the coloring and wheatish texture of my skin offset those particular flaws.

While I waited for sounds of life in the yard below my room, I opened my tablet to the murder file. Under the list of suspects, I added Rex's name, with a note to ask Caroline about the ranch hand's last name. I recalled the scowl on Rex's face as we'd ridden away out of the yard, and the hostility in his voice when he'd warned me about Dakota's temperament. What did the scowl mean—was it directed toward Caleb's behavior? Or was I becoming overly suspicious of everyone?

I unlocked the sliding glass door and slid it open. Clear blue skies and a cool breeze greeted me. I stepped back inside and grabbed my camera. The yard was alive with activity, and the delectable aroma of barbeque sauce and hickory smoke filled the air. Men with cowboy hats and aprons tended to several rotating spits filled with entire slabs of beef. Large pots sat atop propane grills, steam escaping the lids on whatever food was inside.

Rows of tables and chairs occupied gold-colored canopies emblazoned with the Calloway logo and name, along with a covered bandstand and dance floor. In the distance, port-o-potties designed to mimic old fashioned cow-town outhouses had been set up for the convenience of the visitors.

Loud bawling directed my attention to where several tiers of stadium seats had been erected, along with an announcer's stand, all surrounded with moveable railings to separate the audience from the rodeo performance. In the outer pens several young bulls milled about. Pickup trucks of every make and model had begun to arrive.

"Mornin', ma'am. You're up early."

I glanced down at a tall lanky man with a saddle slung over one shoulder and another in his hand. I raised my camera and clicked, then offered a smile. "Looks like a good day for a rodeo."

"Yes, ma'am. It's always fun to watch the young'uns strut their stuff." He nodded. "Catch ya, later, ma'am."

From my bird's eye view, I spotted a pickup truck pulling a trailer toward one of the stock pens adjacent to the arena. A teenage boy alit from the cab and signaled to help the driver line up the trailer to the pen's gate. I lifted my camera, ready to get a shot of calves as they exited the trailer. However, I couldn't help but smile when bleating reached my ears.

Mutton Bustin'.

I recalled my days as a five- to six-year-old when my dad would put me on top of a sheep, I'd lie down and wrap my arms around the wooly's neck, and for six seconds hang on for dear life. There were no losers in those events, and every snaggle-toothed little boy or girl that participated went home with a trophy.

I was reveling about the olden days when the bedside phone rang. I rushed to answer it. "Hello?"

Caroline said, "I hope you weren't sleeping."

"No, I'm dressed and ready. I was standing on the deck watching all the activity."

"Great! Are you up for blueberry pancakes? Sofia makes the best."

I thought about my grandmother's long-time friend Patty Sweet. I was certain no pancakes could hold a candle to Patty's. "Blueberry pancakes are one of my favorites."

Careful to lock the slider and the apartment's door, I carried the camera with me and made my way to the main house where I met Caroline and followed her to a room with a one-hundred-eighty-degree view of the ranch. A polished black walnut, live-edged table had been custom-curved to serve as a dining-observation area for the viewing pleasure of guests.

Caroline said, "Magnificent, isn't it?"

A deep nostalgia swept over me as I marveled at the tall grass prairie dotted with bison, and the rugged Glass Mountains in the far distance. I thought about my deceased cousin, Uma Hoktochee, and regretted that I'd not spent more time with her; and although my grandmother is originally of the Oconaluftee Clan in Cherokee, North Carolina, before me lay the vast lands of my ancestors who had survived the brutal trail of tears.

"More than you know," I agreed and sat where Caroline motioned. Sofia appeared from nowhere. She placed a cup in front of me and filled it with coffee. I inhaled the delectable aroma of hazelnut. The young maid, whose name was still a mystery, followed with a platter of fluffy pancakes. I held my plate and said, "Three, please."

Sofia returned with a tray of platters filled with scrambled eggs, crisp bacon, and sausage, and a crystal carafe of maple syrup. I felt like I was living in the lap of luxury. I recalled Caroline saying she'd give it all up for the safety of her children. Hmm, I mused to myself. She was born with a silver spoon in her mouth, and in spite of Caleb's unlawful past, he had done well for his family; mostly with the financial backing of his father. I surmised that living in poverty, if it came to that, would definitely not be Caroline's style. I double-hmm'd. Maybe I should move her name up a couple of spaces on my suspect list. If something were to happen to Caleb, I suspected she'd be a very wealthy widow.

"Miss…Miss?"

Caught up in my musing, I'd missed the maid's offer to pour melted butter over my pancakes. "Oh, sorry, thank you, Miss…ah, I'm afraid I've forgotten your name."

She offered a wan smile. "I didn't give it, Ms. Waya, but it's Roseanne. Most everyone calls me Rosie."

"Do you have a last name?"

Rosie glanced toward Caroline and shrugged. "Rosie will do."

Another name to add to my growing list. Why didn't she want to give me her last name? I tucked the question away as I loaded my fork and savored the blueberry pancakes. Fluffy and tasty, but they didn't hold a candle to Patty Sweet's.

The panoramic view of the ranch and all the activity was like watching a movie on a big screen. I savored another forkful of food, then asked, "Caroline, why doesn't Caleb let his foremen do the heavy lifting?"

"You know Caleb, Tu—Ms. Waya? He thinks he's indispensable. Of course, Rex and Tully are perfectly capable of running the day-to-day operation."

I didn't miss the far-off look in her eyes and the way she'd nibbled her bottom lip, and I seized the opportunity to ask, "Good foremen are worth their weight. Do Rex and Tully have last names? How long have you known them, and where did they come from?"

She set the cup in its saucer as she turned to look at me. The expression on her face appeared guarded. What am I missing here, I wondered.

Caroline said, "Rex Siegler and Tully Taylor. Both men came highly recommended by Caleb's parole officer. And yes, like Caleb, they're both cons." The tone of her voice changed. "Honestly, maybe it was a mistake bringing you here. Your hyper suspicions are totally out of line and make me uncomfortable. And before you ask, Rosie's last name is Ramos. And if you suspect Sofia, too, her last name is Kai. She is Rosie's aunt."

When Caroline stood, she tossed the linen napkin to the seat of her chair. I knew she was in a snit, but again, why? "Caroline, last night, I made it clear that I would ask tough questions. If you think wanting to know the names of your employees is tough, what about this one, "Were you jealous of Pamela Dorsey and Caleb's relationship? The baby she miscarried—was Caleb the father? And why is Sheriff Coffey enamored with you—have you given him cause?"

Caroline raised her hand and drew back. I grabbed her wrist before she could slap me. I'd hit a raw nerve with my questions. Before she had a chance to race out of the room, Sofia appeared with a gift-wrapped box adorned with a red silk bow. She held the package forward. "For you, Miss Caroline. The delivery man said he was instructed to tell you to open it immediately."

Caroline thanked the woman, who set about to collect the dishes of food. "Leave it for later, Sofia."

"As you wish, Miss Caroline." The maid smiled and left the room.

I didn't bother to disguise my annoyance. "I'm sorry to miss the festivities, but under the circumstances, I think it's best I leave. You can tell your guests my publisher called, requesting that I return immediately and sending me to Canada to interview five-time international bull riding champion Kyle Blue Horse."

"Fine!" Caroline ripped the bow and the silver paper off the medium-sized square box.

I had approached the door and was about to make my exit when Caroline's blood-curdling scream filled the room and echoed in my ears. I wheeled about in time to see a diamondback rattler flip from the box. It hit the floor and immediately coiled, its tail hiked upward and rattling a deadly warning. The snake's hooded eyes exuded pure evil, while its tongue flicked in and out.

In a hushed voice, I warned, "Whatever you do, Caroline, don't move...don't...move!"

Chapter Twelve

Sofia and Rosie had rushed to the doorway. I immediately shoved my hand toward them. "Stop!" and pointed to the deadly viper.

"Holy Mother of Jesus!" Sofia made the sign of the cross across her ample breasts. In a muted tone, she said, "Rosie, light a fire under your feet and go find Mr. Caleb."

The rattler seemed to rear its body upward. The rattles whirred faster. I knew the snake was agitated and kept my eyes on it in case it decided to seek a way of escape. From experience, I knew motivated vipers could glide fairly quickly.

Caroline's voice quivered when she spoke. "Can't I just inch toward the door, Tullah?"

Uh-oh. In her state of fright Caroline had forgotten to use my alias. One glance at Sofia's face, and I knew she hadn't missed the blunder. At the moment, I didn't care because as soon as the snake situation was under control, I planned to get in my rental car and drive to the airport. As far as I was concerned, the sooner the better.

I kept my voice low and calm. "Don't even try, Caroline. As a rule of thumb, rattlesnakes can, at best, strike a distance of two-thirds their total body length. This guy looks to be about three foot long which means you are in its direct line of fire if it decides to strike."

As part Cherokee, I'd been taught that all animals,

even the most dangerous, were God's creatures. As a veterinarian with a degree in forensic science, I'd sworn an oath to save lives, not take them, no matter how perverse or dangerous. I spoke an urgent message to the Great Spirit Father to show me how to save two lives—one human and one reptile.

The room with its beautiful panoramic views was no longer a place of tranquility, rather a den of danger and fear. The viper's flat triangular head seemed to measure our breaths as its tongue flicked in and out.

"Why is it flicking its tongue, Tullah?"

"It's sensing us; collecting information. Please," I implored. "Stay quiet."

She whimpered. "Oh, God, I think I'm going to faint."

The snake hissed as it reared its thick body higher and glinted its slanty eyes toward Caroline. I knew if the snake decided to lunge and strike, it would sink its fangs just below Caroline's knee. In its agitated state it wouldn't be a dry bite but instead the fangs, I feared, would sink deep into her flesh and release an ample supply of venom into her leg.

The once-comfortable room seemed to grow increasingly hot. Sweat pooled in my armpits as I tried again to quell my mind enough to commune with the Great Father Spirit. At that moment my eyes strayed to the linen napkin I'd used earlier. I was close enough to ease my hand ever so slowly to grip the napkin's edge. I thanked the Great Spirit Father for hearing my pleas and for guiding my attention to the cloth. In the language of my mother's people, I spoke to the snake, assuring it that I meant no harm.

It felt as if I were outside my body and watching

myself in slow motion as I bent forward to drop the cloth over the rattler's head and then grasp it behind the neck. The coiled rattler resisted my grip. I commanded, "Caroline, get me a pot or a basket, something with a lid to contain this guy."

At that moment, boots pounding up the stairs echoed inside the high domed roof. The snake coiled around my arm, and my hand quivered while trying to maintain a grip on its neck. Caroline grabbed a gold ice bucket. She lifted the lid. "Will this do?"

I practically shouted, "No, it's too shallow. Hurry before I lose my grip."

Caleb burst into the room; a revolver in his hand. Following him was Rex, holding a long-handled hoe, and Tully with a burlap sack. I was thankful someone had good sense. What did Caleb plan to do if he missed—fill his beautiful hand-polished red oak floor with bullet holes?

Tully opened the sack. As soon as I dropped the rattler inside, he twisted the sack's neck into a tight knot. He grinned as he said, "Hellfire and six ways to Sunday, I don't think I've ever seen a woman capture a rattler. Mostly women just scream and run away. You gonna write about this in your article, Ms. Waya?"

At this particular moment, the only thing I wanted was a shot of bourbon to calm my nerves. I did manage to smile. "I don't think so, Tully. Something's come up, and I may need to leave sooner than planned."

Caleb cast a puzzled, unspoken question, looking from me to his wife. He said, "Rex…Tully, get rid of that thing."

The moment the two foremen left the room, I grabbed the box that had held the snake and looked inside. In my experience with helping my dad solve crimes, I knew culprits usually included warning messages. The snake's musky odor lingered on the scrap of folded brown paper that may have been torn from a grocery sack or a sandwich bag.

"What does it say?" Caroline sat in a chair with her hands clasped in tight fists.

To avoid contaminating evidence, I used the tips of my fingernails to unfold the paper and held it toward Caleb with a caution to not touch. A frown wrinkled his brow. "It's a picture of a coiled rattler. Whoever wrote the note must be illiterate. I can't make sense of this chicken scratch, can you?"

I studied the poorly formed letters and misspelled words. "It says, 'You will never know when I'll strike again.'"

He demanded, "Where did this come from?"

Sofia entered the room carrying a large pot with a lid. "I am sorry, Mr. Caleb. I was so nervous I couldn't think what to put the snake in."

Caleb pointed to the box that I had set on a table. "Who brought this, Sofia?"

The maid shrugged. "I do not know. The doorbell rang. I answer it. I never see this man before. He handed me the box and say to give it to Miss Caroline."

I said, "Was he dressed in a uniform, like a delivery man?"

Again, she shrugged. "No, he was dressed like...like a...regular person."

Sweat laced Caleb's brow. He paced about the room. "Did Rosie see this man?"

Sofia shook her head. "She was in the kitchen stuffin' mushrooms."

The red on Caleb's face deepened to scarlet. I could see his impatience growing. Upsetting the older woman wouldn't help solve the delivery person's identity, and I didn't wish to see Caleb fire her because she wasn't helping to solve a mystery.

To ease the situation, I walked to the carafe and jiggled it. Good, I thought. I lifted a clean cup from the sideboard and filled it with coffee. I motioned for Sofia to sit. When I offered her the cup, she cut skeptical eyes toward her boss.

I intervened. "It's okay, Sofia. Mr. Calloway isn't upset with you, only the situation." I urged her to drink the coffee, hoping a jolt of caffeine would settle her nerves and jog her memory.

I kept my voice to a soothing low as I spoke. "Close your eyes, Sofia, and try to visualize the man. What color was his hair...did he have a scar or a tattoo...were his hands large or small?"

The coffee had cooled enough that she swallowed it in two gulps. She inhaled, and closed her eyes. Caroline looked as if she was about to speak. I lifted a finger to my lips to shush her. I didn't know any words in the Quapaw, and I didn't know if Sofia spoke her own native language anyway, so I simply said softly, "Look into your spirit, Sofia. See what you can see. It is there. Trust me. It is in your mind's eye."

Sofia heaved an exhale. She opened her eyes. "He was dressed like a ranch hand, but he had a star tattooed here." She pointed to her left earlobe. "He wore a black ball cap, but I think his hair was dark. He wasn't tall or short."

She wiped a tear that had dribbled down her cheek. "I am a worthless old woman. I wish I had paid more attention."

I placed my arms around Sofia's shoulders and gave her a hug. "You are not worthless, and on a busy day like today, with all the hustle and bustle happening, no one can blame you for not being able to fully describe the person who left the package."

I shot Caleb an *I dare you to fire her* look.

He said, "I didn't mean to yell at you, Sofia. If you think of anything else about the guy, let me know."

The older woman stood and hustled from the room.

Caleb said, "What's this about you leaving, Tullah?"

"About that. Caroline, in a state of fright, called me by my name. Sofia heard, but I don't think she'll say anything. However," I shifted my focus to Caroline, who continued to sit in silence. "Caroline doesn't like the questions I asked."

At my comment, she came alive. "That's right, Caleb. I've asked Tullah to leave. She's overly suspicious and has virtually pointed her finger at me as being responsible for all of…of this."

Caleb still held the box. I said, "I suggest you report this incident to Sheriff Coffey. Although the box has been handled by several people, he can still pull prints from it that might lead to the delivery guy, and then to the person who wrote the note and sent the snake. Other than that, yes, I'm leaving today."

My attention to detail is what made me an excellent doctor and a competent detective. The other side of my nature lay carefully hidden from public view, controlled by an iron will. Beneath the façade of smooth control lay a volatile set of emotions that could explode like Mount Etna. I had learned long ago that when I gave way to this side of my nature, I exhibited a wildness that could injure those who got in my way—including myself.

"No, you can't." He glared at Caroline. "What did you say to her?"

Caroline opened her mouth to speak, then closed it abruptly. She rose and left the room, slamming the door behind her. Caleb looked after her, shook his head, and said, "Never mind her. I'm asking...no, I'm pleading with you to see this thing through. Whether she likes it or not, I'm asking you to stay."

I arched an eyebrow. "I'm not a wishy-washy person, Caleb. You've played on my sympathy by holding your family's safety over my head. Both of you have repeatedly pleaded for my help, yet you've impeded me at every turn when I ask questions that get too close to answers that neither of you want to give. This isn't high school, where you and Caroline get to be the top dogs on campus, and the kids you bullied turned the other cheek for fear of repercussions.

"The snake was directed toward Caroline. Why? Who has she pissed off—or better yet, who have you screwed over to bring threats and possibly murder down on your family?"

Caleb began to tremble. It appeared his legs had collapsed when he tried to stand. The sight of his suppliant expression sickened me. For a brief moment there was silence.

I bit my lower lip, admitting to myself that maybe I was too hard on him and Caroline. I attempted to smile. It didn't work. I was too tense to smile. I could almost hear my dad's voice whispering in my ear, *You're not a quitter, Punkin. You gave your word.*

With no enthusiasm at all, I said, "Against my better judgment, I'll see this through until we nab the person behind this."

Caleb blew out a breath that signified his relief.

Caroline's expression was contrite when she entered the room. "Tully sent a text saying that Sheriff Coffey is on his way to the house. I've asked Sofia to make a pot of fresh coffee."

She looked at me, and I let my distaste show when she asked if I was leaving. Caleb answered for his wife. "Climb off your high horse, Caroline. Tullah is staying. That is, Ms. Waya is here to enjoy today's festivities while she does a little observing...for the article she's writing." He shifted a questionable glance toward me. "Isn't that right, Ms. Waya?"

My head itched. I wondered if it was from the wig or if the itch was a warning to expect another dangerous incident.

Chapter Thirteen

"Caleb, if you're not sure the sheriff is on the up and up, I'd like to suggest that you give him the box and wrapping to check for prints, but allow me to keep the note." I'd been careful when sliding the paper into the plastic baggie that Sofia had provided. "You can trust my dad's forensics team."

A frown creased Caleb's brow. "I totally agree. From past experience, I know Coffey will find some reason to treat this heinous incident like he's done with all the others—unimportant."

"I have another suggestion—stick close to me. I'm supposed to be shadowing you. Let's make it look authentic; also, if there's another incident, it'll be the two of us against whomever. Also, my guess is that the guy who delivered the snake is still on the premises. How well do you trust your foremen?"

"Rex and Tully are as dependable as they come. Surely you don't suspect them?" This time Caleb glinted his frown toward me. "I mean, what reason would they have to ruin me and harm my family?"

"At this point, I'm not sure who you can trust. It's not so much that I mistrust them, it's that they're both in a position to keep an eye out for a stranger with a star tattooed on his left earlobe. Since Rex and Tully know about the snake incident, you might ask them to notify you immediately if they spot this guy."

"Good idea." Caleb opened his cellphone and sent a text to his foremen. The phone pinged almost immediately. Caleb offered a thumbs up. "It's a done deal, Tullah. Ah, shit. I keep forgetting to call you Ms. Waya."

****

By noon the ranch was a bevy of activity. Chairs were occupied under the canopies, several groups of ranchers huddled together as if in deep conversation, and voices and laughter set a gleeful tone that masked the underlayers of malevolence toward the Calloways.

Caleb and I waited inside the parlor for the sheriff to show while Caroline joined a group of mothers at the sheep pens to help set-up for the Mutton Bustin' event—and, I'm sure, to avoid the sheriff.

When he entered the room, Sheriff O'Neal Coffey was the opposite of what I'd pictured. Instead of a John Wayne lawman persona, Coffey had a rotund paunch that caused a couple of buttons on his shirt to strain at staying closed. I was sure he'd suffer a heart attack if he had to run a mile. However, his deputy Cletus Dodge was the complete opposite. This man was built like a bull and looked as if he could easily bench press a couple hundred pounds.

Caleb made the introductions.

A shudder wafted over me. Instinctively I knew these men were not to be trusted. The eyes are windows into the soul. Coffey extended his hand. I cringed when his sweaty palm gripped mine. Deputy Dodge merely offered a civil nod.

Sofia entered with a tray of coffee. Caleb said, "That'll be all, Sofia. We can serve ourselves."

I chose the same chair I had earlier occupied, and

observed both men while Caleb related the snake incident. He pointed to the box and wrapping paper on the coffee table. "I'm sure you can pull prints that will lead you to the delivery guy, and maybe to whoever was responsible for my father's death."

Coffey motioned to his deputy. "As you well know, Caleb, my office is rather lacking in funds to purchase forensics equipment. However, I assure you that Deputy Dodge will do his dead-level best to make sure the evidence is sent off to Tulsa immediately."

Coffey directed a smile toward me. "I'm not sure this little lady reporter should be hearing all of this. Beggin' your pardon, ma'am, and meanin' no offense, o' course."

I clamped down on the inside of my jaw to avoid slapping back at his intentional insult. *Little lady*, indeed. "I was witness to the snake incident and thought I could help shed some light on the event."

"Now ain't that something. Seems you saved our pretty little Miss Caroline's life." Coffey stepped forward to stand directly in front of me. The stench of stale sweat assaulted my nostrils. He pierced me with a sneer. "I don't believe I've ever seen a—" he snapped his fingers as if trying to think of a special word, "an Indian with blue eyes and blonde hair. What are you? Not Quapaw or Cherokee. Hmm, maybe Italian?" He drew out the word so that it sounded like "Eye-tal-yun."

He reached to take my hand. I purposely lifted the demitasse cup to my lips. A repulsive shiver rippled over me. I peered over the cup's rim. "My ancestry is no one's concern. I'm simply here to shadow Mr. and Mrs. Calloway until after the PBR rodeo in Louisville."

I shot Coffey a sly look. Two could play his game.

"The snake incident will make interesting copy, as well as whatever events take place today, and during Kentucky's Bucking Beast rodeo."

Coffey belly-laughed. "I hope Caleb hasn't been feeding you some kind of gibberish about an unknown person tampering with his bulls."

Deputy Dodge, who'd remained silent up to that point, also guffawed.

I managed to offer a wide-eyed look of surprised interest. I thought to myself that maybe I'd missed my calling and should have majored in theatrics. I shifted to look at Caleb and added amazement to my voice. "Mr. Calloway, is this true? How exciting...please, tell me more."

The expression on Coffey's face spoke volumes. He'd definitely stuck his foot deep inside his mouth. I looked forward to hearing how he'd squirm out of his lapse in confidentiality.

A knock sounded at the door. It opened and Rex walked in. "Caleb, Mr. King is asking to speak to you."

Before Caleb could answer, Coffey butted in. "Afternoon, Mr. Siegler. I trust you haven't missed any check-ins with your parole officer."

The way Rex's jaw clenched and his hands doubled into tight fists expressed his dislike for the sheriff. "Mr. Avery is outside with his wife and sons. I'm certain he'll vouch for me."

"Now...now, no cause to get all riled up. Just doing my duty, Mr. Siegler." Coffey patted his belly. He lifted his nose and sniffed. "Barbeque smells mighty good. When we gonna eat, Caleb?"

"After today's rodeo, about four 'o clock." Caleb walked to the door and opened it. "You know your way to the kitchen. I'm sure Sofia will be happy to fix you a sandwich."

"And when's the rodeo start?" Coffey wanted to know.

Caleb glanced at the wall clock. He grabbed his Stetson off a hat rack. "In about thirty minutes." He offered me a hand. "Ms. Waya, please join me. I'll introduce you to Wade King. He's one of the county's larger cattlemen." He thanked Rex, and we proceeded out of the parlor.

I overheard Coffey tell his deputy to take care of the evidence. Except the way he said it implied that "to take care of" actually meant "get rid of." This thought ramped up my curiosity. Sheriff O'Neal Coffey and Deputy Cletus Dodge had definitely moved up a couple of notches on my list of suspects.

Coffey waddled off in the direction of the kitchen while his deputy beat it outside. I watched Dodge striding toward his patrol car, the box and its wrapping in his hand.

Rex excused himself saying he needed to help Tully and a few other ranch hands get the chutes ready for the young bulls and riders. I followed Caleb to a tall slender man touting a handlebar moustache, Wade King, and was also introduced to Robert Avery, the parole officer, as well as the mayor and several other notables.

It was plain to see that Caleb and Caroline were respected citizens of the community. No one mentioned Caleb's past. Everyone seemed interested in meeting an acclaimed journalist, and each person had a story to share with me. A tiny bit of guilt niggled at me for the ruse. I pledged to myself to find a way to get the story published.

"Tullah?" Caroline's voice interrupted my musing. "Why are you smiling?"

Thinking quickly, I said, "It's a beautiful day. I look forward to watching the children perform."

She sighed. "I wish Maddie and Breck were here. Maddie is becoming quite the barrel racer, and Breck, well, he'd put up a fuss about riding a sheep because he thinks he's like his daddy—a bull rider."

We stopped by one of the food canopies, grabbed popcorn and lemonade, and a program. "C'mon," I said, "let's get a front-row seat before they're all taken."

As we walked, her voice was quiet. "Did Coffey ask about me?"

"Yes."

"What did he say about the snake?"

We'd reached the bleachers and decided to climb to the top row. After we'd settled, I kept my voice low. "You're right about Coffey. He's a genuine sleaze. I'm glad Caleb agreed to let me keep the note, because I don't think Coffey will make any effort to have the box and wrapping paper dusted for prints. He seemed more interested in feeding his belly and harassing Rex than finding out who threatened you in such a dangerous way."

Caroline munched on her popcorn. "He threatened Rex? What happened?"

"It was subtle. He implied that Rex might not be keeping up with his parole meetings." My opinion of the ex-con foreman had shifted slightly, in a positive way. "Rex kept his cool. He handled the situation well."

Caroline emitted a throaty growl. "I wish the earth would open up and swallow that fat pig and his entire damned force." She scooted closer and leaned to whisper, "Do you or your dad have connections that can help us get rid of Coffey?" As if she realized how her question appeared, she hastily said, "I mean legally, of course."

Before I could answer, music blared over the loudspeakers and a deep masculine voice announced, "Ladies, gentlemen, boys and girls, and the young at heart, welcome to the second annual Calloway Youth Rodeo."

The announcement was answered with cheers and an exuberant round of applause. A gate opened and the arena filled with a junior quadrille riding team dressed in red-and-gold sequined outfits.

Again, the announcer's voice rang out over the arena. "These little ladies range in age from six years to twelve years, and are under the tutelage of Mrs. Caroline Calloway and her dedicated team of mothers. I guarantee you will be entertained. Let's hear it for these youngsters and their horses, who practice every day of the week, rain or shine."

Mounted on pintos, palominos, and chestnut horses, a team of sixteen young girls completed an entertaining figure-eight square dance, at full gallop, as they crisscrossed the rodeo area with just inches to spare.

"I remember my days as a quadrille rider. Somehow, my partner and I got out of sync. Our horses collided, and I ended up with a broken leg." I reached down and rubbed my right leg, and with a grin said, "I always know when it's going to rain."

Caroline chuckled. "And the bull riders call us crazy. Does that tell you something?"

During the Mutton Bustin' event, laughter rippled through the audience as one little fellow burst out of the chute hanging on for dear life. The boy was riding his sheep backward and holding on to the tail.

Parents and spectators cheered for the little cowboys and cowgirls as the kids struggled to hang on for six seconds. A couple of stoic little boys refused to cry when the rams they were riding turned tables and butted them in the belly.

And so, the day's events went without incident, until...

Chapter Fourteen

The last event of the day had turned dangerous, and it had been fully meant to send a warning message to Caleb and Caroline.

I could still feel the metallic surge of adrenalin in my mouth. My arms had goosepimples, and as I followed Caroline and Caleb to the house, I pulled my jacket tighter around me. Not all the icy chill rippling inside me was from the weather.

Before the perilous attack, parents had tucked their exhausted children inside the campers of their various pickup trucks. Several teens had curled up in chairs, their heads resting on folded arms, eyes closed. The cooks had cleared away tables and cooking equipment, and under a large canopied dance floor, the band played a slow waltz.

Completely sated from a barbeque with all the trimmings, plus a large bowl of Sofia's blackberry buckle topped with a generous dollop of homemade whipped cream, I relaxed in a chair and nursed a coffee. I glanced around to count heads. Sheriff Coffey and Deputy Dodge had come in on each other's heels and stood chatting. I suspected the cups in their hands held more than coffee.

Robert Avery and his wife cuddled on the dance floor swaying to the music. Rex Siegler stood off by himself. I noted the nostalgic expression on his face and wondered if he was thinking of a special someone.

Mr. and Mrs. King floated around the dance floor, stopping every few milliseconds to speak to various couples.

Caleb held Caroline in his arms. She had changed into a pair of black slacks with a matching black jacket trimmed in gold braid, with her blonde hair now pulled into a neat chignon. Caroline's dreamy smile contrasted Caleb's wary frown.

Sofia and Rosie bustled around the food tables, wiping and cleaning. Deputy Dodge approached the table. He held out his hand. From the vigorous way Rosie shook her head and moved away, I surmised that she had refused his offer to dance. He looked angry, and because he looked irate, I allowed myself to scope the remaining people, mentally counting heads, and trying to recall faces and names. Missing were Baily Strum and Tully Taylor. I dismissed them as still dismantling chutes and helping to clear the grounds.

I glanced at my watch. The hour was approaching eight, and tired from pretending to be a journalist and listening to multiple rodeo experiences, I was ready to call it a night. Yet I still had questions to ask Caleb before leaving the next morning to catch my flight.

Far in the distance, I heard agitated bawling. The working part of my brain told me something wasn't quite right. Dread touched my neck as the ground beneath me vibrated.

Before any of us could react, Rex Siegler's body was tossed into the air. We could only watch with gaping mouths. The scene appeared to happen in slow motion. That is, until two thousand pounds of ugly, misshapen, shaggy creature on four legs plowed through the dancing couples. I saw Caleb shove Caroline out of the way.

Sofia and Rosie dodged under a table, and sleeping teenagers sprang to life, scattering in different directions.

Tully and Baily, along with two other cowboys, raced forward, swinging ropes. A gray Brahma loosed a deep bellow as it lowered its massive head, and its deadly horns caught Tully in the midsection, sailing him back over the bull's massive shoulders.

Sheriff Coffey had drawn his weapon and was shouting, "Get out of the way!" He pointed his revolver and was weaving it back and forth as if trying to focus on his target.

What the hell is he thinking? I thought. How can he shoot into a crowd of frenzied people trying to escape from being mauled by two slobbering beasts?

Caleb and I grabbed metal chairs to stave off the bulls. I yelled, "Someone call 9-1-1. We have two men down!"

At the sound of my voice, an odorous behemoth swung around. Its black beady eyes trained on me. This was a new breed of bull. I surmised a bison and Brahma mix. A killing machine in a brown, hairy body. The beefalo flung its malformed head from side to side, baptizing me in snot and slobber.

The animal charged. With no time to move out of its way, instinctively, I swung the chair back, and with all my might, bashed it against the bull's massive head. The violence of the strike vibrated through my arms. I was certain I had knocked my shoulder out of its socket.

I ventured a quick glance at the loud BAM to my right. Caleb had mimicked my action and had landed a fierce blow to the Brahma's snout, temporarily sending the beast to its knees.

Our actions had stunned both bulls. Men's shouts

and women's screams filled the night. I looked around for a place of safety, knowing it was impossible to outrun a bulldozer on four legs.

At first, I thought snakes were sailing through the air, and wondered if this night could get any worse. Those snakes turned out to be lariats, swung by four young teens I recognized as participants in today's rodeo. The loops found their marks, but the scrawny boys were no match for powerful bulls.

Caleb and I rushed forward. We each latched on to a length of rope to lend our strength in what became a tug of war—humans against beasts, and we humans were losing. Just when I thought the battle was over, and we were about to be gored and stomped, riders galloped to our rescue.

More ropes sailed through the air. Two of our young rescuers grabbed the Brahma by the horns and wrestled it to the ground while the cowboy alit from his horse and hogtied the bovine by its feet.

Meanwhile, the beefalo whirled and pawed the ground. The cowboys on horseback swung their loops, and the bull fought against the ropes. I feared if he charged, it would harm horse and rider. I also wondered how the men would manage to lead two muscled powerhouses back to their pens.

As if the Great Father Spirit had heard my thoughts, the chugging sound of an approaching front-end loader grew louder. The driver shouted, "Mr. Calloway, I'll scoop Diesel into the bucket, and we'll tie Widow Maker to the hitch. We'll get 'em penned up."

Caleb pulled a handkerchief from his back pocket to wipe at the sweat on his crimson face. He looked up at the driver. "How the hell did they get out?"

"Don't know for sure, Boss. Jeff and me checked the gates. Nothing was broken, and one thing for sure, neither bull climbed over its pen, 'specially Diesel. Looks like somebody might've unlatched the gates on purpose."

Caleb lifted his foot to the dozer's wheeled hub to pull himself up to the cab. "Ms. Waya, tell my wife I'm checking on the bulls."

I assured him I'd let her know he was safe. I also watched him twist around until he'd spotted the sheriff and deputy. Caleb yelled out, "Hop aboard."

Above the tractor's roar, I heard him say, "Thanks for the quick thinking with the dozer, Moses."

Caleb then turned and faced the group of men who had come to our rescue, and the remaining guests who had ventured forward now the harrowing action was over. He said, "Men, Ms. Waya and I appreciate your saving our lives."

To the crowd he said, "My apologies for—" Emotion filled his voice and he seemed at a loss for words.

I stepped forward. "It's been an unexpectedly exciting finish to an otherwise entertaining, and fun-filled day, but a very long one. If you will excuse us, I think it's time to call it a night. Mr. and Mrs. Calloway and I thank you for attending, and wish you a safe journey to your homes."

A teen's squeaky voice called out, "Ms. Waya, when will that article come out? I want to make sure to see if my picture is in the magazine."

The adrenalin was beginning to seep from my body. I feared my legs might fall out from under me. Still, I managed a smile. "Fletcher Worth, right?"

The lanky teen in a white cowboy hat offered a sheepish grin. "Yes'm."

"Don't worry, I'll send copies to Mr. Calloway. He'll make sure everyone featured in the magazine gets a copy, and there'll be extras for anyone who wants one." While the tractor chugged off into the night, I waved, excused myself, and headed toward the house.

Sofia met me at the door. She held a mug forward. "I believe your favorite is a Bailey's Irish Cream."

I accepted the drink and asked if she and Rosie were okay. Sofia assured me that neither of them had suffered anything more than having the wits scared out of them.

In spite of the harrowing ordeal, we'd all just experienced, questions filled my mind. An hour later, when Caleb entered the parlor, he seemed to have aged beyond his thirty-two years. His shoulders slumped, there was a visible tic under his left eye, and a blood-soaked right hand was wrapped in a dirty linen napkin.

Caroline had just come to the bottom of the stairs. She raced to her husband. "Oh, dear lord, you're hurt!"

"It's nothing serious, honey. Don't worry yourself."

I asked him to hold his hand forward. He obeyed. I unwrapped the napkin. The deep gouge didn't require stitches, but dirty horns and lack of proper treatment could turn an innocent-looking wound septic.

Sofia stood by. I said, "Please bring a basin of hot water, peroxide, antibiotic salve, and clean bandages."

Within minutes the maid and I had cleansed and wrapped Caleb's wound while Caroline stood by and simpered. My suspect-o-meter was working overtime.

Caroline asked Sofia to prepare a pot of coffee and lace it with bourbon. "If there are any cookies left, we'd like those, too."

Mighty inconsiderate of Caroline, I thought. Rosie and Sofia were probably more exhausted than any of us. Taking the bull by the horns, so to speak, I decided to override Caroline's authority as matron of the house, and said, "Sofia, why don't you and Rosie call it a night. Caroline and I will clean up before we retire for the evening."

Sofia and her niece cast doubtful looks toward Caroline. She merely said, "Of course, Ms. Waya is correct, and there's plenty of food left over for us to reheat. The two of you take tomorrow off, too."

After a few busy but silent minutes in the kitchen, I grabbed the tray of cookies while Caroline carried the coffee carafe. We made our way to the parlor. Caleb said he would join us after he locked up the house and turned out the lights. "It's terrible not feeling safe in my own home."

We settled in our mutual chairs and sat quiet for a good ten minutes. I ascertained that we were all lost in our thoughts. Finally, I asked, "Caleb, if you had to name three people who might want you or Caroline dead, who might they be?"

He thought for a minute, then said, "I don't know, and that's the truth."

"How about a jealous stock contractor, or that mysterious Dangerous Dan, or perhaps a relative of the rider killed by one of your bulls?"

Caleb made the universal shrug. "There's always jealousy amongst the stock contractors. But there's a difference between being a friendly rival pain in the bohunkus and being someone that hates enough to kill. As for the rider who lost his life—that comes with the territory. Bull riders or bronc busters, we all know that when the chute gate opens, there's eight seconds between life and death."

I decided to switch gears. "Did the latches on the gates look as if someone had tampered with them?"

Caleb stood quickly, then sat back down. He lifted the cup to his lips and drank deep before replacing the cup in its saucer. "Before we returned the bulls to their pens, Moses—he was the driver—pivoted the dozer so the headlights focused on the gates. Honestly, I had no idea what I was looking for, and Coffey didn't seem all that interested. He and Cletus chalked it up to a teenage prank."

Although that made perfect sense, I wasn't convinced. "What about you—do you think it was a 'prank'?"

Caleb slowly rose from his chair. He looked a little shell-shocked by today's events. "I think whoever opened the gates did it on purpose. I know every kid who participated in today's rodeo. Several of them are the same ones that came to our rescue. Good kids from good homes, and some of those youngsters are honor students with great futures ahead of them."

"So you think Sheriff Coffey and his deputy are blowing smoke?"

Caleb nodded. "The thing is—I don't know why."

Caroline looked a little pale. "Can't you stay another day, Tullah?"

My head throbbed. I wanted a shower, a couple of aspirin, and a peaceful night's sleep. "My staying another day won't catch the guilty party." I huffed a sigh. "Besides, I have a busy practice, and patients to care for."

She persisted. "I realize we're asking you to put us

first, but…"

"Caroline…" My aggravation meter was about to explode. "My guess is that whoever is behind these cruel shenanigans is waiting until next month to make their big play at the PBR in Louisville. That's when we really need to be on our toes."

"Yes, but what about after you leave…tomorrow… or next week?" Caroline wrung her hands together. "I'm truly afraid."

"If other incidents happen, write them down, in detail."

To take her mind off today's carnage, and my leaving, I suggested she call the hospital to check on Rex and Tully. On her way out of the parlor, she cast me a woeful look.

"Caroline?" My questioning voice stopped her at the doorway, her back still toward me. I said, "Don't worry, I'll have plenty of backup. We'll do our best to nab the person responsible for making your life miserable; and if we can prove it, we'll hit them with murder charges for the death of the bull rider."

Unexpectedly, she walked over and wrapped her arms around me. "Thank you." She glanced at her husband and left the room.

"Caleb?" I stared at him long and hard. "I hope you're not playing stupid with me."

He appeared to choose his words carefully. He clenched and unclenched his fists. "It's awfully hard for a man to change his course. I screwed up. Big time. That's why I moved to Oklahoma. But it doesn't matter how far you go, your past always seems to catch up with you."

His emotional pain was clear as day. I gave him an

appraising glance. "And has your past caught up with you, Caleb?"

He let out a breath. "I've paid for my wild and careless days, Tullah. I've kept my nose clean. I go to church; I work with young guys to help encourage them not to walk down the path I chose." He spread his hands wide, his frustration apparent. "I don't know who's doing this to me and my family. I don't know why whoever it is wants to destroy me."

He sat in the chair, leaned forward and covered his face with both hands. I refilled my cup and sat nibbling on a cookie. It was time to put my thinking cap on.

"Caleb, tell me about the rider who died and those who were injured—the names and as much detail as possible for each one. Also, when did you first suspect the bulls were being juiced up? How did you find out? Did the rodeo veterinarian run tests on the bulls, like drawing blood or testing their saliva?"

I was certain, given time to think, I could come up with a dozen or more questions that might help lead me to the who...the why...and the how. For now, my brain wasn't cooperating.

Caleb sighed deeply. "Not tonight, Tullah." He held up his wounded hand. "With the snake incident, and the excitement of the rodeo, and then the damned bull rampage, I can't handle anything more tonight."

"I'm leaving in the morning. If not tonight, then when? This information is important."

"Why? The man is dead. I can't bring him back."

He was hedging. I knew it and so did he. However, he did have a point. I was also at the point of exhaustion. "Okay. I agree, we're all worn out, mentally and physically. Write it down—every detail, even those you might think are not important. Send it to me by email attachment. The sooner the better."

We both stood. This time tomorrow, I'd be sleeping in my own bed and looking forward to doctoring animals and making barn calls.

Before saying goodnight, I looked at Caleb. It was as if *Guilty Knowledge* was written on his forehead.

Once alone and in the bedroom, I carefully undressed. Earlier, I had spotted a container of plastic trash bags beneath the bathroom sink. I opened one and laid my soiled clothing inside. Once I was home and had access to my chemicals, I planned to test the saliva and mucus for drugs.

Chapter Fifteen

I sat by the Learjet's window seat and stared down at land that reminded me of a patchwork quilt. When the seatbelt sign flashed on, a flight attendant announced to the passengers to remain belted in our seats until the plane had landed. For a strange reason, I felt torn between my vocation and the Calloways. The one thing I wasn't confused about was my innate ability to solve crimes. This one, I admitted, had me puzzled.

My cellphone pinged. A text from my dad announced he was waiting for the plane to land. I answered with, *Lots to tell U.*

I spotted him the moment I walked out of the gangway. Dad opened his arms and embraced me as if I'd been away longer than a few days. And then he held me at arm's length. He pursed his lips. I wasn't sure if he was approving or disapproving of my new look.

I stiffened and sent him a challenging look. "It'll grow out, Dad."

He made a motion as if he were zipping his lips. I returned his non-comment with a playful punch to his shoulder. "Dad, do you mind if we stop by Uncle Charlie's? I'm starved."

He relieved me of my carry-on and satchel. We made small talk as we left the terminal and walked through the parking lot to his truck. I asked if he'd heard from Grandmother.

He chuckled. "She and the girls are having the time of their life. In fact, I think the travel bug has bitten them hard. Her last text said something about the United Kingdom."

He turned and gave me his Dad-look. "The dark circles under your eyes tell me you haven't been sleeping well. I'm all ears if you're ready to talk."

As we arrived at his truck, he held the door while I climbed inside. I hadn't realized how tense I was until I'd settled in the seat and strapped on the seatbelt. Flying definitely isn't my favorite mode of travel. When I stand up, I like to know that my feet will touch the ground.

"I'll tell you one thing, Dad. When May gets here and I go to Louisville, I'm not wearing a wig. The thing not only gives me a headache, but it makes my head itch like crazy."

Dad chuckled. He navigated the traffic like a pro. Of course, he also knows all the back roads. No interstate highways for him. He focused on driving while I admired the countryside. I didn't feel like talking just yet. My mind was filled with a flurry of unanswered questions.

Finally, I said, "Ella kept me up to date about the clinic. Thankfully, there were no emergencies."

He glanced over at me. "Yep. What happened at Caleb's?"

I filled him in on the rodeo and bull incidents while he drove. "Caleb claims he doesn't know who is setting him up for a fall."

"Do you believe him?"

I huffed a sigh. "I'm not sure. There are moments I think he's on the level, and then there are instances when he does or says something, or acts like he's hiding behind a shield, which causes my suspect-o-meter to go haywire."

Dad said, "You're telling me that neither O'Neal Coffey nor his deputy brushed the gates for fingerprints?"

"Exactly. They sluffed it off as a teenage prank."

I opened my tablet and filled him in on my list of suspects. I recanted my original suspicions that included Rex Siegler and Tully Taylor. "Both men were recommended to Caleb by his parole officer."

Dad glanced at me. "Ex-cons. What were they in for?"

I scrolled down to the data sheet I'd created on each person I'd added to my list of possible suspects. "Rex served five years for grand theft larceny and Tully for habitual drunk driving, even with a suspended license, and leaving the scene of an accident. From all accounts, it appears they came from different prisons and didn't know each other until arriving at Caleb's ranch."

"Where were they when the bulls got loose?"

"In full view the entire time, and pretty much run ragged helping with the rodeo earlier." I related how both Rex and Tully had been injured and sent to the hospital. "Before I left this morning, I checked on them. Rex suffered several broken ribs, a punctured lung, and worse, a piece of metal from a chair had pierced his heart. The Brahma's horn had ripped a hole through Tully's large intestine. He was in surgery when I called. He also suffered kidney damage."

Dad said, "Whew! Both men are lucky to be alive."

The two-hour drive from the airport seemed to fly by as I continued to fill my dad in on the details. Conversation will do that. In no time, he was pulling into the Whitehorse Saloon's parking lot. I'd had my fill of barbeque and looked forward to a bowl of Uncle Charlie's prize-winning chili, crispy onion rings, and a large cola with a healthy squirt of lemon.

We strolled into the saloon's dim interior, and I walked into Uncle Charlie's open arms. Just as my dad had done, Uncle Charlie held me by the shoulders and scrutinized my shorn locks. "Who scalped you?"

The twinkle in his eyes told me he was kidding. I huffed an exaggerated sigh. "You and Dad…you're both impossible." I leaned forward and kissed his cheek.

A powerfully built man, part Apache and part Inuit, and my dad's blood brother since sixth grade, Uncle Charlie is a gentle man, and quiet by nature, until he's riled. He led us to our favorite booth and signaled for a waitress. We gave her our orders, and before she left, Uncle Charlie cut me a deep-dimpled grin. "They're not as good as Patty's, but the new owner of Sweets 'n' Eats makes darn good donuts. I have glazed and chocolate covered. Which one do you want?"

I returned his grin. "Both." Which brought guffaws from Charlie and my dad.

After the waitress left to fill our orders, I related my dream about the medicine woman. "She was so real. Like I could reach out and touch her. I didn't want to upset Grandmother or give her reason to cut her vacation short, so I didn't text to ask her what the name Shunkaha means. I don't think it's Cherokee because the medicine woman said he was not of my people."

Uncle Charlie offered a teasing smile. "I'm surprised you didn't Google it."

The waitress arrived with our drinks. I honestly wasn't in the mood for teasing—from anyone. I sucked a giant gulp, which immediately when down the wrong windpipe. I thought Dad was going to beat me to death the way he pummeled my back. I managed to clear my throat.

Uncle Charlie looked contrite. "Sorry, Goddaughter, I didn't mean to tease."

Before I could answer, the waitress arrived again, with our food.

I assured Uncle Charlie he was forgiven.

He said, "The medicine woman was correct. He is not Cherokee. Shunkaha is a Lakota name."

I ladled in another spoonful of chili. "Interesting. She also said his name was the same as mine, and to trust my spirit animal."

Uncle Charlie seemed to drift away. Then he spoke. "Long ago, when I was a small child, and before I came to know Henry, I spoke no English. My mother and father had gone to rest with the Spirits in the great beyond. I was taken to a Sioux Reservation in Montana and placed in a foster home. I learned the ways of the Lakota, and some of their language."

In the custom of the Native people, their explanation for all things was often related in story form. Uncle Charlie's sing-song voice quieted my tension. The knots in my muscles began to relax, and I savored my food and the company of my two favorite men.

"Goddaughter, the name Shunkaha means—wolf."

The spoon was midway to my mouth. "Wolf? Are you sure? Well, of course, you're sure. The medicine woman did say he was not of my people."

It was a little surreal to sit in silence while trying to digest the significance of my family name—Waya and Shunkaha—both meaning Wolf. I managed to say, "She said he would protect me." I shrugged. "I'm not sure how he's supposed to protect me if he's a spirit."

Uncle Charlie said, "Why do you think he's a spirit?"

"Because the medicine woman said he was like my spirit animal."

He touched his chest, and I knew that, beneath his shirt, he was touching his medicine pouch. He said, "I will think on all that you have told me about your dream, Goddaughter, and I will ask the Great Father Spirit to enlighten me."

"Charlie?" Dad's voice hinted of concern. "I think you and I will attend the rodeo when it comes to Louisville. I'm not trusting a spirit to protect my daughter."

I consumed the chocolate donut. "Whoever this threatening person is, he or she means serious business." I related the snake incident. "And by the way, Dad, with Caleb's permission, I kept the note that was inside the box with the rattler. My gut instinct told me Coffey might not bother to try to pull prints off the wrapping paper or the bow."

Dad finished the remains of his coffee. "You have it with you?"

"Yessir. It's in my travel bag."

Uncle Charlie crooked a grin. "You know, if I wasn't an old man, I'd like to ride a bull."

I patted his hand. Then, realizing the time that had passed by, I was happy when Dad asked if I was ready to go home.

He didn't need to ask me twice.

On the way to my place, I sent a text to Ella letting her know I'd see her at the clinic first thing in the morning. She replied that we had light appointments until the afternoon so I should sleep in.

Once we arrived, River, my black Lab, and Rascal, my gray teacup donkey, greeted me with endearing *woofs* and snuffling brays. After giving my dad the plastic bag holding the note, I gave him a departing hug and stood watching as he drove toward the highway.

I gave my animals another hug, opened the refrigerator, and poured myself a large glass of iced tea. Heading into the living room, I relaxed in my recliner with the tablet's murder file and slowly read through the details.

Fact one: Carl Calloway was gored to death by a bull named Diablo.

Question: Was Carl's death an unfortunate accident or did someone want him dead?

Question: How does Carl's death relate to the ongoing threats against Caleb and Caroline?

Thought: Ask Caleb for the last number received on Carl's cellphone, and if there are matching calls from the same number. *Note to self:* Why didn't I think of this before I returned from Oklahoma?

Fact two: There is definite tension between Caleb and Rex Siegler.

Question: Does the tension have to do with Rosie? I could infer that sexual tensions were small potatoes compared to murder.

Fact three: The killer is sending a strong message to Caleb and Caroline.

Question: Who was the delivery guy with the tattoo on his left ear? Is he a ranch hand?

Question: Who hired the delivery guy? Would it be a ranch hand?

Question: Did the two bulls escape their pens or did

someone open the gates?

Question: What will ruining my clothes and testing them for illegal substance prove?

Thought: Trace the chemicals to a supplier—legal or otherwise—and the buyer.

Fact four: Sheriff O'Neal Coffey and Deputy Sheriff Cletus Dodge are up to their elbows in dirty business.

Question: What's in it for them? Money? Or is it personal?

Question: Are there fingerprints on the note?

Fact five: Shunkaha…

At this inopportune moment, River and Rascal raced to the kitchen door and kicked up a fuss. I didn't welcome the interruption. I sighed and went to answer it, hoping it was someone I wanted to see. The mysterious warrior, perhaps?

"Welcome home, Tullah."

Ella embraced me in a generous hug. "We're in between appointments. I wanted to check on you. How was your trip? Oh, and we have two chihuahuas arriving in about half an hour. One is the victim of a porcupine attack, and the other has been in labor for more than twenty-four hours."

I'd been home exactly forty-five minutes, and 'tho Ella was like a sister, I wasn't exactly feeling all warm and fuzzy. I sighed deeply. "Which do you want—the possible cesarean section or pulling out porcupine quills?"

"You look beat, Tullah. I'll take the C-section."

Chapter Sixteen

Blood oozed from the quills that protruded from the poor chihuahua. It was obvious Little Man had lost the battle of a porcupine versus a small dog that tried to live up to its name. I removed more than a dozen sharp barbs and injected Little Man with an antibiotic to protect him against infection, along with enough sedative to keep him asleep and out of pain for several hours.

The afternoon turned out to be much busier than expected. It's not unusual to have walk-in emergencies. Over and beyond scheduled appointments, I went to work to put in what I thought would be about four hours and ended up working well past our usual closing time.

As we finally strolled across the yard to the gate that separated our properties, Ella said, "Do you mind if we chat for a little bit?"

"Sure. Want to come in for a cup of coffee or relax on the porch swing?"

There was a chill to the late April evening. Ella replied, "Coffee, in the kitchen."

Once we were seated with cups of steaming hazelnut in front of us, I waited for a few minutes. Ella looked at me with the weary superiority of someone who had bravely undergone a major milestone. And she had—graduating veterinarian school with honors and becoming my business partner.

"You look like you have the weight of the world on

your shoulders, Ella. What's troubling you?"

She added a spoonful of sugar to her cup. Ella never put sugar in her coffee. I surmised that whatever was eating at her was serious because she was the most upbeat person I'd ever known. Nothing ever seemed to get her down.

At last, after stirring the life out of her coffee, she looked at me with deep concern and heaved a heavy sigh. "I'm just going to say it right out—and be honest, Tullah—are you in love with Andy? If you are, I'll…I'll…"

"What? Whoa!" Her question had come completely out of left field and caught me off-guard. "Whatever gave you the idea I was in love with Andy?"

She shrugged, and stirred her coffee, again. "I'm not sure. I guess it's the way you look at him, sometimes, and the way he looks at you."

"Andy looks at me a certain way? I'm not sure what you mean."

"You know—like you're a special kind of dessert he wants but it's not on the menu. And there are times when you look at him with a far-off wishful-thinking expression."

I laughed. "I've been compared to a lot of things, but never a dessert."

I removed her cup and dumped the syrupy liquid down the drain. I opened a cabinet and removed a bottle of Chablis and filled two wine flutes. I handed her the long-stemmed glass. Then I looked her straight in the eyes and said, "Ella, read my lips. I am not in love with Andy. Sure, when we were kids, I fancied myself as being infatuated with him. That was then. He's a good-looking guy with a great personality. But we're all grown up now, and we're friends. *Nothing more.*"

The tears in her eyes, and her sniffles, cued me.

Oh, boy, this was more serious than I thought. "*You're* in love with him." It wasn't a question. I was stating a fact.

She nodded. "I think he thinks we, he and I, are friends. You know—pals—buddies—someone to hang out with, watch old movies, play chess, but not fall in love with."

I burst out laughing, and then apologized for my gaff. I had kept the best secret in the world. In fact, I'd been so caught up in my busy day-to-day life as a veterinarian and assisting my father with solving crimes that I'd totally forgotten the conversation Andy and I'd had where he'd sworn me to pinky-finger, eat-a-toad-turd, hope-to-die secrecy. How could I keep his secret and dispel Ella's fears? Andy feared Ella only thought of him as a big brother.

I sipped my wine and thought. "Ella, I can assure you the only interest Andy has in me is being a pal."

"But—"

I held up my hand to shush her. "When you get home tonight, take a good long look at yourself in the mirror. You'll see what Andy sees—a beautiful girl dressed in jeans, plaid shirt, and no makeup, and most of the time smelling like…" I wrinkled my nose. "If you want him to see you as an alluring young woman out to capture his heart, you gotta dress the part and act the role. Know what I mean?"

"Um, I'm not sure. Enlighten me."

"Talk to your mom."

"No way! Please, Tullah. Help me."

"Help you! You're totally asking the wrong person."

I draped my hand down the front of my denim shirt. "Look at me. If I knew, I'd have a man in my life."

I really wanted to break my promise to Andy, and tell Ella how much she meant to him, and that he thought she wasn't interested in him. Breaking promises wasn't my style. Too bad he was too shy to make the first move. Every time he mentioned her name his freckles would light up like red Christmas bulbs. Maybe, in my spare time, I could come up with a plan to bring them together.

"Ella, my brain is muddled from dealing with rattlesnakes, bulls gone berserk, crooked cops, and frenemies that speak out of both sides of their mouths. Maybe a good night's sleep will clear my head."

I reached out and patted her hand. "In the meantime, please believe me, Andy is more like the brother I never had. He's not on my radar for anything other than being a great pal."

I walked her to the front door. She hugged me and apologized for her outburst. "Geez, I didn't mean to sound like a silly teenager."

I assured her that such was life, and watched her trot to the gate and open it. She turned and waved, with a smile. "See you tomorrow."

I returned to my chair, opened my tablet, and tried to pick up the thread of my questions about the Calloway case. Soon I realized I'd gone as far as I could go.

The sound of loneliness echoed inside my head. I closed my eyes and allowed the heaviness I caried inside me every moment of every day to come crashing back down. I actually felt the misery descend. After all these years, I still carried the grievous burden and the weight of loss for the only man I had ever loved, other than my dad and Uncle Charlie.

The day before our wedding, my fiancé, Bryce Myers, had been kicked in the head by a fractious stallion. Bryce was funny, kind, and gentle. We'd mapped out our future together, including the number of children we wanted. We'd planned to become veterinarians and open a renowned animal hospital.

I never had the opportunity to say goodbye or to tell him how much I loved him. Bryce had died instantly. From that day forward, I'd buried myself in academics, forensics, and my career. I'd drawn a curtain of privacy around myself, refusing to open my heart to future love opportunities. I had become a widow before having the opportunity to become a wife. In some minute way, I almost envied Ella and Andy.

I thought about my dad and his budding relationship with Dr. Sunny Sanders, Ella's mother. Like me, after my mother's tragic murder Dad had locked away his feelings and, like me, had buried himself in work. I hoped that someday he and I would find the keys to unlock our hearts.

After trudging upstairs and opening the bedroom door, I wondered for the first time if remaining in the home I was born in, and remaining in Enigma, had been a mistake. Opening the door to the bedroom that had once belonged to my mother and father was a reminder of her death, and gave me a little shock.

I walked to the cedar chest at the end of my bed, opened the lid, and rummaged beneath layers of blankets and other items until my fingers found the frames. I withdrew the pictures. After almost fourteen years of being hidden away, the photo of my mother was still unbearable to look at. Tracing a finger across her beautiful face, I could almost see myself in her image. I gently returned the picture to its resting place.

My hands trembled as I stared at the couple in the whitewashed frame. So full of love, so innocent, so filled with hopes for what was yet to come. It was the first and only time I'd been to the beach. Our pre-honeymoon trip to Galveston, Texas. Bryce sat on the wooden rail of a fishing pier, his long legs and arms embraced me against his body, our noses touched. Below our images, he had written, *Love never ends!*

I closed my eyes and recalled his laughter mingling with the mewling cries of seagulls, and waves lapping against the shore. Lifting my eyes, I spotted the blue velvet box sitting in the chest's long tray. Laying the picture aside, I opened the box. Inside lay my rings and the wedding band I'd planned to slip on Bryce's finger as we repeated our vows. I looked at the photograph and rings for a long moment.

Whoever said that time heals all wounds had never met grief up close and personal. I nestled the mementoes of the past in their dark places and closed the lid. I climbed into the bed, and River and Rascal settled on their sleeping mats. I switched on the lamp and picked up the mystery book I'd been reading, though I didn't remember a word I had read.

I lay awake in the darkness for a while allowing my mind to ramble through a myriad of thoughts that ranged from my past life to the present. Across the field, and in the direction of the swamp behind my property, a dog barked—at the moon, at a racoon, at a wandering cat or a derelict dog—who knew?

River raised his head and *woof*ed. For my convenience, and the accessibility of my animals, I had installed a doggie door within the bedroom door. Now, I realized I'd somehow forgotten to shut down their door from kitchen to outdoors. Too exhausted to get out of bed and go downstairs to keep them in, I listened as River and Rascal clattered down the stairs, knowing they were headed outside. River had a barking episode. I didn't mind, this once—the noise was company for my thoughts.

I found myself thinking about Bryce, when he'd moved to Enigma, and how we'd met at the 4-H rodeo. I figured that when I met him, I'd been thirteen and he was seventeen. Now I'd soon turn thirty. Had he lived, Bryce would be thirty-four.

I'd been angry with him when he died. Perhaps, in many ways, I was still upset with him for leaving me. My eyes fluttered shut and I drifted into oblivion. My anger against Bryce slid off my mind, replaced with a more familiar melancholy.

I wasn't jealous of Ella and Andy. I sent up a prayer asking the Great Spirit Father to help me guide them to each other, and to give them an unbroken bond of love. A gust of wind rattled the bedroom window. I pulled the quilt up to my chin. I thought about going downstairs and brewing myself a cup of hot chocolate, but that would mean getting out of my warm bed.

The bedroom doggie door flapped as River and Rascal returned to their beds. I could sense sleep approaching now, could feel it stealing over me. I held onto the thought of Bryce so I could slide under; if I looked directly at the sleep I needed, it would slip away.

Tomorrow, I'd contact my friend, head of the forensics department at the University of Kentucky, and make arrangements to send my soiled clothes with a request to test the bull's secretions for possible hallucinogenic drugs.

At long last, I sighed and surrendered to sleep, allowing it to drag me down into the depths of darkness. The name *Shunaka* rested on my lips.

Chapter Seventeen

He stood in the mists, his raven hair flowing in the breeze, an armor of porcupine quills adorning his bare chest. His faded denims spoke of many washings, and the spurs on his worn boots jangled as he strolled toward me. Two dark tears were tattooed beneath each eye. I was about to ask his name when the alarm clock interrupted my dream.

I glanced around the room, amazed that I had slept soundly through the night, and a shy ray of sun beckoned me to rise and shine. For several moments I lay with my eyes shut trying to recall the man in my dream. River and Rascal were having none of my lolling in bed.

I'm not sure why I had the sudden urge to go for a ride. It was several hours before time to open the clinic. I dressed and, foregoing coffee, I hustled across the yard and to the barn. It was the perfect morning for a horseback ride. I saddled Gandalf, my black-and-white pinto gelding, and set off to the vast acreage behind my property, my loyal pets at my side. The sweet aroma of wildflowers, the earthy scent of soil, and the motion of my horse were calming.

I stopped at the edge of Dolphy's Preserve, a vast swamp where, two years ago, I had discovered the skeletons of eleven murdered women. The swamp is a wild and peaceful place now that the murderer is living out the remainder of his years in a mental institution.

Gandalf stamped his foot and pawed at the damp earth. Impatient, he wanted to run. He was my mother's horse, a Quarter Horse built for speed and agility. She had used him for barrel-racing competition. I loosened the reins, touched my heels to his flanks, and let him sweep me across the swamp's higher grounds in a rhythm of rippling muscles and pounding hooves. I gripped the saddle with my thighs, spread my arms like giant wings, and allowed a primal war cry escape from the depths of my soul.

I let Gandalf run until his neck was flecked with foam where the reins touched him, allowing him to slow at his own free will. I looked back to watch River racing toward me and Rascal pushing his stubby legs to keep up. Dog and donkey flopped to the weedy ground as if welcoming the rest.

I dropped the reins as I dismounted, not fearing that Gandalf would stray away. Horse, dog, and donkey all ambled over to a small stream swollen from the recent spring rains. True to his black Lab nature, and in spite of the chill, River unceremoniously jumped into the middle of the water. Rascal mimicked his buddy. I jokingly scolded my pets for showering me with cold water as they shook chilled rivulets from their bodies.

In the stillness of the marsh, I listened to the trill of songbirds and watched flashes of reds, browns, and blues flit through budding tree limbs. I hoped we weren't in for a false spring, but instead, in another few weeks, the land would be alive with variations of green.

This morning, I had awakened from an unsettling dream. Only the fragments remained—a bare-chested man wearing an armor of quills. There were black images beneath his eyes. I gazed at Gandalf cropping grass and wondered whether the indigenous man in my dream was a visit from the past or from the present.

I have often seen the spirits from the long-ago dead, listened to their chants of war, of births, of death. Today the land before me was empty of ghosts. Mother Earth works her magic to bring sunshine and rain to nourish her children—tiny plants, and microbes invisible to the naked eye. Long ago, my aged cousin, Uma Hoktochee, had explained that this is Mother Earth's gift to us. She also said humans have no magic for this part of the process.

A dark cloud passed over, blocking out the sun, and a chill slithered over me. Shadow Woman hovered, then whispered—*Beware Uya*!

In the ancient ways of my people, I opened my arms to embrace the earth, the wind, the sky, and lifted up a supplication of gratefulness to the Great Spirit Father and asked for his guidance and protection from *Uya*. I whistled for Gandalf.

I settled in the saddle, my mind filled with a mixture of thoughts—Bryce, Shunaka, the Calloways, a promising romance between Ella and Andy, and now another warning about a malevolent being. I turned Gandalf toward home. It was almost time to open the clinic.

"River." I called my dog from the marsh where he'd gone sniffing the trail for rabbits or a covey of quail. He's a hunting dog who now seizes on the scents of evildoers and has more than once saved my life from bad people.

A wind kicked up and blew across the open field, but the morning sun warmed my back through the light jacket I wore. Gandalf rocked my hips with his long-legged gait. I closed my eyes and simply enjoyed the sensation of the sun and movement.

My cellphone chimed, alerting me the call was from Ella. "Gandalf is missing from his stall. Should I be worried?" There was a hint of urgency in her voice.

"He and I are out for a morning run." I enjoyed talking on the phone while sitting on my horse. It could only be better if I had a piping hot mug of coffee.

"Wish I was with you."

I shrugged. "Sorry, I needed a little alone time."

Rascal emitted one of his snuffling brays that sound like a sneeze but loud enough to bring a chuckle from Ella. "Tullah, about Andy and me…just forget all that silly nonsense."

I couldn't help grinning. "Okay, if you say so."

I waited for her to break the silence. In the background, I heard Jeff, our office assistant, greet Ella. And then the office phone rang.

"I'm about ten minutes from the house, Ella. As soon as I unsaddle Gandalf and turn him out, I'll grab a quick shower and hustle on over."

I nudged my horse to a faster gait, with River and Rascal bringing up the rear. Before I disconnected, Ella said, "Jeff brought two boxes of donuts. I'll have the coffee on."

"That boy's a keeper."

We ended our call on a chuckle.

My thoughts were on how to plan a romantic dinner and keep it a secret from my two best friends. Perhaps I could enlist both Ella's Uncle Tiny and her mother to help.

A *woof* from River interrupted my woolgathering. Gandalf stretched his neck and whinnied. "What's going on with you two?"

I leaned forward in the saddle, and stared toward my house. As I drew closer, I didn't see any vehicle or stray dog that would draw the animosity of my pets. But they were clever animals, and I had learned to trust their instincts.

I leaned down to open the gate that separated my property from the preserve. River raced through the opening and toward the clinic. I debated whether or not to leave the gate open and close it later. But if there was an emergency, Ella would have told me.

I closed the gate and trotted Gandalf toward the corral, where I dismounted and led him inside. A great barred owl fluttered to rest on a fence post.

My owl.

I unstrapped the girth and removed the saddle and then the bridle from Gandalf. Normally, he would roll in the dirt, give himself a good shake, then head to the water trough for a long drink. At the moment, he stood close to me instead.

Ella opened the side door of the office. "Coffee's hot, and our first two clients are on the way."

The owl winked at me. He lifted his brownish-gray wings and flew close—the feathered tips brushed the side of my face. A tremor of foreboding swept over me.

Chapter Eighteen

"Why are you frowning, Tullah?"

"Witches aren't real." The words unexpectedly popped out of my mouth.

"*Witches*...are you having one of your empathic episodes?" Ella's Texas twang deepened. I detected the concern in her voice. Her eyes had widened as she scanned every direction of the yard.

Call me superstitious, but I had been weaned on Native American folklore. You could also call me a bit of a history geek. I enjoyed discovering the ways and the pasts of other cultures, their day-to-day lives hundreds of years ago. Their struggles and celebrations. Their beliefs.

"Hey, Tullah, did you hear me?" Her voice sounded a bit testy.

"Yes, I guess I am." I brushed my hands up and down the sleeves of my jacket to ward off the chills. "Give me fifteen minutes to shower and dress." I tried to brush aside her question and my own intuition. "And have the coffee ready...and a couple of donuts."

"You're not getting off that easy. You're spooked. It's written in your face."

She had a point. I was spooked. "It's about the case I'm working on. Nothing for you to get upset over."

"We're friends, Tullah. More like sisters. Everyone needs someone to talk to...even you."

True, except I wasn't much for sharing.

The side door opened and Jeff stuck his head out. "Hate to interrupt, but we have an emergency. A Mrs. Pierson is on the phone and frantic. She found her mare this morning with an arrow through its neck."

Alice Pierson was Enigma's beloved 4-H teacher. I'd known her since fourth grade. I rushed inside and grabbed the phone. "Mrs. P, it's Tullah. What happened?"

"Oh, Tullah, Some fool shot Neda. Can you come?"

"Is Neda standing?"

"Yes, and I have her in the small shower stall to keep her from lying down."

"Great! I'll be there in twenty minutes. And, Mrs. P, call my dad. Whoever did this needs to pay…and dearly."

"What should I do until you get here?"

"How badly is she bleeding?"

"It's a steady drip."

"Stay with Neda. Keep her calm and on her feet. I'm on my way."

Forget the shower. Over my shoulder, I said, "I'm not sure how long this will take. You know where to find me."

Jeff said, "Who would want to hurt a horse?"

"A person without a soul," Ella responded as she followed me to the door. She touched my arm to momentarily delay me. "Tullah, you never answered my question."

I gave her a matter-of-fact look. "Empathic? Call it what you like, but yes, I was sensing a message from a spectral aura."

Ella cleared her throat. "What did it say?"

I grabbed the keys to my fully equipped traveling

medical office on wheels, and before racing across the yard to my truck, I kept all inflection from my voice. "Today is doomsday."

At this point all I wanted was a much-needed infusion of coffee and to get on the road. "I'll check in as soon as I can."

Ella's voice trailed after me. "What does that mean—today is doomsday?"

I turned and back-peddled. "You'll know when I know."

Jeff rushed after me. He held a large to-go cup and a folded napkin. "I'll put this in your truck."

I thanked him for his thoughtfulness. I raced inside the house and up the stairs and shed my soiled shirt for a fresh one before I hurried back downstairs and out the door. I had inserted the key into the ignition before I remembered I hadn't filled River's and Rascal's bowls.

I set my phone in the cradle and said, "Call Jeff."

"Holliday Animal Clinic. How may I help you?"

"Jeff, when you have time, I'd appreciate it if you'd feed River and Rascal. The kitchen door is unlocked."

"You got it, Doc."

I pushed the gas pedal and sped toward the highway. Dad's voice seemed to whisper his usual caution in my ear. *Don't speed, and drive safe.* Nevertheless, I made my turn and burned rubber to Mrs. Pierson's house.

My cellphone played Dad's favorite tune. "Did Mrs. P call you?"

"She did, and I'm on my way."

I concentrated on the road. "Mrs. P doesn't have an enemy in the world, and Neda is so old she can barely swat a fly." I slammed the steering wheel. "Since the town has grown, we've had a rash of calls to treat injured animals…horses, dogs, cows… It's inhuman, Dad."

"I hear you, Punkin. Bored kids with too much time on their hands."

"What'll you do if you catch the person?"

"Charge them with animal cruelty. The rest is up to the judge."

"I'm pulling into Mrs. P's driveway, Dad. I'll meet you inside the barn. And Dad will you grab my portable x-ray machine from the truck?"

"Will do."

I stopped within inches of the barn door and exited my truck. I opened a panel and grabbed my medical case, but that was all, for the moment. I'd need to examine the horse before knowing exactly what supplies were needed.

Mrs. P rushed to the door. "Oh, thank God, Tullah. I think she's dying. I couldn't keep her on her feet."

Alice Pierson was a spritely seventy-five-year-old with a ready smile. Today, she wore a haggard expression, and worry clouded her normally bright blue eyes. She and I raced to the wash station at the end of the barn. The old mare lay on her side, the tile floor awash in red. Mrs. P quickly sat, oblivious of the blood that soaked into her clothes as she lifted her dear pet's head to her lap.

"Tullah?"

"Down here, Dad." His footfalls indicated he was trotting down the barn's wide aisle to us.

Concern and anger laced his eyes as he looked at me. I met his unasked question with barely a perceptible nod. "She's lost a lot of blood, but she has a strong will and is hanging on for dear life."

As a team of three, we worked to encourage the

downed mare to stand. I knew she was in pain and it was easier for her to remain inert than try to stand. I knelt and lifted her head to look into her eyes as I spoke to her, and after my encouraging words, she nickered and I knew she was ready to live.

I stood. "Mrs. P, you stand at Neda's rear. Dad, we'll need your strength to help roll Neda forward, and I'll take command of her head." Speaking in Cherokee, I commanded the old mare to rise.

She let out a loud grunt, and in spite of her obvious pain, she worked with the three of us to gain solid footing on the stall's slick surface. It took several struggling tries to get the mare to her feet.

With Dad's help, I set the portable x-ray machine in place and, thanks to modern technology, I was able to see the arrow had nicked the jugular vein—thus the cause for the leaking loss of blood. What could have been worse was if the arrow had split a vertebra in half rather than the slight fracture I saw was also involved.

Dad didn't care that blood seeped through the knees of his uniform. He knelt and placed an arm around his old friend's shoulders. A sob escaped as Mrs. P leaned against him. "Who would shoot a horse…who would commit such a horrible act?"

Her woeful expression tugged at my heart. She said, "Do what you have to do, Tullah. I don't want her to suffer."

"I won't lie to you, Mrs. P. It's bad, but with your loving care, and a lot of antibiotics, Neda will live to celebrate many more birthdays."

Between sobs and joyful laughter, Alice Pierson enveloped me in a bear hug. "How can I ever thank you, Tullah?"

I returned her embrace, then suggested she let my dad escort her to the house. "He'll need to take a statement from you, especially if you decide to press charges."

Dad helped Alice stand. For a moment, she gazed at her bloody hands and clothing. She spoke as if more to herself than to Dad and me. "Last week it was old Mr. Alvarez's dog, and several days before that, Wanda Scofield's cat."

A diminutive woman that had to strain to look up at my dad's six-foot-plus stature, she said, "We're all old people, Henry. The lowly cowards are targeting us because they think we're too cowardly to report them."

She laced her arm through the crook of his. "Soon as you finish up, Tullah, c'mon to the house. I made lemon scones last night. We'll partake of tea and cookies while I give Henry my statement."

Dad said, "Tullah, preserve the arrow."

"Yessir, I will." And, to my favorite childhood 4-H mentor, I said, "After I tend to Neda, I'll clean up the blood, Mrs. P."

She rewarded me with a tearful smile.

Once I'd carefully removed the arrow and wrapped the bloody object in a sheet of plastic to preserve any fingerprints that I hoped the criminal had left behind, I stanched the bleeding and inserted plugs to close the puncture wounds.

An hour later, I sat enjoying a luscious bite of lemon scone. I waited for the dark Darjeeling tea to perk me up. At first, I thought my former teacher had reached the age where rambling and conversations that tended to wander off into the weeds were unavoidable, but her blue eyes belied such judgment. She was in expert control of her faculties and of the conversation.

"You know, Henry, this was no hunting accident, because hunting season is over. The other day, I was having tea with Mr. Alvarez and Wanda. We were sitting on her back porch when we spotted three boys, way off in the distance. Mr. Alvarez said he thought the boys were up to no good because it was at an hour when they should've been in school.

"Can you describe the boys, Alice?" Dad asked.

She arched her eyebrows. "Not really. These ol' peepers of mine don't see so good anymore. But it looked like they were whacking weeds with long sticks." She perked up for a moment. "Maybe it was bows and arrows."

"Alice, think…do any of your backyard neighbors have teenage boys?"

"I don't know, Henry. All the students I taught are now adults, and most have married and left Enigma for greener pastures. These days, I stick pretty close to my inner circle of friends, and we're all past our prime."

She shifted a concerned look at us. "I've never been afraid of anything in my entire life, but Henry, the older I get, the more concerned I am about protecting myself. Whoever did this to our animals might decide to do the same to us older folks."

There was a hint of desperation in her voice that tugged at my heartstrings. I thought about the owl that landed on my fence post earlier. I had sensed it had nothing to do with Alice Pierson and her friends.

Alice looked at me. She seemed to consider her words. "Tullah, be honest. Will Neda be as good as usual?"

I lifted her wrinkled hands to mine. "I'd never fib to

you, Mrs. P. The arrow nicked a vertebra. Neda's very lucky it was just a nick. She'll be sore, and she may never be able to jump hurdles or race in the Kentucky Derby, but in time, you can take her for an easy gallop."

Alice patted my hand and, with a twinkle in her blue eyes, said, "These days and at our age, 'easy' is about all the speed we can muster."

My phone chirped. After a quick glance at the caller, I excused myself to take the call. Dad also stood. He assured our friend that he'd do all he could to find the culprit and bring him to justice. Mrs. P squeezed our hands in a grateful goodbye.

He followed me outside, down the steps, and to my truck. When I disconnected the call, he said, "From the frown on your face, I take it you have another emergency."

"If only it were that simple." Now I understood why the owl had visited me. I said, "That was Caleb. Rex Siegler just died."

"Hmm. Where was Siegler on your suspect list?"

"At the top with Sheriff Coffey and Deputy Dodge."

Assisting my dad with solving cases had been an interesting education in criminal psychology. I learned that at a certain point in any investigation, everyone is a suspect, even the least obvious. I'd also learned that given the right motive, a person is capable of anything.

Dad said, "I'll have Tiny conduct a deeper investigation into Dodge and Coffey's backgrounds."

"What about fingerprints on the note? Was Tiny able to pull any?"

"He's working on it, Punkin. I can tell you one thing for certain—hiring Andy Kemble and Wayne Ramsey has taken a weight off Tiny's workload."

"Maybe he'll stick around longer rather than retiring early."

"I sure hope so. Next to Charlie Whitehorse, Tiny Goodbody is the man I'd want watching my back when push comes to shove."

I totally agreed. Deputy Tiny Goodbody was Ella's uncle and a loyal, trustworthy and a great friend for anyone to have. I rested my hand on the truck's door handle. "Dad, back to Rex's death. My problem with this case is that it seems the list of suspects and motives is endless." I shrugged. "Everyone on my list seems to have a motive."

Dad gave me a fatherly hug. My stomach growled, and we both laughed. He said, "When did you have *real* food? And I'm not referring to donuts!"

When I scrunched my face into a questioning frown, he scolded, "Call or text Ella, tell her whatever you want to tell her, then get in your truck and follow me to town. I'm buying you a breakfast that does not include sweet confections."

I pecked him on the cheek. "Can I entice you to come to the house tonight to discuss the case, and to bring a plate of chicken wings and onion rings from the Crispy Chicken, and—"

He scoffed. "Don't say…donuts."

"I wasn't. I was going to say…chocolate eclairs."

He belly-laughed. "Punkin, you are a hopeless sweetaholic."

Chapter Nineteen

As I drove home, the possibilities of Caleb's case perked and bubbled in my brain.

The minute I thought about the owl, and the news of Rex's death, a darkness passed over me. Meanwhile, a gentle spring rain pattered against the truck's windshield. I wasn't sure if the chill invading my body was from the weather or from a hovering dark spirit.

I turned off the main highway onto the graveled drive that led to my house and the clinic. I stopped to watch Gandalf, Moon, Banjo, and Ella's buckskin, Jupiter, frolicking in the front pasture. They nipped and bucked and raced away, chasing each other, then hiked their tails and lashed out with their hind feet. As I watched this play, it was as if their movements were choreographed. And then they would race in different directions, stand, stretch their magnificent necks, and whinny. Their method of communication fascinated me. In many ways, I felt that I shared a psychic connection with my animals, but especially with my black Lab. As I approached the clinic and parked next to the side of the office, I pushed my fanciful thoughts aside. Now that Rex was dead, I needed to get serious and focus on my list of suspects.

Jeff walked out the door. I briefly filled him in on Mrs. P's mare and said I would type up the medical report and place it in her file. "How are classes going?"

I inquired.

"Finals are coming up. I'm a little nervous."

"If you need time off to study, Ella and I can handle the office work until finals are over."

He blushed. Jeff was the first in a long line of family members to graduate high school and attend college. He worked part-time as our office assistant. His aspirations were to become a teacher; additionally, he desired to be a positive role model for his younger siblings and a host of cousins.

"I appreciate the offer, Doc. I could, maybe, use the day before the test to get in some extra studying."

I assured him that whatever he needed was fine with Ella and me, and with that assurance he hustled to his old clunker, climbed inside, and waved goodbye.

Ella sat with her feet propped on the edge of a trash can. I grabbed a cup of coffee and joined her at the desk. I also related that I'd given Jeff permission to take time off to study for his tests. She smiled. "You know, he'll soon graduate with his associate degree. What're we going to do when he leaves to attend the university in Lexington?"

"He's a great kid, and smart." I sighed. "He runs this office like a well-oiled machine. He'll be difficult to replace."

Ella agreed. She said, "Fill me in about Mrs. Pierson's horse. It really had an arrow through its neck?"

"It did. That mare's lucky to be alive." I related all the details. "Dad's giving the case to Andy. And speaking of Andy—the last time he and I chatted, he expressed regret that he hadn't been riding in a while. I'm thinking a nice horseback ride and a picnic—make that a romantic picnic—might get the ball rolling between the two of you. I'm sure my dad wouldn't mind if Andy gave Banjo some much needed exercise."

I stopped Ella's protest. "Neither of you has to dress up. However, it would be great if you wore a little extra makeup, and some really nice-smelling perfume. And, I happen to know that his favorite food is parmesan-garlic chicken wings. He's also partial to lemon-filled donuts and ginger tea with honey. You and he also enjoy rodeos. You might suggest getting tickets to the upcoming PBR."

Ella clapped her hands together like an excited child. "Tullah, you are a genius. It's perfect!"

"I must confess I have an ulterior motive for wanting you at the rodeo." I went on to explain that I'd be doing a little undercover detective work. "As of now, I don't have a clue who's behind the threats against Caleb and Caroline. But I do know that the incident with the two bulls getting out and rampaging through the guests was no accident."

I drew a breath, then told her about Rex Siegler's death. "He was number three on my suspect list."

"Gee whillikers, Tullah. Isn't that murder?"

"Yes and no. Technically, his death was the result of being gored by a bull. At this point there's no way to prove otherwise."

Puzzlement draped across her face. "I just don't get it."

"Neither do I, Ella. I've reviewed my suspect list and the facts, over and over, and nothing adds up. Dad's coming tonight. Maybe between the two of us we can figure out the who and the why. Frankly, I'm ready to nab the bad guys and close this case."

"You're a good detective, Tullah. You're also like a

sister to me, and I'm afraid you'll get hurt, or worse."
She gave a nod. "You can count on me being at the
rodeo, and Andy, too, if he's not on duty."

At the sound of an approaching vehicle, we checked
the clock. Ella said, "One 'o clock on the dot. That's my
neuter job." She loosened a little giggle. "It seems
Sparky is really the Romeo of the neighborhood, and
some of the neighbors are in a snit about his 'sparking'
their girly-dogs."

"Ella!" I joined her laughter. "You do have a way
with words."

I was glad the rest of the day was routine, and
relieved when we finally notified our answering service
and then locked the door. I was anxious to discuss the list
of suspects with my dad.

While I waited for his arrival, I opened my laptop
and looked up Rex on the internet. He was thirty-six,
born in Eufaula, Oklahoma. His mother was a waitress
and his father worked as a mechanic. He was the third
child of four, had excelled in baseball and attended his
first year of college on an athletic scholarship until he
messed up his shoulder. His baby sister committed
suicide at age twenty. Between losing his scholarship
and the death of his sister, Rex had turned to alcohol and
drugs. To support his habits, he'd turned to petty theft,
and then after advancing his career to stealing expensive
cars for chop shops, he'd been sentenced to ten years,
served seven, and was paroled for good behavior.

What a tragic beginning to such a short life, I
thought.

River and Rascal set up a ruckus, alerting me that a
vehicle was approaching the house. I closed the laptop
and walked to the front door.

It's rare that Uncle Charlie gets to leave the saloon. I was happy to see him striding up the front steps with my dad, and I opened the door wide. Uncle Charlie held up a large picnic basket. He grinned. "*Barbeque* ribs, potato salad, baked beans, and peach cobbler." The aromas flirted with my nose and stomach.

Dad held up a cooler. "Lemonade and iced tea."

I rushed to set the table and to fill glasses with ice. While dining, we made small chit-chat, with Uncle Charlie relating that Vera, his new waitress, was working out great, and the customers loved her quick smile and wit.

While we enjoyed our food, Uncle Charlie said, "I almost envy Tanti and the gals having the freedom to go on a thirty-day cruise. I can't remember the last time I had time to go fishing." He wiped his mouth with a napkin and grabbed another spare rib.

"Have you ever thought about retiring?"

He held the rib midway to his mouth as if I'd somehow surprised him with my question. In case I've forgotten to tell you, Uncle Charlie has his fingers dipped inside multiple pots in our small but growing town. Not only does he own, operate, and prepare delicious food at the Whitehorse Saloon, and occasionally breaks up a fight, he's Chief of Enigma's volunteer fire department, and until funds were allotted for Dad to hire two new deputies, Uncle Charlie served as an auxiliary deputy, helping my dad and Uncle Tiny many times.

Charlie chugged down a gulp of iced tea, then cleared his throat as if nearly choking. "Retiring, ah, what would I do with all that spare time?"

Dad and I laughed. As if we were one mind, our words echoed when we said, "Go fishing."

Uncle Charlie held up his hands and did a quick finger count. "I figure Henry and I will retire in about ten years." He flashed us a wide grin. "Until then I'll continue to gripe about having no time to fish."

Dad returned the grin and offered his best friend and blood brother two thumbs up.

Once we were completely sated, the table cleared, and the dishwasher filled, we again convened at the dining table. I asked, "Was Tiny able to pull prints off the piece of paper?"

Dad thrummed his fingers against the table. He shot me a direct frown. "Yep, and you're not gonna like it."

"Please don't tell me they belong to Caleb..."

"Nope. Rex Siegler."

All I could do was stare at him with gaping surprise. "Rex?"

Dad arched an eyebrow and nodded. "As I live and breathe."

"And I was getting ready to bump him from the top of my list as suspect number one." At that moment, if I'd had the ability to look inside my mind, I'm sure it would have been crowded with tiny creatures shaped like question marks and scratching their heads. I huffed. "Back to square one."

I pushed away from the table to grab my laptop off the counter. "I did an additional internet search of Rex," and I followed up with the newest information I'd discovered. I said, "Not exactly a pillar of society."

Uncle Charlie had sat quietly, just listening. Then, using my pet name, he spoke, "Little Sister, what about the other feller—the one that also got hurt. Have you checked to see if he and this Siegler guy are connected?"

"Tully Taylor? All I know is what Caroline told

me—that he and Rex had the same probation officer who asked Caleb to hire them." I tapped a few keys on my computer, then opened the murder file and scrolled down until I located Tully's name, and then related the information I'd found on an internet search. "Unlike Rex, Tully was a high school dropout. He worked as a wrangler at several ranches, had a long list of driving drunk offenses and barroom brawls. However, it was leaving the scene of an accident where a death occurred that landed him in prison with a ten-year sentence. The article stated that Tully was so inebriated it took several days for him to sober up, and then he claimed he didn't remember the accident. I guess the judge more or less threw the book at him."

I could visualize the wheels inside my dad's head turning. A true lawman. He said, "Three ex-prisoners on the same ranch with one ex-con being the boss, hmm. Maybe Siegler was resentful of Caleb's success. Maybe with Caleb out of the way, Siegler figured he might be able to step in and replace Caleb." He cocked an eyebrow. "Owning a ranch, being a successful rodeo stockbroker, and a ready-made family…" He shrugged. "You never know the mindset of a criminal."

I glanced at Uncle Charlie to see if Dad's theory held water with him. Uncle Charlie drew a long sip of iced tea before he answered. "Like Henry said, it is difficult to crawl inside a criminal's mind. Envy and jealousy are powerful motives for murder, or perhaps this Tully guy was simply in the wrong place at the wrong time."

Both theories sounded plausible. However, deep inside my spirit a little voice was disagreeing. At that moment, I seemed to drift away. I thought I heard my dad say, "You're frowning, Punkin. You don't agree?"

The dining room appeared to spiral into a dark abyss, and Uncle Charlie was shushing my dad and saying what sounded like, *She's entered the spirit world.*

In a black chamber, I stood on the sidelines and watched a frightful creature—its eyes glowed red, and it snorted puffs of smoke from its nostrils. My feet were rooted to the ground. I could not move. The earth beneath me vibrated. The beast was upon me...River's morose yowl shook me back to reality.

A throb pulsated in my temple. "Wow, that was some loud clap of thunder. Sounds like we're in for a horrific storm."

"Little Sister..." Uncle Charlie wrapped his calloused hands around mine. "There was no thunder. The only storm brewing is in here." He touched my forehead. "River sensed whatever you saw. He was afraid for you. Can you tell us?"

A shiver wracked me. I looked at the incredulity on his and my dad's faces. I didn't want to bring this darkness to my family. I tried to smile. The muscles in my face refused to work. I heard myself stammer, "It's nothing. Really, I saw nothing."

Inside my head I was silently screaming, *I saw myself die.*

I knew the two men I loved the most didn't for one second believe me but refused to push, knowing that if they did, my stubbornness would kick in. Uncle Charlie stood and gathered the picnic basket and empty cooler kit. Taking the cue, Dad and I followed him to the porch.

Dad placed his large hands on either side of my face. "I don't know what you saw when you drifted off into never-never land, Punkin. Whatever it was, no matter how bad, when you're ready, I hope you know you can tell me."

Uncle Charlie relieved himself of the items he held. He too, said, "Little Sister, the Great Father Spirit has not blessed me with the gift of seeing beyond this world. For this, I am glad." He laid his hand on my dad's shoulder, then reached for my hand. "Like Henry, I would walk through fire for you." He touched the medicine bag beneath his shirt. "I will pray for your safety."

I do not cry easily, yet my eyes filled with tears. I wrapped my arms around both men. I could not speak the words in my heart.

Chapter Twenty

With trying to play catch-up from my trip to
Oklahoma, I had neglected to send my friend Dr.
Vaneeta Sunreet, head of forensics at Lexington
University Hospital, my soiled clothes. I immediately
sent her a text with a brief explanation about the attack
and the need to have her test specifically for any type of
hallucinogenic substance in the bull's dried saliva and
nostril mucus.

While I waited for her reply, I pondered the psychic
phenomena I had experience, and I had to admit I was
still shaken to the very core of my soul. No one in their
right mind wants to witness their own death. To distract
myself, I aimlessly stared at the page of the mystery
novel I held.

It wasn't until my phone pinged that I realized I had
drifted into a void of nothingness. I immediately tossed
the book aside and opened the text.

Vaneeta: *Tullah, namaste, good to hear from you.
You do lead a life of unusual adventure. Of course, send
asap! And may the god Vishnu preserve you.*

A sudden relief wafted over me when I answered
that I would overnight the package to her. She
immediately replied with a thumbs-up emoji and, *Give
me a couple of days to run a complete drug analysis. I'll
email the full report to you as soon as I'm finished.*

I rushed to the basement and grabbed a box, scissors,

tape, and an address label, then returned to the hallway and sprinted up the stairs to my bedroom. From the bedside table, I jotted a quick note of thanks, and also invited Vaneeta to visit.

Once the package was ready, I phoned the FedEx office. "Hey, Bob, this is Dr. Holliday. How soon can you pick up a delivery?"

"Evening, Doc. A delivery from your house?"

"That's right—my house, or should I bring it in?"

"No, ma'am, after you saved my Dinky-Do's life, I'll send a driver out right away. Where's the package going?"

I relayed the address. "No problem, Doc. I have a driver headed your way in ten minutes. The package will be in the hands of the receiver before midnight."

"You are the best, Bob."

After thanking him, I grabbed the package, a light wrap, and the mystery novel. Downstairs, I poured myself a mug of coffee, flipped on the porch light, and decided to relax in the porch swing while I waited. River and Rascal settled at my feet, and I opened to the bookmarked page.

I was so caught up in the mystery story that it was River's throaty growl that caused me to look up from the book. I watched headlights bouncing up and down as the vehicle approached my house. As the driver stepped down from the large brown van, I ordered my pets to stay and met him at the steps, package in hand. The entire transaction took less than five minutes, and the driver, along with the box containing my articles of clothing and what I hoped would reveal significant evidence, were on their way to Lexington.

Three days later, I received two unexpected

surprises. My phone pinged, notifying me of a text, and then it chimed, which signaled an email. Ella and I have a special sound if the text is an emergency and requires immediate attention. Since both messages were the generic ping and chime, I ignored them. Dosing an owner's colicky thoroughbred colt takes priority over my personal business.

When I'd finished with the colt, I washed up, repacked my truck, and after getting on the road, commanded my phone to contact my office.

"Hi, Doc," Jeff answered.

"Just checking in. I've finished with the Rockin' Acre's colt. Anything else before I head back to the clinic?"

"As a matter of fact, a Mr. Barstow phoned about his mule. He said the farrier he uses found maggots in the mule's hind hooves. I have him down as first appointment for tomorrow."

"Call Barstow and tell him I'll be there in about forty-five minutes. He's almost to the Dixie County line. I might as well get it done while I'm already out and about."

"Will do. Aah, wait. Ella's signaling that she needs to talk to you." His voice rose with excitement. "You're not going to believe—" I heard Ella shushing the boy.

I said, "Okay, what are the two of you giggling about?"

I knew from the echo that Jeff or perhaps Ella had switched the phone to speaker mode. Ella said, "I wish you were coming back to the office instead of going on another call."

"Why, what's up?"

More twittering.

Like Jeff's, Ella's voice was filled with excitement. "You received a package today."

Jeff said, "A *big* package!"

"Well, don't keep me in suspense. What *is* the really big package?"

Ella snorted. "It'll spoil the surprise if we tell. You've got to see it to believe it."

"The two of you are bad...truly rotten to the core." I joined their laughter. Then added, "Whatever it is will have to keep until I finish treating Mr. Barstow's mule." Then I apologized to Jeff because he had class and would miss out on watching me open the mysterious surprise.

He countered with, "I already have his appointment set for tomorrow morning. Pleeese, Doc."

I had to admit curiosity was getting the best of me. "Okay...okay. You win. I'm about fifteen minutes from the office. And this had better be good."

I could hear the smile in Ella's voice when she said, "Oh, it's good, all right."

With a sense of mild expectation, I drove to the clinic. I had no idea who would send me a large gift. My birthday was several months away and so was Christmas. So many thoughts flitted inside my mind. My eyes drifted to the screen on my phone. I noticed the email icon and hoped it was from Vaneeta.

Deep in thought, I almost missed the driveway to my house and clinic. It seemed everyone was waiting to greet me. Ella, Jeff, River, and Rascal stood outside. I braked to a halt and stepped out of the truck. Ella and Jeff wore wide grins. Even River and Rascal appeared to be smiling.

"Okay, where's this mysterious gift?"

Jeff sprinted to open the side door that led to the

large animal stalls. He pointed to a stall adorned with a large red bow. "I think she's a little shy."

Puzzled, I looked at Ella, who gave me a gentle nudge. "You're just gonna die when you see what's inside."

Given the fact that I'd recently had a vision of my impending death, I wasn't too keen on the word *die*.

I walked to the stall and peered inside. For a moment, all I could do was stare. I finally managed to say, "Is she a patient?"

"No, silly," Ella gushed. She handed me a brown envelope. "I signed for her, and the shipping slip definitely said 'Personal Delivery to Dr. Tullah Holiday.' "

I opened the large brown envelope, removed a smaller envelope, and upon opening it, I did a quick scan to the bottom. The note was signed simply, "Caleb."

"What does it say, Doc, or is it is too personal?"

I glanced at Jeff's freckled face. The tips of his ears had turned red to indicate his embarrassment. "It is a bit personal." I briefly related the nasty stunt Caleb and his buddies had pulled in high school resulting in the death of my beloved mare. "But the note's not so personal that I can't share it with you."

I cleared my throat and read aloud what had been written in a scribbly hand.

Dear Tullah,

She's three years old and green broke. Her registered name is Beladora's Hope. She's a registered American Quarter Horse. I know she'll never replace Venus, but I hope you'll accept her as my sincere apology for the completely juvenile and cruel antic the guys and I pulled on you during our high school years of stupidity. I don't think any of us realized the dire consequences of our malicious prank.

Caroline and I look forward to seeing you at the rodeo. If all goes as planned, there will be more surprises in store.

At that moment, the anger I had nurtured for so many years melted away. I stuffed the note inside the envelope. "Wow, she's a real beauty. I think I'll call her Bella."

Inside the stall stood a gray dappled mare, approximately sixteen hands tall and with perfect conformation. "Caleb must have searched far and wide, because Bella is almost a twin to my Venus."

I reached inside my pants pocket and withdrew a handful of carrot nibs, then opened the latch and stepped inside the stall. The young mare whickered as she accepted the treat from my open palm. I stepped forward and caressed her silken neck, ran my hand down her well-formed torso, and down her flank to lift a hind leg. She didn't object.

I asked Jeff to grab a halter from one of the racks. He handed it to me, and I held it forward for Bella to sniff. Again, she received the attention without hesitation. Actually, she rested her head across my shoulder. "Whoever trained this mare knew what they were doing. She's not the least bit skittish."

Ella said, "How do you plan to introduce her to the others?"

I knew the two geldings would want to assert their dominance. "Gandalf is the dominant leader. We'll move Bella to the center stall. Let's place Gandalf and Banjo on either side of her. Moon is so docile I'm not worried about her. We'll place her in the stall facing Bella."

Ella expressed concern over her gelding, Jupiter. We agreed to place him in the stall directly across from Bella, and shift Moon to the next one.

I faced the young mare. "There'll be a little spirited back-and-forth barn conversation before we turn all of them out to the corral. It won't be any different than when we introduced Jupiter to the group."

Ella expressed her doubt. "Maybe you'd better give all of them a little lecture in that secret language you use when horses are fractious."

Giving one last affectionate pat to the newest addition to my animal family, I left the stall. Bella thrust her magnificent neck over the gate; again, she whickered, worry and doubt reflected in her large brown eyes. I placed my hands on her broad jaws and leaned to touch my forehead to her face. In my mother's language, I whispered assurances that her new family would fill her with joy.

Chapter Twenty-One

Jeff bade us goodbye and wished us a great weekend. Ella and I strolled toward my house, and I invited her in for a glass of wine. She grinned and with a sly look said she needed to get ready for tomorrow.

I stupidly missed the cue and asked, "Ready for what?"

She sounded a little breathless, or perhaps a bit giddy. "Andy and I are going on a date, and it's not horseback riding. We're driving to Lexington for a movie and dinner at the Seafood Palace. So I'm taking your advice and pampering myself. You know, girly stuff like polishing my nails and, um, shaving my legs. I'm even wearing a dress."

I arched an eyebrow and smiled at my friend. "Good for you. Have fun, and I'll look forward to hearing all about it—every detail." I recanted. "Well, maybe not every detail."

Ella laughed and waved as she skipped across the yard and through the gate that led to her house.

The wind had kicked up and a few drops splattered on the ground. I whistled to my pets and dashed to the carport and then into the kitchen. I opened the refrigerator and fished out the containers of leftover spare ribs and potato salad. I also treated myself to a glass of Merlot. To avoid the loneliness that surrounded me, I carried my meal to the front porch swing and allowed the patter of raindrops, and my pets, to keep me company.

My thoughts turned to the beautiful gift from Caleb. Although his reason for gifting with the mare was plausible, my empathic senses were working overtime. I don't consider myself a psychic. However, I do seem to be more sensitive to the energy and emotions of others, and that includes the nonliving, plus the ability to commune with animals.

I closed my eyes, and except for the pattering of rain I emptied my mind of all thoughts. Caleb's face floated before me. I recalled the way he had stared at me, looking hard and very cold for a split second; then suddenly his demeanor had changed.

I also recalled the way Rex Siegler had warned me about the temperament of the horse Caleb had selected for me to ride that particular day. It was as if Rex was apologizing. I allowed myself to drift farther into my memory until Caroline's voice coupled with the rising wind. She had remarked that there were times when Caleb acted like two different people. She had also scolded him about his excessive drinking.

The solution to the who and why mystery of this case teased my senses. I could almost reach out, grab hold of the answers, and reel them in. As the answers began to fade, I heard myself say, "No-no...don't...go."

My phone chirped. I looked down and saw I had a message from an unknown caller. The area code wasn't familiar, and if it were a client with an emergency, my service would have contacted me. I chalked it up as a spam call.

The spring shower rapidly developed into a fierce storm. Lightning lit the sky in a rhythmic dance to the tune of rolling thunder. When River and Rascal tried to seek safety in my lap, I decided to move indoors. Once I'd cleaned my dishes and replenished my wine glass, I settled in my favorite spot—the recliner.

Opening my laptop, I chastised myself. In the excitement of receiving a beautiful and valuable gift, I'd forgotten to check my email.

The message from Vaneeta sent a rush of excitement through me. It read:

Tullah—I think you'll be most interested in the results of the drug analysis. Your suspicions were correct about possible drugs. The samples I extracted from the bovine saliva and mucus presented with ample amounts of anabolic steroids. My full report is attached.

I must apologize for ruining your clothing. I can return the items, but honestly, the shirt and pants are no longer wearable. It's up to you.

I immediately responded, expressing my thanks for her quick reply to my request, and not to worry about my shirt and pants.

I phoned my dad. "Hey, Punkin, what's up?"

"Vaneeta emailed the drug analysis results. It's as we suspected. The bulls, at least the one that tried to bulldoze me, had mucus and saliva that tested positive for anabolic steroids."

"That's illegal, isn't it?"

"Theoretically, yes. Legitimately, no."

"That's not much of answer."

As a veterinarian, I know that though there is no anti-doping policy for livestock in the Professional Bull Riders tour—the major leagues of bull riding—or in the rest of the rodeo world, the use of anabolic steroids in bulls is nevertheless unapproved and illegal.

"Do you think Caleb is the guilty party?" Dad asked.

"The big question is—why would he be juicing up his own bulls? Caleb is still on probation. Why would he put himself in the position of going back to prison if he got caught?"

"The long and short answer is—money. The competition to be the best stock contractor and supply the best-of-the-best bucking stock is fierce."

Dad's comment made sense. "I agree. But in Caleb's defense, maybe one of his competitors is the guilty party."

"You've got me there, Punkin. At the rodeo or at the party, were you introduced to other stock contractors?"

"Sorry, Dad. Except for the sheep, all the animals used at the junior rodeo were supplied by Caleb. I met several ranchers and their wives, but no one that was specifically pointed out as a competitor. Also, Caleb and Caroline were on the dance floor when the two bulls crashed the party. Another question—who let them loose?" I hastened on. "My guess is that Caleb has an employee that's out to get him. The question is why?"

Dad countered with, "Sounds reasonable. The rodeo is next week. You might want to give Caleb a call to get a rundown on all his ranch hands."

"We can rule out at least two—Tully Taylor is still in the hospital, and Rex Siegler is dead."

Before we said our goodnights, I told my dad about the young mare and Caleb's note. Since it was too late to contact Caleb, and there was nothing I could do until morning, I went upstairs and readied for bed, then grabbed my mystery book. I slipped into the story, hoping that somehow or somewhere among the pages I'd find a bit of detecting that would help with my own case.

It'd been a long day. I was too tired to turn out the light when I felt the book slide from my hands and land with a gentle thud on the floor. I closed my eyes and allowed sleep to engulf me.

There are times when I wished I didn't dream. I found myself fully dressed for riding. What I didn't expect was a handsome stranger standing in my kitchen. Coffee perked, and the aroma of cinnamon apple muffins teased my appetite.

"How did you get in?" I asked.

"You forgot to lock your doors."

I grew alarmed. "Did you hurt my dog and donkey?"

A dimple on his tanned cheek deepened as he smiled. "I may hurt a lot of things, but never animals or beautiful veterinarians."

"Who are you and why are you in my house?"

He cocked his head to one side. His liquid blue eyes darkened. His smile faded. "Shadow Woman sent me."

I knew then that I was dreaming.

"Am I going to die?"

The dimple in his cheek deepened when he crooked a smile. "Not if I can help it."

He didn't wait for another question. Instead, he said, "From what I understand, you have a friend who is guilty."

My temper cranked up. "If you mean Caleb, I don't believe you."

"Believe what you wish."

This tall, handsome stranger dressed as a cowhand wasn't at all sympathetic.

"I need to find the person out to hurt Caleb and his family," I practically yelled at him.

"So you think he's not guilty?" He smiled.

"Everyone is guilty of something; even those who seem the most innocent."

I almost felt as if he were mocking me. I helped myself to coffee and a muffin. "Are you avoiding telling me your name?"

"Aho, you forget so easily. Shadow Woman has already told you."

I bit into the muffin. "If you're going to talk in riddles, then get out of my dream and let me sleep in peace."

His voice hardened. "Ask your friend about the drugs. Ask him about his father—accident or murder? Caleb knows."

I demanded, "What kind of asinine statement is that?"

"It's the right kind." He reached down and spun the rowel on his spur. "What's he hiding, and why is he lying?"

"Caleb is innocent. He gifted me with a beautiful dappled gray mare. What you are saying is nonsense."

"If you believe he's innocent, then why are you so angry? Remember, to get the right answers you must ask the right questions, and if you don't succeed, ask again, and again."

The aura around him began to fade.

"Wait, don't go. I have more questions."

"You will know the answers in due time."

I asked, "Who is the man with the tattoo on his ear?"

"He is of little importance."

I swallowed a gulp of coffee. "That doesn't make sense. If you know the answers, then don't keep me in suspense."

His smile was a million watts. "We will meet again,

soon."

"Where…when?" I despised the pleading in my voice.

As his essence trailed off, I was certain he had said—*at the rodeo*.

In a wisp of smoke, he disappeared. I awoke to the sound of the doggie door flapping back and forth, a signal that River and Rascal had left the bedroom. My brain was humming with questions that begged for answers.

Chapter Twenty-Two

Last night's storm brought life to Enigma. I cradled a mug of coffee as my feet pushed the porch swing to and fro. The landscape was alive with pops of color that ranged from lavender to pink to white. The freshness of the air and the sweet scent of wildflowers tantalized my nose as I gazed at the vastness of my front pasture.

The man in my dream stood out fresh in my mind. I closed my eyes and willed his image to come into view. Tall and straight, he was a warrior. Dark hair curled just beneath his black felt Stetson. He spoke in a soft, cultured voice, like a man who never had to speak loudly to be heard. My emotions were getting a workout. I drew a breath and cautioned myself. Real or not, he was not a man to be tampered with. Oh, but how I wanted to feel his touch, his lips, his—

Damn! The phone rang. I glanced at the number. It was the same area code and number that had called last night. I decided to let it go to voice mail. When the ringing persisted, I practically yelled into the phone, "Hello!"

A voice I didn't recognize said, "Tullah?"

"Who is this?"

"Please don't hang up. It's me—Rosie—Sofia's niece."

"How did you get my number?"

The young maid from Caleb's house whispered,

"When I heard Caleb call you Tullah, and then Caroline did the same thing, I decided to do a little snooping when I cleaned your room at the ranch. I found the plane ticket with your name on it." It sounded as if she stumbled on the words. "I looked you up on the internet, Dr. Holliday. You are a veterinarian, not a reporter."

Roseanne Ramos hadn't been particularly forthcoming when we'd first met. In fact, she'd sent my bullshit meter into the red zone.

How dare she rifle through my belongings! My voice was gruffer than I had intended. "Are you going to rat me out; is they why you're calling?"

Morning light slanted through the oak trees, creating an ethereal essence over the pasture. I gathered myself and walked inside to freshen my coffee. There was a garbled discussion on the other end of the line. Finally, Rosie said, "I'm calling because Caleb and Caroline are in danger. And…and I know who sent the snake, and why."

The news about Caroline and Caleb's safety was old news. however, the statement about the snake reached out and grabbed hold of my attention. "Rosie, are you where you can talk freely?"

"Yes, I'm not at home, and I'm not using my cellphone. In fact, I'm at the church. I have confessed my sins to Father D'Angelo. I am using his phone."

Smart girl, I thought. "Do you mind if I record our conversation?"

"Will it get me in trouble?" The doubt in her voice was obvious.

"I promise it will not. However, I must tell you that my father is a sheriff. He's honest to the bone." I added, "All of his deputies are loyal to him, and just as trustworthy. And, Rosie, if you need protection, I assure you my father will see that you get it."

Before we began, I had to ask, "Rosie, are you in love with Caleb?"

She hesitated. "Yes, but not in a sexual way because he can't...I mean because of things that happened to him in prison...he isn't able to...you know, perform."

She hastened on as if not wanting to delve further into the topic of a relationship between her and Caleb. While I waited for her to continue, I made a mental note to contact Caroline. My phone call would be twofold— to thank her and Caleb for the beautiful mare, and a follow-up on what happened to Caleb in prison.

I pressed for an answer. "Why do you think Caleb and Caroline are in danger?"

Her voice had an edge to it. "Be patient, Dr. Holliday. In the end, you will understand."

I am a direct and to the point person. Talking in circles tries my patience. I sucked in a breath to calm my agitation.

Finally, she said, "Rex wrote the note and he sent the snake."

I refuted her statement. "Rex is dead. Isn't it a bit convenient to put the blame on a dead man?"

Rosie countered. "What you say is true, and what I say is also true. I'm telling you because Aunt Sofia says since you are one of the People, we can trust you."

Almost to herself I heard her whisper, "Oh, Lord, forgive me." It wasn't said so much as a prayer but more like an afterthought of there being no turning back now. She said, "Like I said, Rex wrote the note. He paid Danny Chicken Boy to deliver it."

"I'm assuming this Danny is the guy with the tattoo

on his ear?"

"Yes, but he isn't very smart. He suffered severe brain damage from a gang beating when he was in prison. To earn a little money, he simply does what he's paid to do. Basically, he's harmless. I know this because he is my cousin."

She continued, "Dr. Holliday, what I have to tell you is like a long, truthful story. Please, just let me tell it without interruptions. Okay?"

I agreed. After all, I was recording her information and could relisten to it if needed. I pulled a notepad toward me to jot down her name and today's date. I also planned to write down questions to ask later.

She began, "Sheriff Coffey and Cletus Dodge are dangerous men. They are small fish in a large pond. They terrorize the young girls on the rez and bully our young men with threats of imprisonment. They harass us for no reason. We pay protection money to keep them from setting fire to our crops, shooting our animals, and worse. My people can barely afford to support themselves."

Interesting, I thought as I broke my promise to listen quietly. "Are you saying Coffey and his deputies are puppets, and their strings are pulled by a higher-up authority?"

"That's one way of putting it."

"Why target Caleb?"

"Because he refuses to kowtow to them. That is why his father was murdered, and why Caleb sent his mother and children away."

Hmm, *murdered*. Noteworthy.

"Do you know names?"

"No, except Rex was not who he seemed."

"Were you afraid of Siegler—is that why you pulled

away from him at the dance?"

"Yes, to both questions. One day, before old Mr. Calloway's death, I saw him and Caroline in the pool house, and they weren't swimming. I wasn't spying. I was collecting dirty towels." Her voice lost a bit of softness. "I hoped he'd die, and I'm glad he did."

"Did Caroline or Rex see you?"

"Both. Caroline was nearly hysterical, begging me, offering me money, to stay quiet. Rex just laughed and laughed. He said he could service both of us. He made a grab for me, and I scratched his face, then ran away."

I didn't see the relevance to the line of information Rosie was feeding me and steered the conversation back to the reason for Caleb's fear. "Do you have proof that Carl Calloway was murdered?"

"I only know what I saw."

Okay, so much for that. I continued. "Why does Caleb mistrust the sheriff?"

She huffed an impatient sigh. "Because Caleb's father was being used as a mule to transport drugs."

This piece of news stunned me. "Fill me in on the details, and do Caleb and Caroline know?"

"Yes."

"How did Caleb's father get tangled up in such a vile and dangerous venture?"

"Dr. Holliday, Caleb tries to be a good man, honest. He didn't willingly choose to get involved."

She said the battery on the cellphone was beeping and she needed to plug it into the charger. I waited for what seemed an eternity until she said, "Are you there?"

I assured her that I was ready to hear the rest of her story. The word *motive* was flashing behind my eyelids. Rosie cleared her throat and began again. "Carl—that is,

Mr. Calloway—was on the verge of losing the ranch, the stock, all of it. In addition to supporting a couple of high maintenance ex-wives, and a current mistress, he apparently made too many risky investments that didn't pay off.

"A person whose identity and name I don't know made a deal to wipe out the debt if Carl would hide cocaine inside the stock trailers. You see, it was easy to transport the drugs across state lines because apparently the agriculture inspectors at the weigh stations don't inspect the interior of trailers filled with dangerous bulls."

I wasn't buying her story. "Uh-huh, but what about drug dogs?"

I could almost hear her teeth grinding. "I don't know for sure. I was listening at the parlor door and heard Coffey say that the coke would be layered between the flakes of hay. With all the fresh manure and bull urine and sweat, the dogs wouldn't be able to detect the drugs. He also said that once the animals arrived at the rodeo yard and were safely unloaded, then Rex or Cletus would supervise the transferring of the hay bales to the buyer and then collect the money."

While she talked, I envisioned what she was saying sounded like the plot in a mystery novel. I said, "Rosie, forgive me for interrupting, but how do Caleb and Caroline figure into all this?"

My coffee mug was empty. As badly as I wanted to refresh it, my kidneys objected. I crossed my legs and waited for Rosie to continue.

"I'm getting to that. Just, please, be patient." The scold in her voice was evident as she continued. "When Caroline couldn't satisfy Rex's needs, he'd come after me. I hated him. He made my skin crawl. On the night of Mr. Calloway's death, I'd told Caroline if she didn't tell her sex boy to stop pestering me that I would rat her out to Caleb.

"She slapped me, called me a whore for hire, and grabbed a butcher knife and threatened to slit my throat. She has a temper, but never anything this drastic. She actually chased after me. The only safe place I knew to hide was the bull barn. Caroline began to hate everything about the ranch—especially Caleb because he couldn't perform in the bed, and Mr. Calloway because he controlled the money.

"I was hiding in the hayloft when Caleb, his father, and Caroline walked in with Coffey, Dodge, and Rex. There was another man. I didn't see his face. I was afraid they might kill me if they spotted me."

I said, "Did you recognize his voice?"

"No, sorry."

"That's okay. Continue. What else happened?"

"There was an argument, with Mr. Carl Calloway refusing to haul any more drugs. He threatened to go to the authorities. Coffey laughed and said *he* was the authority. Then Mr. Calloway said he meant federal marshals. That's when I heard the gate to Diablo's pen rattle. Caleb spewed cuss words. I could hear fists on flesh. Caroline screamed. Rex must have slapped her because he said if she didn't shut up, he'd hurt her worse. That's when he threatened her that he'd go public with photos of them doing the...ah...doing the nasty in bed.

"Somebody fired a gun. I don't know who. I had to clamp both hands over my mouth to keep from crying out. Diablo and the other bulls were going crazy. The unknown man yelled, 'You S-O-B, nobody lays a hand

172

on me.' He told Coffey and Dodge to take Caleb and Caroline to the house, and if they didn't keep their traps shut, he'd cut off the heads of their children and feed them to the vultures. Then he told Rex to take care of the old man.

"When Rex asked how, the faceless man told him to use his imagination, but to make it look like an accident."

Rosie's sob touched my heart. I heard Sofia consoling her niece, and the priest murmuring a prayer. I said, "If you need to take a break, Rosie, I'll understand."

Between sobs she said, "I need to tell it all." She blew out a sigh. "I fumbled around and managed to peek over the edge of the hayloft. Mr. Calloway fell to the ground when Rex slugged him. I think the blow must have knocked him semi-conscious.

"Some hay fell through the cracks and drifted onto Rex's head. When he looked up at the hayloft, I scooted farther back. The next thing I heard was Diablo bellowing and old man Calloway screaming for help. I lay flat on the floor and tried to look between the slats. That's when I saw Rex lift the chain on Diablo's gate. At one point, I saw Mr. C's body tossed in the air like a limp doll."

In my mind's eye I saw exactly what had happened to Carl Calloway. After Rex had decked the old man, he apparently opened the gate, allowing the already enraged bull to escape. Carl Calloway never had a chance.

I've witnessed death in both animals and humans, and I've experienced several close calls. Yet I cannot imagine Carl Calloway's terror and pain as he was being brutalized.

"Where was Rex all this time?" I asked.

"He left. I'm not sure how long he was gone. When he returned, he was with Baily Strom." For a moment her sobs intensified. "I wanted to help the old man. Diablo just kept mauling him.

"Sometimes, I close my eyes at night and I can still hear the old man's screams. Anyhow, Baily tossed a loop over the bull's head and Rex started whacking him on the head with a shovel handle. Between the two of them, they managed to get him back in the pen. It was Baily that called 9-1-1.

"I stayed in the loft until after the body was removed, until I was certain I could escape without being seen."

She was correct. Carl Calloway had been murdered. The problem was proving it. Rex Siegler was dead. Coffey and Dodge knew how to dispose of evidence, and who was the unidentified man? I logged all of this in my memory. Later I would transfer the information into my murder file, as well as informing my dad.

"What else, Rosie?"

"At first, Caleb refused to transport drugs. That's when things started happening. His bulls became extra mean. Two riders hurt, one rider dead. Even then, Caleb refused to transport drugs. Next it was the pet dog and then the goat. It was to let Caleb and Caroline know the children's lives were being threatened."

I said, "That's why Caleb's mother and the children fled to Florida."

"Dr. Holliday, Caleb and Caroline love their children more than life. I've heard Caroline arguing with Caleb, pushing him to do Coffey's bidding. She thinks doing this will keep them safe, and will put the ranch back on its feet even though Caleb is on probation. I don't know much about the law, Dr. Holliday, but I do know that if he gets caught transporting drugs he'll go back to prison."

"Rosie, is there anyone Caleb can turn to—like his probation officer?"

She made a sound of disgust. "Robert Avery is in Coffey's pocket, and before you ask, so is the medical examiner, and the local veterinarian. This is a small county where honest people turn a blind eye to corruption. We all know what will happen to us if we don't."

"Rosie, I'd feel better if you and Sofia were somewhere safe. If you have a car, get in it and head to Kentucky. Don't worry about clothes or a place to stay. We'll figure that out when you get here. And, please stop calling me 'Dr. Holliday.' 'Tullah' will do."

"That's very kind of you, Tullah. Unfortunately, all we have is my uncle's beat-up old truck that wouldn't get us as far as the next county." She added, "I think we are safe as long as no one knows about this phone call."

"Trust me, Rosie, the only person I'll share this conversation with is my dad. In the meantime, go about business as usual. I'll see Caleb and Caroline next week at the rodeo in Lexington."

"What do you plan to do?"

"I'm not quite sure. Whatever happens, I'll make sure Coffey, Dodge, and anyone else involved in this drug operation will be taken down. I'll also try my best to protect Caleb from going back to prison."

We both said an uneasy goodbye. The call had worn me out. One part of me wanted to warn Caleb that he might face arrest, and the other part knew I had to protect the lives of two innocent women and a priest.

Chapter Twenty-Three

After a much-needed visit to the bathroom, I telephoned my dad and gave him a brief rundown of my discussion with Rosie. "With her permission, I recorded the conversation. Shall I come to the office, or do you want to come to the house?"

He said, "I'll stop by the Whitehorse. Charlie said he was whipping up a batch of his prize-winning chili. I'll spring for lunch."

"Don't forget dessert."

He chuckled. "I don't know where you inherited your sweet tooth. It certainly wasn't from me."

While I waited for Dad's arrival, I opened my laptop to the murder file, which I'd transferred back from the tablet. My fingers flew across the keys as I typed all the details from the phone call. What's the old saying, *Time flies when you're having fun?*

Time did fly, but I wasn't having fun. By the time I'd saved the information, River and Rascal had set up a fuss and were dashing out the doggie door. I met Dad on the front porch and helped him carry in our lunch. While we sat around the table enjoying bowls of chili, we listened to Rosie recounting the details of Carl Calloway's death.

I switched off the phone while Dad refilled our cups with coffee. His comment was, "I didn't know Carl that well. I do remember Caleb as a teen. Cocky, headed for trouble, all of which was nurtured by an absentee mother and a father who probably wasn't the best role model for a son."

Dad washed down the last bite of his second glazed donut. With a smile, I teased, "What was it you said about me not inheriting my sweet tooth from you?"

We both laughed. I wiped off the table and set the dishes in the dishwasher. "This seems like an impossible case, Dad. The rodeo is next week, and I don't have a clue how to help Caleb. He wanted me to find out who was juicing up his bulls to make them extra dangerous. However, he's omitted a plethora of details."

Dad propped his elbows on the table and steepled his fingers together. He shot me a look—a *You're not going to like what I'm about to say* look. "Punkin, have you considered that Caleb is lying, that he's actually the principal player in this scheme?"

After wiping my hands on a kitchen towel, I rejoined him. Huffing a sigh, I said, "Yes, sir, I have."

"And?"

"Because of our past history, I discounted my feelings as being prejudiced against him and Caroline. I'm trying to keep an open mind about them both."

I sat silent for a moment. I knew Dad was waiting for me to pull my thoughts together. I related the incident at the ranch with the unmanageable horse Caleb had selected for me to ride, and how Caroline had scolded him about his drinking and said he often seemed to be two different people.

"Dad, setting Caleb aside for a moment, let me tell you about the dream I had last night."

"I'm listening."

After briefly reminding him about the vision where

Shadow Woman visited me, I related the details of the dream. "This spirit or person said he would be at the rodeo and would let no harm come to me. What harm, Dad? This puzzles me because I've done nothing to cause Caleb or Caroline or anyone associated with them to want to hurt me."

Dad's voice deepened. He practically growled his reply. "Anyone dares harm you, and I'll forget I'm a lawman."

He glanced at his watch. "Tiny's off duty in a half hour. I hate leaving good company." He stood and wrapped me in a bear hug, then kissed the top of my head. "Give Caroline a call. Feel her out. Let's see if she unknowingly corroborates Ms. Ramos' story."

Although I'm on the high side of approaching thirty, I still have a little girl's need of her father's protection. "Good idea. I'll do that today."

I walked him to the front porch and thanked him for bringing lunch. Before he left, Dad said, "Since my authority doesn't extend to Lexington, I'll give Sheriff Cal Saunders a call to alert him of a possible drug drop at the rodeo."

"Good idea, Dad. I'll touch base with you after I talk to Caroline."

We waved goodbye, and I watched until he drove out of sight before I entered the house. On my way inside, I placed a call to Caroline's cellphone. There was an urgency in her voice when she answered. "Hello, Ms. Waya, it's nice to hear from you."

Whatever was wrong, I knew I had to play along in case someone was listening. "Caroline, please call me Chenoa. Are you free to chat?"

"Not at the moment. I have company. I was just

getting to serve *coffee* and cake."

Smart girl. Coffey and possibly Dodge were there. "I'm sorry to bother you. Perhaps when your company leaves, I'd appreciate it if you or Caleb would return my call. I need a little more information for the article I'm writing."

Before we disconnected, I searched for a way to let Caroline know that I understood why she couldn't talk. "Coffey and corn dodgers aren't exactly friendly to a girl's diet."

I breathed a sigh of relief when she chuckled. "They certainly aren't. I'll try to return your call in about an hour. I'm not sure if Caleb will be here. He's unavailable at the moment."

As soon as we disconnected, I phoned my dad. "What's wrong, Punkin?"

I glanced at the clock, and understood the concern in his voice. The phone call with Caroline had taken less than five minutes, and Dad had barely had time to reach his office.

"Nothing, I hope." I relayed the conversation I'd had with Caroline. "There's no one she can trust or call for help."

"Yeah. I could put in a call to a buddy who's a federal marshal. But we have no evidence to prove that Coffey's visit is nothing more than social, or a follow-up on the bull incident at the party."

As much as I hated to agree, Dad was correct. I felt helpless.

To take my mind off a situation I couldn't control, I decided to bide my time by making friends with my new horse. Whistling up River and Rascal, I skipped across the yard with them. All of the horses greeted me when I entered the barn. As was their routine, River and Rascal followed me from stall to stall as I treated all the horses to carrot nibs.

I grabbed the curry comb, brush, and hoof pick. Once I finished grooming Bella, I moved to Gandalf's stall. He had belonged to my mother, and then there was Moon and Banjo, my grandmother's aging pinto and my dad's appaloosa. Each horse held a special place in my heart.

By the time I'd completed the grooming chores, had fed and watered, and forked fresh hay in the stalls, I was ready to call it a day. Checking the time on my phone, several hours had passed since speaking with Caroline. She had not called back. Needless to say, I was concerned.

Racing to the house, I rushed through a quick shower, one ear cocked so as not to miss hearing the phone ring. After I'd dressed and poured a fresh cup of coffee, I settled in my recliner and was dozing when my phone chimed.

I grabbed it. "Hello?"

"It's me. Caroline. I can talk now."

"Are you where no one can hear you, and are you sure there are no bugs?"

"I'm in my daughter's bedroom. She doesn't have a phone or a TV. I'm also seated by the window where I can see if anyone approaches the house."

I felt an instinctive urge to hide what I was thinking. I wiped my mind of ugly thoughts and decided to focus on the questions I would ask without betraying Rosie.

"Caroline, in lieu of all the strange events that took place when I was at the ranch, I have more questions to ask."

"Caleb isn't here. I'll have him get in touch with you when he returns."

"It's you I need to talk to."

There was a hesitancy when she said, "O-kay."

"I already know Tully Taylor and Caleb share the same parole officer. Are there any other ex-cons working for you?"

"No one except Rex, and he's dead."

Caroline was smart. As much as I wanted to delve into her relationship with Rex, I swallowed those questions. "What about Baily Strom?"

"Baily is a retired bull rider." She chuckled. "You saw him at the junior rodeo. He was the clown. Baily is also a professional rodeo clown, and works exclusively for the Triple C brand. He's married and is putting a couple of kids through college. He and his family are as good as they come. I'd trust Baily with my life."

I crossed through his name. We discussed several other hands until I was satisfied I could cut to the chase with tougher questions. "Caroline, a couple of weeks ago, you commented that Caleb often acted like two different people. What did you mean?"

She burst into tears. What she said made no sense at all. "I hate these awful turquoise boots. They're ugly...I'm ugly...the world is ugly."

I mustered up a calm voice. "Caroline, you're not making sense. What does this have to do with Caleb?" I wanted to say more but decided to wait.

"Nothing. Oh, Tullah, I'm tired of all this bullshit. I hate this ranch and everything it has become. I miss my children. The ranch isn't safe for them. And...you asked about Caleb. He *is* two different people, and the bad Caleb is getting worse every day."

I was surprised by her outburst. "I'm listening, and I won't judge."

"When Caleb was first released from prison and we came to the ranch, he had terrible nightmares, and still does. He'd wakeup screaming. I finally convinced him to see a psychologist. Dr. Lund diagnosed him with post-traumatic stress disorder."

In my psychology courses we had studied PTSD. I've witnessed it in both humans and animals after being subjected to long-term abuse. I said, "Is that why Caleb drinks so much?"

"Not at first. It was only after the mess that his father got us into." She hesitated. "And things I've done."

I waited until her sobs subsided. "I'm still young. I have sexual needs. You understand, don't you?"

I reserved comment. Those unpleasant thoughts I'd tucked away moments ago reared their ugly head. I clamped my jaws together. After all, I had promised not to judge.

She continued. "The long and short of all this is that our once active sex life became a duty, with Caleb barely able to perform. The more he neglected me, the more he drank and the more I nagged, blamed, and threatened. I'm ashamed to admit that I had an affair with Rex. Rosie caught us, and I actually threatened to hurt her if she went to Caleb.

"It was Rex who told me what happened to men in prison. I didn't believe him because he'd been inside and there was nothing wrong with his performance. After Rosie caught Rex and me, I dared to ask Caleb if that had happened to him.

"Oh, Tullah, I'll never forget the look on his face. It was like all the blood drained out of him. He finally managed to say that was the only way he'd survived. That by becoming the gang's *boy*, they protected him from other gangs. After he told me, he went to the bathroom and threw up. When he returned, he said to never ask him about prison again and that he was moving out of the bedroom.

"I'll never forget his words. He said, 'Caroline, I stopped loving life a long time ago. Don't ask for a divorce because I'll never let you have Mattie and Breck. Without them, I'd go insane. Maybe in time I'll become a man again. Until that time, for better or worse, you're my wife. I want to love you like a man—like a husband. Right now, I just can't.' And the most horrible part was that he threatened to kill himself if that day never came."

Tears don't come easy to me. Yet I found myself searching for a paper towel to dry my eyes. I didn't trust myself to speak.

"Tullah, are you still there?"

"I'm sorry, Caroline. I can't imagine the hell Caleb has suffered, and it's still haunting him." I walked to the coffee machine and popped in a pod of chai tea. While I waited for the tea to brew, I asked, "Do you know who sent the snake?"

She didn't hesitate. Anger laced her voice. "Rex. He tried to blackmail me by threatening to tell Caleb about our affair. I beat him to the punch and told Caleb. He practically went insane and threatened to kill Rex if he ever touched me or Rosie again."

"Were Rosie and Caleb involved?"

"I thought they were. I was wrong. She was the little sister he never had. I'm ashamed that he turned to her when I refused to listen to him. She became the broad shoulder I should have given him. I think that's why I became so angry—not at her but at myself."

"All that aside, Caroline, I sense you know more about Carl's death than you let on. Be honest, and tell me."

Except for a few minor details, what she related correlated with Rosie's account of the murder. It appeared Carl's death would remain listed as an unfortunate accident.

"Caroline, where is Caleb?"

"I don't really know. When he has a PTSD episode, he saddles one of the horses and rides off into the mountains. Sometimes he's gone for several hours, other times for days. When he left this morning, he packed his saddlebags with canned goods and two bottles of bourbon.

"Tullah, I begged him to let me go with him. I promised I wouldn't nag, that I wanted to be there if he needed to talk, yell, or just rant." Her voice hitched. "He merely touched my face, kissed me on the cheek, and said not to worry."

"How long has he been gone?"

"Two days. The most he's stayed away is a week. But because of the rodeo in Lexington I'm hoping he'll return soon. Caleb may be a lot of things, but he's never reneged on a rodeo stock contract."

"Caroline, I have to ask, were Coffey and Dodge pressuring you to convince Caleb to haul drugs on this trip?"

"Yes. Coffey says they know where Caleb's mother and the children are, and if we want to see them alive he'd better agree to transport the goods. He didn't give them a good answer, Coffey says, when they talked to him about it a few days ago."

"So Caleb didn't agree, or did he just stall them off?"

The length of time she took answering clued me as to Caleb's answer. Still, I needed to hear it from Caroline. Several seconds passed before she finally said, "We're between a rock and a hard place. We've over-extended ourselves, and with that added to Carl's bad investments, we're not only in the red, but the financial hole is so deep I don't think we'll ever see daylight."

"Is that a yes, Caroline? Caleb agreed to haul a load of drugs?"

She had softened her voice to the point that I had to strain to hear her say, "I'm not sure."

My frustration grew and my scalp itched. I despise cat-and-mouse games. "What does that mean?"

Chapter Twenty-Four

"It means I don't know." She snapped the answer. "Caleb stopped confiding in me a long time ago. Personally, with Coffey's threats to harm our children, coupled with our growing debt, I believe Caleb feels pressured to accept."

"I'm sorry," I said. "Do you trust me?"

"Of course. That's why we contacted you. Except I apologize for not being completely honest about our reasons. What do you have in mind?"

Caroline had admitted she trusted me. However, I'm not sure my feeling was mutual. I said, "At this point, I don't have a concrete plan. I'll discuss what you've told me with my dad. And I'll touch base with you and Caleb at the rodeo."

"In the meantime, what should I do?"

"Go about your usual routine. If Caleb doesn't show up soon, let me know. And, Caroline, Bella is beautiful. She is a treasured gift."

After we disconnected, I prayed that a spiritual creature would make itself known to help me snare the unwary—and those who are ambitious for the wrong reasons.

After talking with Caroline, I felt an overwhelming sense of doom. For lack of anything better to do, I trudged upstairs and slumped across my bed. When I closed my eyes, what I saw frightened me. "Oh, hell," I said. "Oh hell…hell…hell!"

Behind my eyes filtered light was blocked out by large vultures. Native Americans believe these ominous black carrions are "pallbearers" from the sky. Death was coming, and it scared the hell out of me.

River nudged my hand with his nose and whimpered. Neither he nor Rascal are permitted on the bed. I supposed River knew I was in a particular mood. I didn't scold when he climbed on the bed and settled next to me. I stroked his broad black head. "Why me, River?" I asked self-pityingly. Although my grandmother says my empathic senses were gifted to me by the Great Father Spirit, I often question why I was chosen.

It didn't take empathic senses or a degree in forensics psychology to suspect that Caleb was experiencing mental turmoil or possibly undetected health issues. The fact that he'd given me an extremely expensive gift, his confession to Caroline, and now disappearing on horseback into the unknown sent warning signals to my brain. All the signs were there. Whether he was aware or oblivious, I sensed that Caleb was dying.

Empathic powers don't mean I can foretell the future. It simply means that I am extra sensitive to certain auras, and I'm in tune with the spirit world which often visit me in dreams. I don't exactly remember curling into a ball and drifting to sleep.

I blinked slowly awake and found that I stood in the middle of an arena. The sounds of bellows echoed all around me. The gates to all four bucking chutes opened. Snorting bulls charged. I tried to run but I couldn't get my feet to move. A black bull burst from another chute. A masked rider clung tightly as he and the massive beast raced toward me.

I met the rider's distressed eyes. I thought he mouthed, "Forgive me."

Someone was flying through the air. Was it me...or the rider? I struggled out of deep sleep with River nudging with his wet nose and making whimpering sounds. I managed to blink myself awake.

I glanced at the clock. It was four in the morning. I knew on some level that the crying I heard came from me, and I rubbed my face, a little unsure of my surroundings. When I woke enough to shift to a sitting position, I gathered River's quivering body in my arms, hugged him, and then eased him to the floor with full assurances that I was okay.

I yawned and stretched the kinks from my body. Remembering the dream, going back to sleep was not an option. What lingered with me still were the images of the malevolent bovines and that of the rider atop a charging black bull. The haunted look in the faceless rider's eyes chilled me to the bone. I knew for dead certainty someone was going to die. But who—me?

I had prayed for a sign to help me solve this mystery; instead, I'd received a series of dreams warning that I was in danger. The omen was so out of left field that I almost choked. My little donkey kept bumping my hand. I patted his head. "C'mon, Rascal, I need coffee."

I crawled off the bed and headed for the kitchen, where I replenished River and Rascal's bowls with food and water. I put the coffeepot on, then removed a box of donuts from the refrigerator and slumped into a chair to wait. Only the aroma of the coffee and the allure of a waiting sugary donut kept me upright.

As the coffee began to encourage my brain cells to

move a bit, I commenced to formulate a plan of action. I finished off a second glazed donut, refilled my cup, and strolled to the living room to sit in my recliner. I carefully set the mug on the side table, opened my laptop to the murder file, and made a few notes.

I was glad today was Sunday. It meant meeting Dad for our usual family breakfast at Sweets 'n' Eats; except grandmother and Patty were still enjoying their cruise.

To bide my time until then, I decided to take Bella out for our maiden ride. Caleb's note had said she was green broke.

In the morning's ebbing darkness, I could make out the lush green pasture beyond the barn, and in the distance my small herd of belted Galloways, the Oreo cows, roamed. I entered the barn and flipped on a dimmer light so as not to startle the horses. As is my usual routine, I greeted each animal with a handful of carrot rounds.

Not certain how Bella would take to the saddle coupled with my weight, I decided to ride her with a bareback saddle pad with stirrups. I led her from the barn. Bella didn't shy or balk when I led her through the gate that opened to the pasture. Before swinging into the saddle, I gently rested my foot in the stirrup while adding the pressure of my weight. The moment I started to swing my leg over her back, Bella decided to walk off. I checked her immediately to let her know she'd made a mistake. I also rewarded her with kind words and a pat to her silken neck to reassure her that she wasn't being punished.

We moved from a walk to a canter to a trot and into a gallop. The fresh green of new grass, and the distant lemony scent of magnolias was electric. Bella didn't hesitate to respond to each of my commands. After a full run, I settled her to a walk and left behind me the magical moments of moving as one with the horse. I needed to recall other comments Caroline had made about her husband.

I had witnessed first-hand his change in personality, changes in his mood and behavior. I had also attributed his impaired judgment to his excessive drinking. Caroline had verified that Caleb suffered from PTSD. While I accepted the fact that his anomalous behaviors were linked to his mental state, I couldn't help but wonder if Caleb was using drugs or if he was suffering from a biological malaise. Either way, this case was beginning to frustrate me. Except for Coffey and Dodge, I had no solid suspects, plus the mystery man who had ordered the death of Carl Calloway.

By the time Bella and I arrived at the house, the morning sun was shining through an accumulation of billowy clouds. A bevy of questions filled my mind as I brushed her dappled gray coat. Rewarding her with a handful of sweet oats, I turned her into the corral and then opened the stall doors to let the other horses join her.

I climbed on the top rail, ready to jump in if the two geldings and the mare decided to bully Bella. But except for a few friendly nips and squeals, she was accepted as a member of the herd.

"Good morning." Ella smiled up at me. "She sure is a beauty."

I'd been so engrossed in my thoughts and watching the horses Ella's voice startled me. "She's a dream, that's for sure."

Before Ella and I departed for the house, Bella

trotted up to me and laid her chin on my knees. I scratched her forehead. Maybe it was jealousy or maybe it was the scent of carrots in my pocket, but either way, the other horses joined us.

Ella laughed. "You have spoiled them rotten."

Crossing the yard to the house, Ella gushed over the happy details about her date with Andy. Caleb was heavy on my mind as I listened.

We entered through the kitchen door. Ella said, "Have you figured out who is injecting Caleb's bulls with anabolic steroids?"

I huffed my frustration. "My problem with this case is that it seems the list of suspects and motives are endless. I'm having problems connecting the dots." I excused myself to shower and get ready to meet Dad and Uncle Charlie for breakfast.

When I returned, Ella sat relaxed at the table, flipping through a rodeo magazine. She held up a picture of a barrel racing scene. "Brings back fond memories. I miss those days."

I took a long slow breath through my nose. "Yeah, me too."

We walked outside and climbed into my truck. To take my mind off the case, I asked, "So, did Andy kiss you?"

She gasped. "Tullah, do you think I'm a kiss-and-tell kind of girl?"

We both laughed at her double-sided response.

Chapter Twenty-Five

Twenty minutes later, I'd dropped Ella at her mother's house and walked into Sweets 'n' Eats. Since the growth of Enigma's population, the small pink building had become a town favorite. At the door of the crowded café a waitress greeted me, and she led the way to where my dad and Uncle Charlie sat.

Flipping open her order pad, she asked, "What'll you have, Dr. Holliday?"

Soon we were enjoying golden-brown waffles topped with butter and slathered with maple syrup, together with hazelnut coffee. After the general chit-chat ebbed, we sat for a few minutes in silence. Finally, Dad said, "I contacted Sheriff Saunders and apprised him of a possible drug dump at the stockyard as well as other information you provided me. By sheer coincidence, he has a son-in-law who's a nurse at the hospital where Tully Taylor is still a patient."

I nearly choked on my coffee at this unexpected but exciting bit of news. "In Tulsa?"

Dad nodded.

"Don't keep me in suspense."

Dad crooked one of his mischievous grins. "Naturally, the son-in-law couldn't legally question Mr. Taylor. However, Cal—that is, Sheriff Saunders—decided he needed a short vacation and flew to Tulsa to visit with his daughter and new grandson, and take care of a little legal business."

To tamp down my giddiness, I stuffed my mouth with the last bite of waffle. I waved my empty fork toward Dad to show my impatience. He said, "Turns out Mr. Taylor was as forthcoming as an overflowing artesian well."

"I'm all ears, Dad."

He lifted the bill from the table, then motioned toward the door. "Let's take this to the office."

The noise level in the room had risen to the point that shouting was required to converse with the people sitting at the same table with you.

Uncle Charlie snatched the bill from my dad's hand. "You paid last time, my brother. You all go on. I'll catch up with you."

Dad and I moseyed across the street to his office where we were greeted by his deputies. I purposely decided to tease Andy. "Ella's at her mother's, if you're interested."

I love it when his ears turn bright red, which enhances the color of his freckled face. His face practically shone with enthusiasm. Deputy Ramsey looked up from his desk and said, "Messages on your desk, Sheriff. Nothing important."

After making myself comfortable, I waited until Dad had glanced through the phone messages. He tossed them aside, leaned back in his chair, and propped his long legs on his desk. "What's on your mind, Punkin?"

"Nothing much," I said without thinking.

"Can't fool your ol' man. You have that far-away, deep-thought look on your face, like you're visiting never-never land."

"It's Caleb. The whole prison experience has broken

him." I related my dream about the masked rider. "I'm afraid he's about to cave and agree to haul the drugs."

"Knowing he'll go back to prison?"

I explained about the Calloways' financial situation. "Between Caroline, Coffey, and suffering from PTSD, I'm convinced Caleb'll crack under the pressure. In his mind, I believe he doesn't see any alternatives. Which brings me to what Sheriff Saunders found out."

Dad walked to the coffeepot and poured two cups. I accepted mine with a smile. Dad said, "According to Cal, Taylor was reluctant to open up because he feared for his life."

"Someone's really slapping us in the face, Dad. How did Sheriff Saunders convince Tully to talk?"

I listened carefully as he began to speak. "Cal was almost certain Tully Taylor's name was familiar. After searching through his file of old warrants, he discovered that Taylor had an outstanding warrant for jumping bail and skipping town. According to the report, he was caught driving north in a southbound lane of traffic. Fortunately, no one was seriously injured in the massive pileup he caused. Taylor posted bail, then never showed up for his hearing. For other infractions, he landed in a correctional center in Atoka, Oklahoma. The man doesn't seem to understand that drinking and driving is against the law."

I waited patiently while Dad swallowed a sip of coffee. He continued. "When Cal threatened to send Taylor back to prison, he said if he talked, he'd be a dead man and asked for protection in return for information. Mr. Taylor was well enough to be discharged from the hospital. Cal arranged with local authorities to have him released into his custody."

"Where is Tully now?"

Dad said, "Resting in a Kentucky county's lockup courtesy of Sheriff Cal Saunders."

"Has he had an opportunity to question Tully?"

"Yep. Taylor's information coincides with the conversations you've had with Caroline and Ms. Ramos."

"But Dad, that still doesn't prove Caleb's father was murdered."

Dad gave me that look that said to be patient. He continued, "Taylor claims a man referred to as Mr. B is behind the entire operation and ordered Carl's *accidental* death when Carl realized he was in too deep and refused to haul more drugs.

"Actually, Rex Siegler tried to coerce Taylor into joining the drug-hauling scheme. Even though Taylor was offered big money, he also refused to be a party to injecting Caleb's bulls. He told Cal that Caleb had been good to him, had treated him like a regular guy, not like an untrustworthy ex-con, because Caleb knew how tough it gets for ex-cons on the outside.

"Taylor claims that one night he was in town and was jumped by four masked guys. They beat him within an inch of his life. Before passing out, he was doused with whiskey to make it appear he was drunk and had broken parole by going to a bar and getting into a fight. He said when he came to, his parole officer was squatting next to him. According to Taylor, Avery played the good guy and let him off with a warning."

"Uh-huh. Does that mean Tully thinks Robert Avery is in cahoots with whoever is behind all of this? I mean, Rosie did say no one dared buck the system if they wanted to live." My question earned a cockeyed frown from my dad.

He continued. "Taylor also said he recognized Cletus Dodge's voice telling him to either cooperate or it'd be fixed where he'd go back to prison, along with the warning that accidents often happen on the inside."

I asked, "Does Tully know who this Mr. B is? And why would Siegler turn against Caleb? After all, Caleb had done him a favor by giving him a job, a roof over his head, freedom from four walls, and a paycheck." I shrugged. "I don't get it, Dad. Why?"

His voice was casual. "Some guys never learn they're not above the law, and there's always the lure of easy money. As for this Mr. B, Taylor doesn't know him. Except the night of Carl's death, Taylor remembers seeing a black Escalade with a government license plate, and a heavyset bald guy in a western-style business suit getting into the car. Unfortunately, it was dark and he didn't see the guy's face."

"Not to doubt Tully, but how did he know the license plate was for a government vehicle?"

"Easy. The tag light."

"Geez, Dad, can this case get any more bizarre? Are we talking about a senator or congressman calling the shots?" I sat quiet, trying to make sense of the mishmash of words and images inside my head. I worked to align them in an orderly fashion.

"By the expression on your face, I can see the wheels turning inside your brain. What're you thinking?"

I hated these crazy moments and often mistrusted the unknown powers that often bedeviled me. "Questions, Dad. Lots of questions."

"And the answers will possibly lead us to Mr. B's

identity." He pulled a pad of paper from a desk drawer and said, "Fire away."

I hesitated. "Although Rex and Tully were incarcerated in two different prisons, it appears that all of the people involved in this case are connected to the Oklahoma penal system."

I ticked off my thoughts. "According to Caroline, Carl bought off most of Caleb's sentence. Question one: who in the system would Carl contact to arrange such a deal?

Dad scribbled on the pad. He glanced up. "My guess is O'Neal Coffey, and if not him, then his deputy Cletus Dodge."

"Good answer. I agree."

I continued with question two: "Did Carl have an ulterior motive for getting an early release for his son?"

The answer to that question wasn't as easy as the first one. We thought about that while sipping coffee. Finally, Dad said, "It certainly wasn't for fatherly love. The Carl Calloway I remember loved money, booze, and women more than his son."

Dad's stare rested heavily on the notepad in front of him. He kept nodding slightly as he mulled over the answer. For a moment he appeared to have drifted to sleep.

To redirect his attention, I cleared my throat. "Dad, I think that when Caleb won the prison's championship bull rider's buckle two years running, someone approached Carl with the idea of using him to front the moving of drugs."

The synapses in my brain were rapid-firing. "To keep himself clean, Carl sacrificed his own son to do the dirty work while Carl raked in the dough. Caroline said it was Carl's idea to buy the ranch, the breeding stock, and set Caleb up as a rodeo stock contractor."

Dad leaned forward, one elbow propped on his desk. "Charlie and I are old-time rodeo guys. From experience, I can tell you it takes years for a rodeo stock contractor to earn a reputation for supplying topnotch, money-making bulls. The competition is fierce."

I nodded my agreement. "Write this down, Dad. Carl is overwhelmed with debt. Someone approaches him with the idea of employing prisoners who, to avoid consequences, will keep their mouths shut about the drug operation. We can rule out prison guards because they're peons. That means a higher authority, a person with a stellar reputation and above suspicion. Whaddya think?"

"I think you're a genius." We both laughed. I thanked him for the compliment.

Dad picked up his phone. He scrolled through the directory. I listened as the phone dialed the number. He said, "Sheriff Henry Holliday calling for Captain Emmett Howard."

I sat patiently listening to two old friends exchange greetings. Dad switched the phone to speaker mode. He related the shortened version of our case to the Kentucky Federal Marshal. "That's right, Emmett. We're thinking the head honcho is possibly a warden. He's bald, heavy set, drives a black Escalade."

Howard responded. "Oklahoma, you say. Yep, I've got a contact in Oklahoma's northern district." Disgust larded his voice. "There's nothing I despise more than dirty officials, and there's nothing I enjoy more than bustin' their asses. I'll do some checking and get back with you. Give me a few days. How d'you want it? Phone call, email, fax—you name it."

Dad said, "An official document."

"You got it, pal." Howard ended by saying, "I hear the National Beast Buck-Off is next weekend. Maybe I'll just mosey on down to Lexington. This ol' cowboy is gettin' tired of ridin' a chair."

After disconnecting the call, the dimple in Dad's cheek deepened to a pot hole, but then his brows knitted together. "I'd rather you didn't attend the rodeo next week. I don't need a crystal ball to tell me you might be in danger."

I felt a twinge of pain behind my eyes. "Dad, I promised. Besides, as a veterinarian, I have a responsibility to make sure Caleb's bulls are drug free. If not, then I'll report it. We don't need another rider injured or worse."

I glanced at my watch. The morning was slipping away. I was actually surprised that my service hadn't called with an emergency. It felt good to have a Sunday free without interruption. I stood to leave, and Dad came around the desk to escort me to the door.

Chapter Twenty-Six

The week seemed to pass by at a snail's pace. There were no emergencies to help while away the days.

Thursday morning finally arrived. I was up and ready by daybreak. I gave some love to River and Rascal, with an admonishment to guard the property and to look out for each other. I shot Dad a quick text to let him know I was on the road.

He answered back that he and Uncle Charlie would meet me on Friday. While driving, I thought about the job ahead of me and was glad I'd have my dad and Uncle Charlie around. It made me feel safer. In a sense, I regretted getting involved with Caleb and Caroline. They were the little fish in a big pond. Finding the mysterious Mr. B would be like trying to find a certain fish in the Mississippi River. The facts, as I had recorded them in my murder file, rolled through my brain like it was a computer.

Two hours later, after checking into a hotel, I pulled into the Alltech Arena parking lot, finding the section that was filled with the contestants' vehicles. Stock trailers of all makes and conditions, from battered bumper-pulled trailers with peeling paint to elaborate gooseneck rigs, and the more affluent semi-trailers that could haul up to twenty-five bulls, were all expertly packed closely together. In a sea of trailers, I quickly scanned the names of the stock companies and didn't spot a trailer with the name Triple C Stock Company on it.

I found a place for my custom vet truck and parked. When I stepped out, I felt a little intimidated by the vastness of the place. I looked around for the stock pens where the bulls were kept, and paused in confusion. A tall, well-built cowboy turned up suddenly out from a line of trailers, leading a beautiful black-and-white pinto. "Lost?"

"Yes." I pointed to my truck. "I'm the new veterinarian, here to check the bulls. Can you direct me to the office?"

"What happened to the regular guy?"

I shrugged. "Don't know. I'm just responding to a request." Which was stretching the truth a little. "Who are you?"

"I'm one of the pickup riders and headed that way," he said with a smile. "Follow me."

I fell into step with him. "First time at the Alltech?" he asked.

I answered at once. "Not since I was about five years old. My mother used to barrel race." I laughed at the surprise that flickered across his handsome face. "I'm just getting my feet wet with a professional rodeo circuit. Still feeling my way around."

"That right?" he drawled. His eyes were ice blue. "I'm Clay Wolfchild. Welcome aboard. Maybe I can give you a hand. I know most of the stock contractors." His was the soft cultured voice of a man who never had to speak loudly to be heard.

I looked at him quickly. *Shunkaha*? I remembered the dream I'd had. Could this be the wolf that Shadow Woman said would protect me? "Wolfchild, are you…?"

For a split-second anger seemed to spark in his eyes. "Yeah, I'm an Indian. Lakota Sioux, to be exact."

I followed him across the parking lot, walking rapidly to keep up with his long strides. A sudden longing took hold of me. I couldn't help my thoughts. What would it be like to sit beside him in my porch swing, sipping wine, in the stillness of a Kentucky night? I shivered.

Be careful, Tullah Holliday, I warned myself. He's just showing you to the bull pens and the rodeo office, not trying to swoop you off your feet. I saw I had touched a nerve, and reached to grab his arm. "I didn't mean to offend you."

I lifted my gaze and reached out my hand. "I'm Dr. Tullah Holliday."

Wolfchild grinned, his teeth very white against his bronze skin. He clasped my hand with the strength of a bull rider. "Holliday, like the infamous outlaw." It wasn't a question.

I shot him an annoyed glance. I thought, Oh, here it comes, the stupid question about who's my huckleberry.

A hint of humor touched his eyes but he didn't smile. "Me Indian. Us noble savages know a lot of stuff about paleface history."

I kept my gaze locked on his, and stated evenly, "I'm taking it that you don't believe in being politically correct. It isn't 'Indian' anymore, it's 'Native American.' "

"Is that so?" Wolfchild offered a patronizing smile.

This man was no ordinary pickup rider. In my high school years, I'd kept up with the rodeo world. I was aware that the stars in that world drew crowds of groupies. He was definitely a star. There would be plenty of women for Clay Wolfchild. Easy women, who would ask for nothing more than his notice, at any price. I vowed to keep my distance from him.

He interrupted my thoughts. "Hey, we're here. If there's anything I can do to help you out, well, everyone knows me."

My brain whispered, Yep, I'll just bet they do.

Before we parted ways, I asked, "Do you happen to know Caleb Calloway, the owner of Triple C Stock Company?"

His eyes veiled. Wolfchild fell silent for a moment. I stood there, my mind reaching for answers to questions without blowing my cover. I couldn't come right out and ask him if Shadow Woman had sent him to protect me. If I did and he knew nothing, I'd come across as a looney, and we'd already gotten off to a tenuous start. For now, it was best to stay silent and alert.

He arched his heavy eyebrows. "Yep, he's the one with the killer bulls. You'd better be extra careful. Calloway's got a bull that won't hesitate to horn you. Don't ever get in the pen with Diablo."

A shiver rippled over me. I decided to play innocent. "I must admit that my expertise is more with equine than bovine. What's makes this Diablo so dangerous?"

"Diablo seems to have an innate ability to outguess the moves from the riders that draw his name. So far, he's unridden." Wolfchild hesitated for a second. "I pity the poor cowboy that draws Diablo tomorrow. I'd bet ten thousand dollars the poor sucker doesn't make the eight seconds, and…" His voice trailed off.

"And what?" My curiosity peaked.

"Forget it. I spoke out of turn."

"You owe it to the riders if you suspect someone is

tampering with the bulls."

Wolfchild shot me an indifferent look. He turned to walk away.

I wanted to say, *But 'a real man' doesn't walk away from his responsibilities.* Instead, I said, "Ah, but you and your horse will be there to rescue the downed riders—right?"

He kept walking. I called him back. "What's your horse's name?"

"Domino."

"Then you'd better not ride Domino tomorrow night or any other night."

Wolfchild's shoulders went rigid. He cut a wary eye toward me as he ran a hand down the pinto's neck. He kept his focus on me, his voice snide. "You got something against Tobiano Quarter Horses?"

I listened to his plaint. "I'm a veterinarian. I know horses, and yours is in pain. Look at how he's holding his left foot off the ground." I softened my voice. "With your permission, may I examine him?"

Wolfchild nodded his go-ahead. I walked to the gelding and ran my hand down his beautiful swan neck and along his withers. When I lightly pinched the trapezius in Domino's shoulder, he flinched, flared and flicked his ears, and tried to back away.

Anger flittered across Wolfchild's face. "What did you do to my horse?"

Ignoring his question, I spoke to the animal and continued my examination without replying to the question. Except for that one spot, the gelding stood patiently. I directed Wolfchild to touch where I pointed. "You'll feel a knot where the saddle's pommel swell rests. The nerve is pinched. Domino is in pain, and bearing the weight of a saddle, and you, only aggravates the muscle."

The patronizing looks he'd given me earlier melted into genuine concern. He said, "He seemed fine when we left home. How did this happen, and what treatment do you recommend?"

I suggested he stable his horse. "As soon as I check in and present my credentials at the office, I'll come by and administer a little horse chiropractic treatment, a cortisone shot, and an ice pack, and recommend four to six weeks of rest. After that, Domino should be good as new."

"I don't understand how this happened, Doc."

Only my close friends used that title. Clay Wolfchild was neither friend nor foe. At this point I was certain there was more to him than met the eye. "It's *Doctor*."

I continued. "Another horse could have kicked him, or perhaps Domino bumped his shoulder while you were traveling." I assured him that with proper care and rest, his horse would heal.

Wolfchild thanked me. He gave the pinto an affectionate pat on the shoulder, which caused the horse to flinch. The worried look in Wolfchild's eyes was genuine. He led the horse across the parking lot.

I called out, "Hey, Mr. Wolfchild, do you happen to know a person named Shadow Woman?"

He smiled. "Call me Clay. Mr. Wolfchild is too formal for an ordinary cowboy. And no, to your question. Who is she?"

"Never mind. It's not important." Curiosity itched my head. As I made my way to the rodeo office, I was determined to find out more about Clay Wolfchild, a Lakota Sioux with blue eyes.

Chapter Twenty-Seven

I wasn't expecting Dad and Uncle Charlie until the next morning. Although I didn't much care for socializing among strangers, I decided to accept the invitation to the Stetson Club at the top of the Alltech's three-hundred-and-sixty-degree glassed dome. A party might be the perfect place to eavesdrop on conversations involving illicit rodeo activities.

The club was filled with sponsors, their guests, and other dignitaries of Lexington and the rodeo. The main lounge was furnished in Western décor, complete with a wall of mounted longhorns and photos of various champion bull riders. I stood at the wide entrance, observing. Women of all sizes and shapes were dressed in western attire. No matter their ages, every woman was in skintight clothing, and most wore either gold or silver lamé pants. I felt a little dowdy in my black slacks and black paisley floral shirt with white pearl snaps down the front.

Scattered around the room were a number of contestants, easy to identify by their new denim pants, their youth, and their health. Older men wore western-cut suits, most were overweight, and appeared less *used* than the guys who actually rode the bulls.

Bartenders were busy behind a long bar, and several attractive girls dressed in very short skirts and western shirts moved among the crowd, balancing trays of drinks.

Everyone seemed to talk loudly, perhaps to override the band, which played country-western music.

I recognized Alberto del Toro, the current reigning champion, in the center of an admiring group of fans. A familiar voice said, "Lost?"

Clay Wolfchild stood at my side. I laughed. "Seems like you're always around to help me find my way." He took my arm and led me into the room, threading the way toward an open space along one wall.

A man and two women watched us approach. Clay greeted them loudly. "Evening, Tank. Bev, you're looking quite fetching tonight." He hauled me around by the arm to face them. "Dr. Holliday, I'd like you to me Mr. and Mrs. Tankard Stockwell. He's the stock contractor that furnishes the sorry animals us poor cowboys have to ride. And this is his wife, Beverly."

Beverly Stockwell was an attractive woman of about fifty with hair right out of a blonde-dye bottle. Although she was beginning to lose the last blooms of her youth, I knew she must have been stunning in her heyday. Tall and shapely, she wore a pair of lilac pants and a deeper shade of pink shirt decorated with gold thread. Despite the fact that she was not as slim and firm as some of the other women, her lush figure would catch the eyes of most men.

"Hello, Dr. Holliday." Bev's voice had a husky tone to it, as if she had smoked too many cigarettes, but her smile was genuine. "Are you from Oklahoma or North Carolina?"

"Please, call me Tullah. Neither. I'm a native Kentuckian. Why do you ask?"

The woman's overly rouged cheeks flushed. "How presumptuous of me. I apologize." She continued. "You look very Native American." And then as if she'd further embarrassed herself, she said, "Of course, you could be Italian or—or…" She glanced from her husband to Clay Wolfchild.

Her husband laughed. "I think you'd better stop before you dig yourself into a hole you can't get out of, darling."

Beverly smiled, but I thought her tone held a barbed prejudice. Tank Stockwell's brown eyes showed immediate discomfort. He towered over his wife's short stature. He shot his wife an odd look.

"No offense taken, Mr. and Mrs. Stockwell."

I felt an intense unease. It seemed as if the Stockwells and Wolfchild stared at me, waiting for me to reveal my heritage.

I looked directly into Clay's teasing blue eyes but addressed my response to Beverly. "You are very astute, Mrs. Stockwell. I am proud of my Cherokee heritage. My mother and grandmother are from the North Carolina Waya Clan."

To break the tension, Tank said, "What a coincidence. Two wolves in the same room. Who would've thunk." Before either of us could respond, he hastened on. "Clay, you riding this year?"

Clay grinned. "Naw, I've been on donkeys that's got more buck in them than some of those scrubs you hauled in today."

Tank scowled. "What about one of Caleb Calloway's bulls?" He cocked an eyebrow. "I've got money says you can't go eight seconds with Diablo."

Beverly scolded her husband. "You know Clay is still on the injury list." Then she squealed. "Look who's coming!"

Oh, crap! I thought as my heart sank. Baily Strom strolled toward us. The one person Caroline said they trusted. I prayed either she or Caleb had revealed my true identity to him. Mostly, I hoped they'd cautioned him to keep my identity a secret. I barely heard Beverly say, "Most important man in the show. Do you know who he is, Tullah?"

"I don't believe we've met."

She introduced us. "Doctor Tullah Holliday, I'd like you to meet Baily Strom. Currently works for the Triple C Stock Company."

His dark eyes crinkled into a frown. Relief washed over me when he nodded with a slight wink. He stuck out his hand. "Pleased to meet you, ma'am."

"I didn't see their stock trailer when I arrived this morning." He scowled. "There was a bit of a delay. I 'spect they'll roll in here before midnight."

Tank slapped Baily on the back. "Why, if it ain't Baily Strom. The best rodeo bullfighter around."

"Oh, come on, Tank!" Baily protested.

"It's a fact. You can get a rider off a bucking bull with pickup men, like Clay, but them bulls ain't afraid of no horse. They go for one just as quick as they'll go for a man. And when a man gets on a bull, two things are for sure gonna happen." He held up his hand and counted off, his face serious. "One, he's gonna get bucked off or he's gonna go to buzzer an' then jump off. That ain't no maybe, that's a hard fact of life. And number two, when he does hit the dirt, that bull's gonna try to stomp out his gizzards, and that's another fact." He slapped his leg. "Got me a gimp leg. I oughta know."

Baily looked at Clay. "You well enough to compete?"

Wolfchild flushed slightly, and shook his head. "Nope. I'm riding pickup."

"Good to know you and Domino will be there to watch my back." He wagged a finger at Tank. "Now, that's one horse that isn't afraid of bulls."

Wolfchild regarded me with sharp attention. "I'm afraid Domino is temporarily out of commission. According to Dr. Holliday, he's got a pinched nerve." His eyes shimmered a little. "I've never heard of chiropractic treatments on a horse, but whatever she popped in his shoulder sure did help."

I glowed on the inside from the compliment. He continued, "She's got a good eye. She spotted right off that Domino was in pain."

Beverly motioned a roving waitress over and grabbed a shot glass and a beer. She downed the shot's amber liquid, grimaced, and slapped the empty glass back on the tray. Then she guzzled half the beer and pointed the glass toward me. She slurred her words. "Everybody knows Calloway juices his b-bulls." She hiccupped the word."

Clay was instantly alert. "Tank, maybe Bev's had a little too much fun for one night."

Baily regarded the woman with sharp attention. "Meaning no disrespect, Mrs. Stockwell, but I don't abide that kind of talk about Caleb. He's as straight as an arrow. Anybody says otherwise'll deal with me."

I decided to weigh in to alleviate the mounting tension. "That's why I'm here. I've been hired to test *all* the bulls. That includes Red Simpson's, Tex Guerrero's, the Calloway bulls, and yours, too, Mr. Stockwell."

An awkward silence fell, so heavy I felt that I'd committed some sort of terrible social blunder. Tank

Stockwell's face reddened, and his wife's lips drew into a hard line. I felt Baily shuffling his feet. Glancing at him, I saw he was staring at the door. "If you'll excuse me, I'd like to speak to Waco Longley." He tipped his hat. "If I can be of any assistance, Doctor Holliday, let me know. Bucking bulls are dangerous critters." Baily shot Beverly a hard look. "Juiced or not."

I cautioned myself to keep my mouth shut. Rodeo isn't a sport. It's business, and that means money is at the center of it. There are egos, too. Everyone wants to be number one—the star. Fortunately, rodeo people like to talk—especially about each other.

I thanked Baily and watched him weave his way through the crowded room. I looked at Clay and said, "Who is Waco Longley?"

"Another bullfighter—better known as a rodeo clown. Like Baily, he's a former competitor, and like Baily, got hurt and had to retire. But it's men like them that put their lives on the line to keep the bulls at bay until the pickup riders can get in and haul the downed man to safety."

Amid her loud protests, Tank had gripped his wife by the arm and was escorting her toward the door. I wanted nothing more than to escape to the peace and quiet of my room. My ears were vibrating from the combination of voices shouting to be heard over the band's music. As if trying to break the rigidity of the moment, Clay said, "Hey, let me get you a drink, Doctor Holliday. What'll it be?"

I sighed. "It's Tullah, remember? And, just a cola, please."

He stared at me in surprise. "You against alcohol?" He slapped his hand against his leg. "Dang! I just put my mouth in another bear trip, didn't I?"

I cocked my head and smiled. Then wondered if I was flirting. "I'm merely heeding the warnings from both you and Baily about how dangerous the bulls are by keeping a clear head."

He waved a waitress over. "You got plain ol' colas on that tray?"

She looked at him as if he'd grown two heads. "You're kidding, right?"

"No, ma'am. I never joke." He took my arm. "Never mind. We'll get our own."

"If you don't mind, I'll meet you on the balcony. This noise is offending my ears."

He pointed across the room and laughed. "Don't get lost."

Tempted to stick out my tongue and giggle like a smitten school girl, I refrained, and once I was outside, the fresh air was a relief from a room filled with cloying perfumes. I stood gazing at the stars.

Clay joined me at the arched door that led to the outside balcony. "Penny for your thoughts." He handed me a tall glass filled with ice and cola.

"Who are you, Clay Wolfchild?"

He sipped his drink. "I'm not sure what you mean."

"You're not an ordinary rodeo cowboy."

"Who do you think I am?"

"I'm not sure. Does *Shunkaha* mean anything to you?"

"Sure. In Lakota it means wolf. That's partly how I came by my name."

"Do you ever have visions about protecting people?"

He laughed. "What you're asking me sounds like a

scene from a soap opera. What about you—do you have visions about protecting people?"

I wanted to say, *Yes*, and that I had visions about dead people, too. Instead, I switched from what appeared to be a dead-end subject. "Why did Beverly Stockwell say that Caleb Calloway injected his bulls? I'm assuming it would be to make them buck harder, or to make them extra dangerous, right?"

Clay rolled the glass between his hands as if searching for an answer. "It was the alcohol talking. Don't pay her any mind." His gaze made me uncomfortable. Finally, he said, "Earlier you said you'd been hired to test all of the bulls. Who hired you, and why?"

"At this time, my employer has requested that I not reveal his name."

"Be careful, Tullah, I'd hate to see you get hurt."

"Is that a threat?"

"Not from me. Amateurs think rodeo is an exciting sport. If you're new to the circuit, then let me assure you it's a dog-eat-dog business. Competition doesn't always happen in the arena between man and beast. If you get my drift."

I set my glass on a table. "You know, I'm getting a little tired of the veiled threats." My temper was about to explode, and I'd decided it was time to leave. I excused myself and walked into a room filled with people. I was almost to the exit door when I heard a loud yell and the crash of chairs. I turned in time to glimpse a man sailing backward as if he'd been shot from a cannon.

"C'mon, Billy Bob!" I heard a woman shout. "Whip his sorry ass."

I saw a man in his early thirties pick himself up and

spit on his hands. Lowering his head, he charged like a bull straight at a tall wiry cowboy who met him with a flurry of blows. The crowd was yelling, and as the two men flailed away at each other, I also noticed the varying reactions from the crowd. The rodeo people apparently loved a good fight and egged on the two fighters. But nervous apprehension covered the faces of the wannabes. When the two brawlers landed at the feet of a balding man with flabby jaws and dressed in an expensive western-cut suit, he said, "This is too much for me. Barbarians! Let's get out of here, Louise." He grabbed the older woman next to him and hauled her toward the door.

The fight moved from one point to another as the battlers continued to pummel each other with wild punches, until the tall man wilted to his knees and came to rest flat on his back.

Somebody shouted, "You whupped the daylights out'n him, Billy Bob!"

Billy Bob raised his hands in triumph. He reached down and offered his hand to the fallen foe. "C'mon, Butch. I'll buy ya a beer."

I moved toward the door. My arm was hooked by a strong hand. "Hey, we ain't met, little lady." A huge man with broad shoulders pulled me toward him. "Friends call me Yuma 'cause I'm from Arizona."

He was a rough-cut cowboy with a receding hairline and a scar lacing his weathered cheek. Whiskey fouled his breath. His calloused hand cut into my arm with unnecessary force. I struggled to pull away. "If you'll excuse me, I was just leaving."

He jerked again. I nearly bounced off his rock-hard chest, and couldn't help the small squelch that escaped my lips. He slurred his words. "Aaw, don't be like that. The party's jes' gettin' started."

I pushed against his chest. "I said—let go!"

Clay didn't hit Yuma. He simply stepped forward and brushed him aside. Yuma lost his balance and fell hard on the tile floor. With the agility of a younger man, the cowboy sprang to his feet and, without hesitation, sent a tremendous blow toward Clay's face.

Clay sidestepped the punch. "The lady said she didn't want to dance." He took my arm and motioned me toward the door.

A flash of motion caught my eye. I had enough time to turn my head and see Yuma lifting a chair over his head. Someone from the crowd yelled, "Clay, watch out!"

A frown appeared across Clay's face like a white slash. The punch he landed to Yuma's face was lightning quick and hard enough to drive him backward, blood spurting from his nose.

Clay cupped my elbow, and I followed him to the elevator. He said, "Now that you've had a little taste of life on the rodeo circuit, what do you think?"

I managed a smile. "First, thanks for coming to my rescue, and second, I think I'll stick with private practice."

We rode the elevator to the parking lot. Clay escorted me to my truck. "That big bully won't try to get even, will he?"

Clay seemed to weigh his answer, then simply said, "Nope."

"Goodnight, Clay. See you in the morning."

I showered and readied for bed, surprised at how the violence at the party had shaken me. I lay awake, my mind dwelling on the people I had met, and on the conversation about Caleb and his bulls.

Chapter Twenty-Eight

I had entered that stage between wakefulness and peacefully drifting to sleep when my phone chimed. Thinking it might be from my dad, instead I opened a text from Caroline advising that she and Caleb had checked into the hotel. She gave me their room number and said to meet them at seven for breakfast.

I answered with a request to have Caleb meet me at the stock pens at six. I was almost too wired to sleep. In less than seventeen hours, the arena gates would open. Spectators would clamor to find their seats, and activity behind the scenes would be tumultuous. Nerves and tempers would run high. I set my clock to make sure I was up and dressed to check Caleb's bulls for steroids before the frenzy started.

My restless night consisted of images of a snarling wolf interfaced with visions of Clay Wolfchild disturbing my sleep. The computer side of my brain refused to retire to sleep mode. By the time my alarm beeped, I awoke groggy and feeling out of sorts.

Up before dawn, I dressed, and equipped with my medical bag, left my room. Badly in need of coffee, I filled a to-go cup to carry with me as I drove the short distance to the arena. At the security shack, I presented my credentials and was waved through by a guard who looked as grumpy as I felt.

A bit of nostalgia filled me as I recalled my college

days, when I had competed on the college barrel-racing team. I wandered through the arena's large doors. Even empty, and slightly ghostly, as it were, I sensed something deadly. Breath stalled in my throat when a large gray wolf stood in the center of the arena. I asked, "Why are you here?"

The image disappeared in a spiral of dust when a tractor chugged through a dark cavern of doors and into the dimly lit arena, pulverizing the earth into powder. The driver was an older man with a shock of white hair and a drooping mustache. He lifted one hand in a languid manner of friendship. I waved back and continued on my journey to the stock pens.

I thought about the old man with a cowboy hat that looked as ancient as him. He had nothing to worry about. He couldn't get hurt riding a machine. Not like a cowboy on top of a two-thousand-pound keg of dynamite—especially one that had been injected with a substance to increase its volatile nature. No, the old man needn't worry that getting bucked off a horn might puncture his lung, or his head smashed by a hoof.

I wondered why bull riders would put themselves in such danger. The answer was easy—for the thrill, the challenge of man against beast, and hoping to survive until the eight-second buzzer, which meant racking up the dollars.

I strolled down a long aisle that ran between the pens, and nearly jumped out of my skin when a voice said, "Can I he'p you, ma'am?" He glanced at the bag in my hand. "You the new vet everybody's been talkin' 'bout?"

The tractor driver's eyes were warm and honest.

"Word travels fast. Yes, I'm Dr. Holliday, and you

are?"

"Jordy Wells. I was a real buckaroo in my day. Now the only thing I ride is that danged putt-putt." He slapped the side of his faded denims. "Aaw, well, it's a living."

"Pleased to meet you, Mr. Wells. I'm here to certify the bulls are in good shape and fit for performing."

We stopped at a pen to look at a creamy tan bull that was eyeing us. The old wrangler said, "This is Buttermilk. He looks peaceful enough, but he's a cowboy stomper, for sure. Always hate to see a young greenie on top of him. Billy Bob's riding him tonight, so it's all right."

The livestock section was beginning to come alive with animals being moved from pen to pen. "Do you travel with the rodeo, Mr. Wells?"

"Wish you'd call me Jordy, and yes'm. Me and Ace-High Sumter, that's the owner, we go back to the days when we were young whippersnappers, only he made the big bucks while I got the stuffings stomped out of me. Then I was a rodeo clown 'til I got too old and decrepit to outfox the bulls."

"I imagine you know the characteristics of each bull."

"Yes'm, I do."

We continued our walk from pen to pen, with Jordy pointing out different traits, and how to know which bull was a good bucker or a dud. I didn't spot any unusual salivating, nasal discharge, or erratic behavior that would signal the influence of an illicit drug.

As we approached the end of our tour, I said, "I don't see any Triple C stock."

"For the past two rodeos he's kept his bulls separate. 'Spect he'll show up soon." He turned to walk away.

"And you heed what I'm telling you, young lady. Any one of these boogers might look all calm and cuddly, but once that gate opens, they're out to hurt anyone in their path. With that being said, Mr. Calloway has a Bramish named Diablo. A small, wiry black 'un with horns pointed straight out like pitchfork tines. He'd sooner hook you than look at you. And, Dr. Holliday, you stay away from Yuma Washburn. He's topnotch at riding bulls but won't win no prizes for being a gentleman."

I trusted what Jordy Wells had advised. "You didn't say why Mr. Calloway keeps his bulls apart from the others."

A stream of brown spittle landed on the ground. Jordy drew a sleeve across his mouth. "Sometimes, I talk too much."

"It's important that I know, Jordy. I suppose you've heard the rumors that his bulls are being injected with a substance to enhance their performance."

He seemed to mull over whether to ignore my question and return to his tractor work, or to answer me. After glancing around, he said in a lowered voice, "I can't say for certain, Doctor. Mr. Calloway's stock is fairly superior to some of the other contractors. Some are a might envious of him takin' home top dollar all of a sudden, like."

"What do you mean by 'all of a sudden'?"

Jordy reached up and scratched under his hat. "Oh, he had some up-and-comers, but mostly mediocre ones, not money makers, if you catch my drift. Then, six rodeos ago, he showed up with Diablo and Jackknife. Sam Toms, nice young kid, drew Diablo. Sam didn't last more 'n two seconds, and that bull was on him like fleas on a dog. Messed the boy up bad. Seemed like it took forever to get Diablo off him.

"It was after the last rodeo, when the rider was killed, that rumors started flying that Mr. Calloway's bulls were abnormally muscled, and more vicious than the other contractors' bulls, and Mr. Calloway was raking in the greenbacks."

The area was beginning to get busy. Hired hands arrived pushing dollies loaded with sacks of feed and bales of hay. I lowered my voice also. "Uh-huh, what you're saying is that another contractor might be out for revenge?"

"Like I said, I talk too much." He adjusted the battered cowboy hat lower on his head. "Gotta finish raking the arena. Boss wants some fancy circles, as if the bulls give a sh…" He let the expletive drift off. I bit back a smile to keep from embarrassing the old-timer. He'd walked a few feet when he turned back. "You tread careful. Rodeo folks don't abide by too much prying into their business." There was a sad cast to his face. "Heed what I'm telling you. If you hear hoofprints and feel the ground vibrating, don't look back, 'cause something might be after you. Run like hell and find a high place to shinny up."

Jordy excused himself and ambled toward the arena to resume his efforts to groom the dirt floor. I continued observing bulls, looking for signs of out-of-the-ordinary behavior. A couple of times, I asked men dumping grain into the bins for permission to bag samples of the feed. I was met with some resistance even when I held out my lanyard to verify my identity.

I asked one such handler, "Are all the bulls fed the same grain?"

"Every stockman I know supplies his own feed and

hay." He cocked his head to one side and cast me a chilling look. "Listen, lady, we heard about you replacing the regular vet. He never went around accusing our bosses of doing anything wrong or wanting to test the feed."

He pointed a pitchfork toward me. I stepped back. He grinned. "Better be careful. Accidents around a rodeo happen all the time."

"Is that a threat?"

He slung several flakes of hay into the pen of a black-and-white spotted bull wearing a Circle Six brand. "Take it anyway you like." He moved on to the next pen.

I made a mental note to research the owner's background and reputation. I glanced at my watch. It was nearing seven and neither Caleb nor his bulls were anywhere in sight. My phone chimed—a text from Caleb.

Me: "Where are you?"

Caleb: "Pulling in now."

I stepped into the sunlight and spotted a gold semi-truck emblazoned with Caleb's brand backing up to an unloading chute. Behind me, a large brown Charbray bull battered the side of its metal pen. Two handlers rushed over. One man flapped his arms up and down to make the bull back away from the fence while the other guy grabbed a water hose to cool down the agitated animal.

A woman appeared from nowhere to stand beside me. "Howdy, I saw you at the party last night. I'm Cherry Popp." Maybe it was the expression on my face that caused her to say, "Yeah, I know. My mother had a weird sense of humor."

I offered my hand. "Dr. Tullah Holliday. Nice to

meet you, Cherry." I was about to ask her a few questions when Billy Bob walked by sporting a black eye from last night's fight and winked. Her homely face lit up. She responded by blowing him a kiss.

"I gather the two of you are an item?"

A sadness covered Cherry's face. "Not likely. Bobo is a fine fella, and an ace when it comes to riding the full eight seconds." She frowned. "But there's one cowboy I think he'd let a bull stomp to death without lifting a hand."

Her voice trailed off as she stared past me. I turned in time to see Caleb stepping down from the cab of his truck. A shiver ran over me when I asked, "Who?"

"There he is now—Mr. High-and-Mighty Caleb Calloway."

It seemed all of the bulls had become agitated, and the entire back area was in motion. "I don't understand. What has Billy Bob got against him?"

There was little compassion in her eyes when she spoke. "I guess you've heard about the rider that got killed."

I nodded.

"His name was Jasper Corbin. He was Billy Bob's little brother and my fiancé."

Now I understood the change in her demeanor. "I'm so sorry. I know what it's like to lose a loved one, but riders know bull riding is dangerous. How can Mr. Calloway be held responsible?"

A look of pure rage clouded her eyes. "Everybody knows Caleb doses his bulls."

"Who are they—where's the proof?"

"There isn't any proof. Diablo's too dangerous to get near, and so is Jackknife."

We both jumped when a deep masculine voice yelled over a bullhorn, "Hey, Cherry, how about running over to the commissary and getting us some coffee and donuts? Three black and three with cream. A dozen donuts will do."

Cherry's bit of information put a new spin on who might have it in for Caleb. She and I parted ways. I strolled to where Caleb stood and watched the bulls sprint down the long silver trailer's ramp. Gates had been strategically placed to guide the animals to their individual enclosures. Midway to his pen, Diesel tried to hook the cowboy that was flagging the animals through.

I expressed surprised to see the beefalo. "I thought he was too young for competition, and not built for riders."

Caleb pulled a handkerchief from his back pocket. He removed his hat and wiped inside the sweatband. "By rodeo standards, he's old enough. This is a test run to see how Diesel performs. I'll be the first to admit that it'll be a challenge for a rider to stay on, but that's the name of the rodeo game."

With all eyes of suspicion on him, I wondered why Caleb would take such a chance. I couldn't help my own doubts. "You were supposed to meet me over an hour ago. What happened?"

He avoided my question. "I don't know about you, but I'm starved. Meet you at the restaurant, and run interference for me. Caroline's a little upset with me."

"I will after I examine your bulls. After all, that's why I'm here—right?"

Without answering, he raced to help a couple of handlers when Diesel tried to climb out of his pen.

Chapter Twenty-Nine

After a tedious hour, I managed to collect enough saliva and mucus from Caleb's six bulls without being kicked in the head or horned. I stored the vials of secretions in a cool-pack and headed to my truck and the drive to the hotel. By now the sun was shining, the parking lot was filled, and the lobby overly crowded. I needed a shower, a triple dose of coffee, and a stack of pancakes slathered in syrup to improve my mood.

I was about to punch the elevator button when my dad's voice stopped me. After a round of hugs, he and Uncle Charlie rode to the eighth floor with me. Fortunately, we were the only occupants of the elevator car, and I was able to give them a quick rundown of last night and this morning's events.

Dad's only comment was that he didn't like the threats against me. Uncle Charlie's face was grim. He said, "If anyone tries to hurt you, I'll turn into one bad Apache."

I listened intently while Dad and Uncle Charlie filled me in with Sheriff Saunders' news. "It appears we've opened a dirty can of worms, with O'Neal Coffey and his lacky, Cletus Dodge, being major players in a vast drug operation."

"Were there drugs in Caleb's stock trailer?"

Dad nodded his answer.

The elevator doors opened and two maids rolled

their carts toward us. They communicated in Spanish, so we had no way of knowing if they would understand anything we might say. We rode in silence until they left us at floor number five.

Uncle Charlie lowered his voice. "The marshal is still working with his informants to uncover the identity of Mr. B."

We stepped out when the elevator doors opened. "Does Caleb know you're here?"

Dad said, "He does. That's why he was late meeting you. I'll fill you in later." He pointed to the small metal box in my hand. "Is that the goods?"

I met his serious look and nodded. "My medical bag and testing kit is in my room. Until I return from breakfast, I'll lock this in the safe."

"How long will it take to get the results?" Dad wanted to know.

"It's a simple litmus test. For six bulls…about an hour, maybe less, once I get started. I've also collected samples of grain used by different ranchers. What doesn't show up in the litmus test may show up in the feed samples."

"You're the only one I trust to get and give honest results." Dad squeezed my shoulder.

I looked at my watch. "I'm meeting Caroline and Caleb for breakfast. Join us?"

The dark circles under Dad's eyes concerned me. He said, "It's been almost twenty-four hours since Charlie and I've had sleep."

Charlie yawned. "Yeah, we're getting too old for these late-night shenanigans."

I scanned the card over my room's key reader to open the door. Before I entered, I asked, "Is Caleb in trouble?"

"So far he's cooperating." Dad shrugged; his dark features impassive. "It depends on the results of your tests."

"Dad, did he haul the…goods?"

With a simple nod, he affirmed the answer.

When I opened the door to my room, a rodeo schedule had been slipped under my door and lay on the floor. I tossed it onto the bed and headed for the shower.

Thirty minutes later, I strolled into the dining room. Caleb stood, waved me to where he and Caroline sat, and pulled out a chair for me. For the next ten minutes the three of us discussed the riders and the possible bulls they'd draw to ride.

A waitress arrived with our food. I noted the slight tremor in Caleb's hand when he attempted to slice the slab of ham on his plate. The pallor on his tanned face stood out. He pulled a prescription bottle from his shirt pocket and washed down two pills with a slug of coffee.

"Are you ill, Caleb?" I asked.

He grinned. "Ask me no questions and I'll tell you no lies."

Caroline shot her husband an angry glare. "Caleb Calloway, what are those pills?"

He demurred with a smile. "Let's change the subject. I'm worried that a greenie will draw Diesel. He's a whole lot of bad for an inexperienced rider."

The slur to Caleb's words was evident. Caroline scolded, "Have you been drinking?" She leaned over to sniff his breath. "You promised." She was suddenly angry. "If you think I've got nothing to do but drop everything and come running every time you get in a jam, you're sadly mistaken. I'm done, Caleb. You're no better than your alcoholic, conniving father."

She stood and tossed her napkin on the table. "I'm going back to the ranch, and don't expect me to be there when you get home—if you get home."

Caleb declared, "You're always trying to run a man's life, but you're not going to run mine."

Caroline looked at me, and bit her lip. "I'm sorry, Tullah." She apologized.

I stood to go after her. Caleb grabbed my arm. "Let her go."

"But…"

"She'll get it over it. She always does."

I returned to my seat and saw that his face had grown even more pale. "What's going on, Caleb?" I noted the pill bottle still clutched in his hand.

He practically growled the excuse. "I've got a massive headache. Give it a rest, okay?"

The dining room had grown quiet. Caleb grinned suddenly. He stood and bowed to the curious onlookers. "Ladies and gentlemen, I'm Caleb Calloway. I've got the best fighting bulls in the country. If you haven't bought your tickets to the rodeo, get 'em. I guarantee my bull, Diablo, will take home the fourteen-million-dollar purse."

I sat there unable to speak. First, at the exorbitant amount of the winnings, and second, by making such a brazen announcement, Caleb left himself wide open to be hustled by every scammer and thief within hearing distance.

He'd grabbed my hand and held on to it. His were clammy, and I tried to pull away. Instead of releasing it, he held tighter. His eyes were fixed on me, and I had no idea what he was thinking. My mind raced, searching for reasons that would explain his odd behavior, but nothing came.

And then his eyes gleamed and sarcasm laced his voice. "I used to be a rodeo star, and I was pretty good, too. In fact, I've got the silver buckles to prove it. If I'd stayed with it, I might be giving Alberto del Toro, bull rider extraordinaire, a run for his money. But I became a stockman instead. I'm asshole in debt, and I'm not just talking about a mortgage. My ol' man owes people—his death didn't wipe out the debt."

A hint of futility lit his eyes, and he quipped, "That's about to change. I've got to prove I'm still a man—to myself; the hell with Caroline."

I stared at him. "Caleb, isn't it against the rules that stock owners can't compete as bull riders?"

He looked at me with an innocent gaze. He tsked. "Tullah, you're way behind the times. The rules changed a couple of years ago. We both know that riders randomly select the bulls they're gonna ride. Except for del Toro, those selections will begin about an hour before show time. And chances are, I'd never draw one of my own bulls."

Rumor had it that no one except Alberto del Toro would pick Diablo to ride in tomorrow night's competition. The last night of the rodeo, with del Toro and Diablo, the killer bull, would be the biggest crowd draw.

Caleb released my hand. He tossed his napkin on the plate of untouched food before him. When he stood, I noticed his eyes seemed to cross, and he wobbled as if losing his balance. He offered a sheepish grin. "A little too much hair of the dog. Nothing a couple of hours' sleep won't cure."

His gait was unsteady as he walked out of the dining room. A waitress came over to ask if I needed anything. "A to-go box and a large coffee, please."

Chapter Thirty

I finished breakfast in my room. The pancakes and bacon had lost their flavor. And, the results of each test soured my stomach even more. The sample of feed for the bull from Circle Six ranch showed traces of jimsonweed; not sufficient to drive a bull crazy enough to kill. I didn't consider it a big deal because the weed could have been harvested when the hay was baled in the field. However, traces of peyote, and other barbiturates showed positive in several bulls owned by other stock contractors. Much to my relief, all six of Caleb's entrants tested negative, which proved he hadn't doped his bulls. I opened my laptop and made notes identifying pen numbers and stock owners.

I had slept fitfully and decided to treat myself to a nap before tonight's opening ceremonies. I was drifting off when the bedside phone rang. I rolled over and mumbled into the receiver, "Dr. Holliday."

A raspy male voice said, "You gotta get to the pens. It's chaos down here."

Completely alert, I asked, "What's happening?"

"The bulls are goin' crazy."

"I'm on my way."

The question of who'd placed the call was left unanswered with a loud click. Fully dressed, I scrambled to the bathroom and splashed sleep from my eyes, grabbed my medical bag, and headed out the door. For a split-second I thought about waking my dad and Uncle Charlie. Considering their level of exhaustion, I instead hustled to the elevator. In retrospect, I should have listened to my gut instinct.

When I arrived, I wondered if someone was playing a joke. I had expected to see handlers being mauled by killer bulls. But the animals milled about as if not having a care in the world. Then I stopped abruptly. Spotting Randy, a Circle Six cowboy, I said, "Hey, what's going on?"

The cowboy tossed a flake of hay into a pen. "Whaddaya mean?"

His face paled a little when I explained about the call I'd received. "If this is a prank, I'm not laughing."

"You've been had, Doc." His voice was brittle with anger. "Some creep is putting the squeeze on all of us. All along we thought it was Calloway. We'd get calls threatening to put a hurtin' on our livestock if we didn't use our trailers to haul drugs."

"Did you call the police?"

"Hell, no! This sorry sapsucker knows who we are, where we live, and the names of our kids. 'Sides, most of us have started totin' forty-fives. I catch that sucker near my boss's livestock, or my young'uns, I'll stop his clock."

"Do you know who *he* is?"

Randy's lips curled into a snarl. "That's the problem. We don't, and we can't keep watch on the stock 'round the clock."

He nodded toward a pen. "Calloway's paying the price. Don't know when it happened."

"What do you mean, 'he's paying the price'?"

The Circle Six cowboy pointed. "You'll need to put

ol' Do'em In out of his misery. When I got here this morning, I heard the bull bellowing, which ain't unusual, 'cept his bellow didn't sound natural. I went over to look." Disgust lined the cowman's face. "Bones were sticking out of both front legs. That's one bad bull. Don't know how anybody could've got close enough to bust up his legs."

I rushed over to the pen and, not waiting for the handler to unlock the gate, I climbed over. Even in a state of extreme pain, the bull struggled to stand. Bones protruded from the skin of both forelegs. I looked up at the cowboy. "Has Caleb been notified? I'll need permission to put the bull down."

"I'm here. What's going on?" Caleb rushed to my side and knelt. His face was tight. He looked mad enough to bite somebody. "Oh, hell! Do what you have to do, Tullah. No need for him to suffer more than he already has."

I felt tired and disgusted, and angry with myself that I hadn't awakened my dad. Then I rationalized that there was no way I could have predicted this malicious attack. I've never enjoyed euthanizing an animal. Tears filled Caleb's eyes. He lifted the bull's head and that's when I spotted the dart embedded deep under the jaw. The bull had been sedated, making it possible to enter his enclosure. "Caleb, give me your bandana." I nodded toward the projectile. To preserve it as evidence, I carefully wrapped it inside the cloth and stored it inside my medical bag.

I opened my phone and called my dad. After filling him in about the situation, I apologized for disturbing his sleep. "Dad," I said, "I never saw a guy hurt so much over a bull. Caleb's really torn up over this."

"Yeah, it could've been worse. They could have broken Caleb's legs." He ended by saying he'd notify Sheriff Saunders.

When Dad and Uncle Charlie arrived, I handed him the bagged dart, then excused myself. My work here was done, unless another similar incident occurred. As soon as I returned to my room, I sent Caroline a text to contact me. Two hours passed with no response. I decided she was ignoring me. I punched in her number. My call went to voice mail. *Caroline—Caleb needs you. Someone broke both legs on one of his bulls.*

If that didn't get her attention, I didn't know what would.

At six that evening, I returned to the holding pens. The entire area in back of the chutes was in motion. Stock was being moved up the line. A stout cowboy attired in a black-and-white cowhide vest over a starched white shirt, with high-heeled boots and a white peaked-crown cowboy hat, was a blur in motion. He walked continuously down the line of chutes, prodding animals, asking cowboys if they were ready, signaling arena hands to bring up more flank straps, more chute ropes, more snagging hooks.

Pickup riders walked prancing horses around the back lot to calm their jitters. I got a little too close and the rear end of a black horse bumped me. The cowboy yelled, "Ma'am, if you don't stay out of the way, you're gonna get hurt."

I offered an apologetic smile and continued my observations. Clay Wolfchild rode a sorrel with a blonde mane and tail in circles. His voice was quiet and calm as he spoke to the nervous horse. I waved, and Clay acknowledged with a polite tip of his hat. I was glad he'd heeded my advice about not riding Domino.

The cowboys were just as active, I observed. They were constantly milling around the chutes in a tireless, nervous manner. Some chewed gum, not slowly and methodically, but quickly in nervous spasms. They worked and reworked their already perfect equipment, taking off their hats and wiping the sweatbands. They squatted, they stood, they got up and walked around—and did it all over again.

This nervous energy transferred to the animals. Metal rails rang and vibrated as het-up bulls rammed their massive heads against the bars. I'm not sure what happened. One minute I was caught up in the excitement, and the next minute the world around me moved in slow motion. Inside my brain I heard the old tractor driver's voice reminding me to run like hell and find something to shinny up if I felt the earth under me vibrate.

It was the wolf's howl that caused me to turn. A flash of motion caught my eye. I had enough time to turn my head just as a red Charolaise bunched its muscles and catapulted over the holding pen's top rail. It was as though I was alone with nowhere to escape. Pens filled with killing machines lined both sides of the dirt aisle.

The dream where Shadow Woman had visited me had become a reality. I stood still and faced the beast. Its eyes glowed with malice; he pawed the earth, sending showers of dirt over his broad shoulders. In my mother's language, I spoke to the bull, saying that I meant him no harm. Strings of slobber drooled from the red bovine's mouth, and with a menacing bawl, he lowered his head and charged. I thrust my hands forward and screamed, "*Shunkaha*!" My plea was answered with a wolf's growls.

The impact drove me into a wall of metal bars. For a moment I wanted to giggle at the absurdity of arms flapping up and down like wings of a flock of gabbling birds as wranglers tried to distract the bull. A massive gray wolf sprang onto the red monster's back. In my state of shock, I was certain the wolf had morphed into…Clay Wolfchild. The last thing I remember was hearing a putt-putt-putt, and the world went dark.

When I opened my eyes, I was lying on a stretcher. Dad, Uncle Charlie, Clay Wolfchild, and Jordy Wells stared down at me. My face hurt when I tried to smile. "What happened to the wolf? I hope it wasn't harmed."

Uncle Charlie said, "Shunkaha was not harmed." In the way of the Native brothers, Clay Wolfchild and Charlie clasped arms. Uncle Charlie said, "I thank you, my Lakota brother, for saving the life of my goddaughter."

Dad explained that Clay had leaped on the bull's back and spurred it away from me, and it was Jordy on his green tractor who maneuvered the bull back to its pen.

I tried to nod, but my entire body protested the slightest movement. Two EMTs lifted me into the ambulance. Dad was adamant that he was riding to the hospital with me; and I argued that I didn't need medical attention.

An EMT swabbed blood from my face. "You're fortunate, Dr. Holliday. It could have been worse. A few stitches to close the gash over your eye, and you'll be good as new—unless the doctor wants to keep you overnight for observation."

I lay quiet. Although my mind filled with questions, I was in too much pain to reason out the answers. I was also annoyed that Caroline had not returned my call.

After several hours at the hospital and every x-ray possible, the doctor declared the worst I had suffered was a mild concussion, a few bruised ribs, and the cut over my eye, which required a plethora of stitches. Dr. Frier had succinctly advised that I be an overnight guest at his hospital.

I shifted my gaze from Dad to Uncle Charlie, then to Wolfchild, and then back to the doctor. "Not on your life. I don't intend to miss the last night of the rodeo."

"I must recommend you stay overnight for observations."

When I refused, the doctor put his hand out and smiled. "I'm here if you need me."

For the next ten minutes the other three men tried to talk me out of going back to the hotel. There was an edge to Uncle Charlie's voice when he spoke. "Little Sister, you are as muleheaded as your old man. You're in no shape to be running around the rodeo trying to look after Caleb Calloway. That's why there is rodeo security. Let them do their job."

Pain reverberated through my head when I snapped out my reply, "Then somebody needs to teach them how to do their jobs. Where were they when the legs of Caleb's bull were being smashed to smithereens?"

Dad looked at me steadily, then said, "Clay, meet us at the hotel. My daughter has a unique gift for solving puzzles. But before she busts a gusset, I think we owe her an explanation."

Chapter Thirty-One

Once we were settled in my room, Dad ordered room service. I popped three extra-strength acetaminophens. Although my everything hurt, I refused to go to bed, opting to relax on the sofa. I needed to hear whatever it was that Dad and Uncle Charlie were withholding.

I promised to close my eyes and rest until the food and Clay arrived. Visions of Clay and the wolf disturbed my psyche. I couldn't figure out why he was the focus of my empath senses, unless—I tried to shake away the thought—unless he was Mr. B. No, that didn't make sense. Deliberate or otherwise, Dad would never invite a criminal into our lives.

I experienced a wild and frightening moment of complete disorientation, fear sweeping over me as I tried to figure out why I was in a dark alley. A flock of vultures waddled around a form. All I could make out was a pair of silver-toed black boots; as the carrions closed in for the kill, a cloud lit the alley, illuminating the shadow of a wolf walking on its hind legs.

Dad's voice said, "Let her sleep."

Cold water had saturated the towel wrapped around an icepack for my head. Only when I reached up and yanked it away did a sense of presence come ebbing back. I sat up slowly, trying to keep my head as still as possible. I thought about the broad head of the bull ramming me. The thought coupled with the act of sitting up brought a grunt, and at once I was aware of a movement to my left. Clay said, "Feeling better?"

"Better than what?" My voice sounded thick and slurred. I blinked and tried to get up, but Dad gently pushed my shoulders down with a command to stay put.

He said, "Which do you want first—a donut or coffee?"

I groaned. "Don't make me laugh, Dad. It hurts." Then I said, "Both."

He wheeled a cart over and removed the warming lids. "How about lobster with all the trimmings, then donuts." Just like he'd do when I was a little girl and ran a fever, he placed a napkin over my lap, only this time he handed me a tray laden with delectable seafood instead of chicken noodle soup.

When I twisted my head slowly and it didn't feel like it would fall off, I watched Clay watching me as he wolfed down his plate of food. I said, "Thank you for saving me."

There was a hint of humor as his eyes focused on me. "All in the line of duty, ma'am."

Dad removed my empty plate. He refilled our cups with coffee, and sat in a chair next to Uncle Charlie. I felt like a specimen under a microscope. "Okay, who's going to tell me what's going on?" Then I pierced Clay with a look. "You are not a cowboy. Who are you, and why are you here?"

He looked at my dad and winked. "Yep, she's feisty all right." Then his face grew serious.

Dad smiled wanly at Clay as if to say, *I told you so*. "Tullah, meet Detective Clay Wolfchild Bannister, from Dallas, Texas. He really is a cowboy, former bull-riding champion, and currently on medical leave."

I knitted my eyebrows together. How did my dad know this detective from Texas? As if he'd read my mind, Clay said, "To answer the question you didn't ask, Tullah, Sheriff Saunders is—was—my father-in-law. He's still like a father to me." He released a woeful sigh. "About a year ago, my wife and I were in the right place at the wrong time. I took a bullet to the spine. It's been a long journey to get back to riding horses. My wife…" His voice trailed off. "Cal knew I was getting cabin fever. He didn't have to ask twice if I'd do a little undercover work for him, posing as a rodeo pickup man. We're well aware of stock contractors being blackmailed into hauling drugs across state lines, and into Canada, and prisoners being used as pawns."

My body throbbed as if I'd been ridden hard and put up wet. I popped two more pills. "What about Caleb?"

Clay nodded toward my dad. "Henry apprised us of your involvement with Calloway, and that he'd put himself and his family at risk by refusing to be strongarmed. We also know about Carl Calloway's so-called accident."

I clamped down on my lip to keep from spewing anger, maybe because I'd been kept out of the loop about Wolfchild's true identity, maybe because Caleb's bull had been brutalized, and maybe…maybe because I didn't like the stirring in my nether regions when I looked into Clay Wolfchild Bannister's molten blue eyes.

I said, "I tested Caleb's bulls. None of them were doped. Is that why his Brahma was hurt, because he stood his ground against these crooks?"

Dad shook his head, then tried to smile. "Partly. The

other was to send a signal to those involved, that Caleb is a dead man."

I felt my mouth forming a question. Dad answered before I asked. "Caleb used his burner phone to contact me, asking for help, and swearing to put these guys away. His parole officer is part of the operation; albeit supposedly under duress. Avery claimed that Mr. B is holding Caleb's mother and two children. The message was that if Caleb didn't deliver the goods, he'd never know where to find their bodies."

I spewed, "Monsters!"

Clay nodded his agreement. "That's when we offered Caleb and his family witness protection if he cooperated with setting up a sting."

Uncle Charlie chimed in. "That's why Caleb was late this morning. He rolled in and parked in a specified location per verbal instructions from O'Neal Coffey. Unbeknownst to Coffey, we'd put a tap on Caleb's burner phone."

Dad picked up Charlie's end of the story. "What Cletus Dodge and two prisoners out on parole found was a trailer filled with slick manure and bags of confectioners' sugar."

Clay chuckled. "Yep, and Caleb's bulls had feasted on an overload of sweet feed."

I clutched a pillow to my ribs to keep them from hurting when I laughed because cows are notorious gluttons when it comes to feed infused with molasses, which causes an explosion of diarrhea.

Clay continued, "Loaded with arrest warrants, we waited until the men were inside and ripping through the hay bales." He couldn't contain his laughter. "There was a lot of slipping and sliding and cussing as they hustled to unload the trailer."

Dad slapped his hands against his knees. "And the rest is history. Sheriff Saunders and his deputies, all trying to keep from gagging, read them their rights and hauled them off to jail."

After our laughter subsided over visions of drug mules being slathered in stinky cow dung, Dad sobered. "Although he's not completely out of danger, Caleb insisted he was riding tomorrow night. He's confident he'll win the purse."

I merely shook my head. "There's more to it than the money." I related the shifts in Caleb's moods, his personality, and the physical anomalies I'd observed. "I'm not sure if he's mentally ill or physically sick. Whichever it is, he's convinced that winning tomorrow night is the cure."

And then I asked, "What are the chances of finding out who Mr. B is?"

Clay scooted to the edge of the chair. "A few years back, we had a case where an accountant and a lawyer were arrested. We suspected their boss, a prominent politician, was the head honcho in a human trafficking trade. Both namby-pambies were too afraid to talk. So we took a little field trip to the Supermax prison in Livingston, Texas. Everyone knows the prisoners there are so violent they spend twenty-two hours of their day in solitary confinement."

A devious grin deepened the crevices in Clay's cheeks. "The accountant sharted his drawers before we even entered the building, and the lawyer, a guy with a girly name, started singing like a canary."

Clay tapped his temple with a forefinger. "I'm thinking Cletus Dodge might enjoy a little observation trip to a federal pen. With him being a deputy, he's well aware of how much federal cons *admire* and *respect* ex-lawmen. I'd bet money names will roll off his tongue in hopes of cutting a deal for a less dangerous environment."

I leaned back against the stack of pillows. A weariness was overtaking me. I don't remember much after that.

Chapter Thirty-Two

I stood in the shower, allowing hot water to cascade over my aching body. Mechanically, I toweled off, then brushed and blow-dried my hair before plaiting it into one long braid. I glanced at the clock. It was nearly four, and the rodeo ceremonies would start at seven. For a long time, I sat in a chair, thinking hard about Clay Wolfchild. I'd known him for exactly twenty-four hours, and yet without trying he'd wiggled his way into my dreams. There was no room for him in my life, and he was a widower, no doubt still grieving for his young wife. I got up and dressed in black denims and a teal silk shirt. I adorned my ears with turquoise studs that had belonged to my mother. Taking the advice I'd given Ella, I spritzed cologne on my neck and wrists and added a light layer of pink lipstick to my lips.

The phone rang. It was Dad, announcing that he and Uncle Charlie were outside my door and ready to escort me to the dining room. We dined on fried chicken, mashed potatoes, buttermilk biscuits, mixed greens, and warm pecan cobbler topped with vanilla ice cream.

Uncle Charlie grinned as he patted his stomach. "Eat all of that, and you'll be fat and pretty like me."

I shot him a lazy look and stuffed my mouth with sugary goodness. "You'll get no arguments from me on that score."

In the crowded dining room, we kept our

conversation light and quiet. I did say, "I'm concerned that Caroline hasn't returned my call. You don't suppose she's in trouble?"

Dad wiped his mouth and lifted his coffee cup. "I called her. She'd checked into another hotel to cool off. I gave her the shortened version of what happened yesterday. She promised to meet us in the VIP section at the stadium."

I didn't know if I was relieved or angry at the news. Dad paid our bill, and Uncle Charlie and I followed him outside to the truck. I said, "I'll be glad when all of this is over and I'm back home in Enigma."

"By the way," Dad said, "Tiny phoned a few minutes ago. The prints on the arrow that you extracted from Mrs. Pierson's mare belonged to a kid from Dixie County. Tiny apprised Sheriff Malachi Dotson of the incident. Malachi picked up the kid, who ratted out his two snot-nosed buddies. All three boys have juvie records. Tiny stated that Mrs. P, Mrs. Scofield, and Mr. Alvarez are willing to press charges."

I refrained from nodding my response because to do so would cause sparkles of pain behind my eyes. Instead, I said, "I wish I could muster up some sympathy for the boys."

After we rode the short distance to the arena, Dad parked and we made our way to the ticket gate. Dad flashed VIP tickets and his badge. We were flagged through, with a personal escort to prime seats situated over the bull pens and with a great view of the bucking chutes. I was surprised to see Caroline seated next to me, and next to Caroline sat Cherry Popp. There was a sad cast to Caroline's heart-shaped face. The silence between us was strained.

She said, "It's about time for the balloon to go up."

Finally, the voice of the rodeo announcer blared over the loudspeaker, welcoming the audience to the rodeo. When that was over, he said, "Cowboys, cowgirls, and little buckaroos, on tonight's program is the champion of all champion riders, and bulls all vying for fame—and, of course, a purse of several million dollars." He introduced the pickup riders and explained their role and the importance of riding well-trained horses.

Clay Wolfchild appeared relaxed in the saddle, physically imposing. The smooth muscles of his shoulders and chest arched, clearly outlined beneath the thin cotton shirt, and he exuded a sense of latent power. He was, I thought suddenly, like a magnificent, untamed stallion, wild and immensely powerful.

The announcer interrupted my thoughts with, "Our first rider up is…"

There was a pause, and then a crackling scratch as if he'd covered the microphone. He said, "Bear with us, folks. We've had an unexpected change in riders."

Another pause.

The announcer said, "It appears our first rider, Alberto del Toro, was severely injured this morning and unable to compete. Our thoughts and prayers go out to Alberto. But, ladies and gentlemen, his replacement rider is…"

I held my breath. I hadn't thought he'd actually go through with it, and I prayed the replacement rider wasn't Caleb. Caroline reached over and gripped my hand when the announcer finished by saying, "Caleb Calloway, and he's no stranger to the rodeo. No sirree, he's a two-time gold buckle bull riding champion. Tonight, he hopes to last the full eight seconds on a bad-to-the-bone bull named Diablo."

Pregnant gasps filtered through the crowd. Evidently, those that followed the rodeo knew of Diablo's reputation. The announcer interrupted my musing. "Like I said, Diablo is a killer. Ladies and gentlemen, let's hear it for Caleb Calloway and Diablo!"

I thought Caleb looked nervous as we watched him settle onto the bull's back. He pulled his hat down, his face tight and pale, then nodded. The chute gate swung open, and Diablo exploded. He hit the dirt kicking, and Caleb's head whipped backward at the charging jolt.

Caleb stuck on, but Dad declared, "He was off-balance coming out of the chute. He won't score high."

I watched the timer on the scoreboard, and prayed. Two seconds...three seconds...three and half seconds...tick...tick! Mid-buck, a bullhorn struck Caleb in the face. Blood splattered. Caleb managed to adjust his balance without losing his form. It seemed a lifetime had passed before the eight-second buzzer sounded. His face a bloody mess, Caleb catapulted off Diablo's back, landing hard on his knees.

Dressed in his garish cowboy clown outfit, Baily Strom galloped in on a toy broom-handle horse, taunting the bull to entice its attention away from Caleb. Instead of heading toward the exit gate, Diablo turned and stood still. If was almost as if he was reading the crowd.

Clay trotted his horse over to encourage the bull to turn to the gate. Diablo did the unexpected. He lowered his head, pawed the dirt, let out a bellow, and charged, hitting Clay's sorrel gelding mid-center and knocking the horse off its feet. The bull then charged toward Baily, who dove inside a safety barrel.

The crowd roared, which seemed to incite Diablo,

and like an egotistical star he strutted around the arena. Then the worst happened. He raced toward Caleb, and in one awful moment caught him in the chest with a horn and flung him into the air. Caroline stood and screamed. I stood, and Dad grabbed me. "You can't save him, Punkin."

Caleb rose from the arena dirt, took a few steps, then motioned to the sidelines that he was hurt. Before he collapsed, face down, it looked as though he had waved to Caroline.

Helpless, we watched in horror as Caleb was mauled by the massive head of the same vicious animal that had killed Caleb's father. Riders on horseback and on foot raced to the rescue. I snatched myself from my dad's grip and rushed to the aisle, then leapt over the rail. By the time I kneeled to examine Caleb, I knew his injuries couldn't be fixed. Hopeful, I began CPR until the first responders arrived. Refusing to give up, the team worked for over an hour before reluctantly agreeing that Caleb was gone.

****

With Caroline's approval, the rodeo association sponsored a public memorial service to honor Caleb. His death seemed to have had a profound effect on rodeo fans and bull riders. After the service, his body was sent to Arcadia, where he was born, to be buried in the family plot alongside his father. Due to his aggressive nature and the fact that his reputation as a "killer" had progressed, Caroline requested that I euthanize Diablo.

While I agreed with her assessment of the bull, I denied her request and recommended she contact a more amenable veterinarian.

A month after the funeral, I sat in the porch swing,

enjoying an iced tea and flipping through a new veterinary medical magazine. River and Rascal alerted me to the sound of a vehicle. I watched as dust arose following a very expensive white sports car down the driveway.

I was surprised when the door opened and Caroline stepped out. We exchanged pleasantries. I invited her inside and offered her a refreshment, and we sat at the kitchen table. I had the distinct feeling that the wealthy widow's visit wasn't exactly social.

She opened her purse and handed me a white envelope. "I thought this might interest you, Tullah."

I removed the letter, unfolded it, and scanned the contents of an autopsy report. Although I didn't know the nature of Caleb's illness, the report confirmed what I had expected—the causes of his tremors, unexplained mood swings, forgetfulness, and slurred words were attributed to an inoperable, stage-four glioblastoma brain tumor. I refolded the report and handed it to Caroline.

She said, "I didn't know Caleb was seeing a doctor until I was cleaning out his office and found appointment cards. I spoke with the nurse and explained about his death, then asked for an appointment to speak with the doctor in person."

She seemed to drift off for a moment. I waited until she collected her emotions. "Tullah, the doctor said that by the time he'd first seen Caleb and conducted all the tests, the prognosis was less than a year. He also showed me the waivers Caleb had signed, refusing chemo and radiation." She sighed. "If I'd only known, I wouldn't have harped on him so much about his drinking or the awful tirades he'd pull. Why didn't he tell me?"

Although I had no true answers, I hoped to set her

mind at ease. "I believe Caleb wanted to die a hero rather than wasting away, suffering his last days in a hospital bed." I reached over and patted her hand. "Caleb was the best kind of hero, Caroline. You and the children can be proud of him. Not because he rode a dangerous bull for eight seconds, but because, like all good heroes, he refused to be cowed by a gang of bad guys."

My answer seemed to gratify her. She offered a weepy smile and went on to explain that she'd sold the ranch and livestock. "The children and I have moved to North Carolina to live near my parents. I invited Caleb's mother to join us. She decided to remain in Florida with her sister."

I wondered about Rosie and Sofia. She said that in his will Caleb had generously provided for them. Caroline stood. I followed her to the porch, where we promised to keep in touch. We both knew that, no matter our declarations, we were frenemies and this was our last goodbye.

Epilogue

Funny how we count time and wished the law worked faster. However, it takes time to follow all the leads, and more often than not they're dead ends. For dedicated lawmen like my dad, Sheriff Saunders, and the federal marshals, never giving up is part of their vocabulary.

After more than a year of arrest warrants, trials, and confessions, a lead finally produced Mr. B's identity—Hubert Bigelow, Regional Director of Wardens, scum of the earth. Apprehending him and making the arrest stick were two different animals. As my dad explained, "It's complex, and we needed to follow the letter of the law to keep from screwing up."

Detective Clay Wolfchild Bannister had volunteered to go undercover posing as a major player in a Chicago drug community. According to his arrest records he had killed off most of his competition before a member of his own gang ratted him out.

Supposedly hailing from Oklahoma, Bannister aka Lucky Lanksy, was extradited to a federal correctional facility in Caddo County. His transporting officers were none other than Cal Saunders and Emmett Tewksbury, Federal Marshal.

After proving that he wasn't a foppish dandy and could put plenty of "whup ass" on any of the yard prisoners, Clay aka Lucky was summoned to the warden's office and offered an early out—an opportunity to work on a ranch, earn mega dollars—and all he had to do was transport drugs and keep his mouth shut.

Due to my work schedule and the location of the hearing in Texas, I wasn't able to attend Bigelow's trial. I got to relive it through Dad.

Dad had arrived at my house loaded with barbeque sandwiches and chocolate eclairs. We settled around the dining table, and I listened to him recount what he'd witnessed on the day of judgment for Mr. B.

"Yep, it did my soul good when Cletus Dodge outed O'Neal Coffey and his entire corrupt department. We also arrested Robert Avery, who fully cooperated by supplying the files of men recruited by their local wardens to work as drug mules. Avery was given a light sentence and promised witness protection for his testimony.

"Needless to say, the District Attorney's office has worked diligently and 'round the clock to make sure there were no loopholes in any of the issued warrants."

I didn't contain the excitement in my voice when I asked, "What was Bigelow's reaction when the jury foreman read the 'guilty' verdict?"

Dad humphed. "At first, he threatened the judge. That was a mistake. Judge Elena Topaz isn't easily intimidated. She stared that fat slob in the face and said, 'Mr. Bigelow, unless you want me to add another twenty years to your sentence, you will sit down and shut up!'"

I laughed and clapped my hands. "I hope she threw the book at him."

"Yep, twenty-five years with no special concessions. In other words, he won't spend his years in a prison resort with golf courses and catered meals."

I retorted, "Creeps like that deserve every bad thing given to them. How did Bigelow respond?"

Dad merely shrugged. "He appeared okay until the guard put the cuffs on him and started to escort him from the courtroom. That's when he broke down and cried like a baby, pleading for Judge Topaz to have mercy. She simply signaled the guard to take him away."

I hesitated to ask. Dad beat me to the punch. "Out with it—what's on your mind, Punkin?"

I said, innocently, "What happened to Clay Wolfchild?"

Dad gave me a lazy look. "Conveniently, Lucky Lansky was killed in an attempted prison escape. In reality, as far as I know, Clay is still one of Dallas's finest detectives. Why do you ask?"

The éclair I bit into had lost its appeal. "No reason. He was the only one you hadn't mentioned."

The last time I had spoken to or seen him was at Caleb's memorial service. Clay Wolfchild Bannister had given no indication that he was attracted to me, and that was twenty-four months ago, but who was counting.

Dad helped me clean the kitchen. As he situated his cap on his head, I noted his sideburns had grown grayer, his blue eyes seemed sadder.

"It doesn't seem fair does it, Dad?" I followed him to the porch.

He said, "What doesn't seem fair, Punkin?"

Anger filled me and breath hung in my throat. "Justice. It's been years since Mama was murdered, and her killer is still out there. Crooked lawmen, dishonest government officials, drug pushers, all caught, tried, and behind bars. Why not Mama's killer?"

Dad wrapped his arms around me. He rested his chin

on top of my head. "Someday, Punkin. Someday."

With that, he walked down the steps to his 4Runner. I watched as he drove down the long driveway. Feeling a little melancholy, I decided to sit in the swing and listen to nature. River and Rascal settled at my feet.

The hackles on River's black neck rose. The growl in his throat was low and deep. I scanned the yard and didn't see what had worried him until a great barred owl deftly lit on the porch rail. It was my owl. I knew because it had one yellow eye and one brown eye.

"Why are you here, owl?"

It blinked, and hooted. Rascal, my miniature donkey, turned his little gray butt toward the bird and kicked at it.

Undeterred, the raptor blinked again. The Cherokee believe owls are messengers of good and evil. This wasn't the first time this particular bird had visited me. I spoke to it in the language of my mother's people. "Wise bird, what news do you bring—good or evil?"

River growled again, the hackles on his neck prominent in the waning light. Within minutes a single shadow became two. The sky darkened, and thunder rolled. I was certain the spirit warriors had risen from the earth and danced among the grasses in my front pasture.

The owl fluttered its wings and soared upward into the darkness. I stepped off the porch to watch the stars, trying to discern the meaning of the raptor's visit. A star shot across the sky, and I distinctly heard my mother's voice say, "It's time."

Moonlight fell across my path, and I was left wondering if I had imagined that my mother had sent me a message. I beckoned my pets to come, and we entered the house and locked the door; remembering Dad's words, *Someday, Punkin, someday.*

My empathic senses were telling me the day of reckoning was coming soon.

Turn the page for an excerpt from
the next exciting Doc Holliday Mystery
from

Loretta C. Rogers

TO CATCH A KILLER

The Final Chapter

Prologue

Death is the ebb and flow of life and eventually comes to all of us. Murder is the deliberate and willful act of taking a life.

Fourteen years ago, my mother died. She was murdered. Someday, I will find the resources to give up my career as a veterinarian and become a full-time seeker of the person or persons who took her life.

Her name was Josie Waya Crow Holliday. She was an artist of Native American history and visiting New York to display her work at a major museum. She was found in an alley. I cannot bear to describe the condition of her body when my father, my grandmother, and I had to identify her.

Over the years, my father has made numerous trips to New York, only to be treated with flippant irreverence by the NYPD, who give him no respect as a law enforcement officer or as the bereaved husband who desires to bring the killer of his wife to justice.

The day I find my mother's murderer is the day that person will beg to be put out of their misery.

Chapter One

I knelt to brush away the damp leaves and debris that had gathered around the tombstone, and then I laid a bouquet of purple cornflowers on my mother's grave. I missed her presence with an aching intensity and I missed how she had listened to my hopes and dreams, and even my despairs. I will never forget the night we received the call from the New York Museum director informing us of my mother's murder.

I sat on the damp earth and traced my finger along the letters of her name: Josie Waya Crow Holliday, Beloved wife, daughter, and *Etsi*.

In the Cherokee language, "Etsi" is the word for— mother. Once her remains arrived at the mortuary, Grandmother and I honored *Etsi* in the Cherokee way. We first washed her body and scented it with lavender oil. We wrapped her in white linen before placing her inside the coffin. Grandmother tucked an eagle feather into her daughter's hands because the Cherokee venerate the eagle as a sacred bird. And because she was born of the *Waya* clan, the image of a wolf was etched into the tombstone to watch over her.

It gives me comfort to talk to her. "The years have passed, Mama. In a few months I will celebrate thirty years of life. I was barely sixteen when you went away. Grandmother says the Great Spirit Father needed you more than Dad and me, and even her. I don't understand.

We…I…needed you…here on earth.

"You didn't get to see my prom gown, or watch me compete, as you did, in barrel-racing events. Even though I knew you were not there, I looked in the audience for you when I graduated from medical school."

I continued talking, telling her about Gandalf, her black-and-white pinto. "He's nearly twenty now, but he still has the spirit of a wild mustang, and there are times when he is as wily as his name." I allowed myself a small chuckle.

The squish of wet grass drew my attention to a pair of shiny black boots. I looked up to see my dad approaching. After all these years, and even with his recent marriage to Dr. Sunny Sanders, lines of sadness still etch his face. He removed his Stetson. Threads of silver lined his brown hair. At the age of fifty-six, he was still ruggedly handsome, still my hero, and still sheriff of Enigma.

I stood. Dad placed an arm around my waist and drew me close. He coughed to clear the huskiness in his voice. "She will always be in my heart, Punkin."

I brushed a tear from my cheek. "It seems like yesterday that we got the call. Fourteen years, Dad, and the NYPD has let the case go cold." Anger laced my heart. "If Mama hadn't been a woman—a Native American woman—the police department would have been all over the case like a squirrel gathering acorns."

Dad looked down at me. He brushed another tear from my cheek, then murmured, "She would have been proud of you."

I shrugged with a weary gesture. "But I haven't honored her by finding her killer."

"Josie was a gentle soul. She loved nature, and all things beautiful. She adored you." He tilted my chin upward for me to look at him. "Finding her killer would be a dangerous journey, even if he or they are still alive. Your mother would never expect you to put yourself in danger because of her."

"But, Dad—"

"No buts, Tullah Josie Crow Holliday! Losing your mother was painful enough. I could not bear losing you too. Promise me you will forget this notion of avenging your mother. Promise!"

As I did when I was a child about to tell a lie, I placed my hands behind my back and crossed my fingers. I stood on tiptoes and kissed his cheek. "We should go. A storm is coming, Dad."

Across the cemetery, a curtain of rain moved toward us as we raced to our individual vehicles. Dad yelled above the sheeting drops, "Meet me at Tanti's. Sunny and she are preparing lunch."

I waved and climbed into my truck. I watched Dad pull away in his 4Runner. I'm not sure why I decided not to immediately follow. There is something calming about the rain and the music it makes. I rolled down the window, and as I listened to the rhythmic thrumming, I was startled to see a female cardinal with her orange-black wings and red beak perch on the hood. She shook herself as if to expel raindrops from her tufted crest and feathers. I was even more surprised when she hopped toward the windshield, then pecked on the glass.

Over the years, I have learned to embrace my empathic gift and to heed the messages of the animals and other spirits that visit me. A flash of lightning frightened the little red bird away, and left me wondering why such a delicate creature would seek me out during a thunderstorm.

I engaged the ignition and drove to meet my father for lunch. I had barely reached the wrought iron gates when a warrior on a rearing pinto horse caused me to slam on the brakes. In a blink the apparition disappeared.

What did these visits mean? My grandmother and Uncle Charlie would know.

A word about the author...

Loretta C. Rogers is a Native Floridian and lives in Central Florida with her husband and rescue dog. When not writing, Loretta enjoys traveling, reading, and working crossword puzzles. Reading is a pastime she enjoys best.